The Grey Area

A Joseph Gleason novel

ISBN: 979-8- 9881862-6-7

Copyright 2025, Joseph Gleason

Published by WinSource Publishing
Tacoma WA 98402

Chapter 1

His eyes blinked, searching for any scrap of light. Every limb was stuck in its place. His head pounded, making it hard to think.

"Hello?" He was trying to look through the dark, barely managing more than a whimper. Was he dead? Dead and waiting for some sort of transfer to what comes next? He couldn't remember anything from before. If this was a transfer to whatever is after, it didn't feel like the way to the pleasant one. His breathing was rapidly getting out of control as anxiety gripped its fingers around his heart. His brain felt like it was dormant but starting to flicker on slowly. Paranoia mixed with his panic like a weight pressing down on him.

That's when the thrashing started. Almost unconscious and uncontrollable, adding to the confusion and cluelessness.

Light filled the room and blinded him for a minute. There were voices in the shuffle, but he couldn't make out what was happening. People, he thought, it had to be people. So, he wasn't dead after all. As his eyes began to adjust, he made out two people pushing through the doors. One walked straight toward him with no hesitation. The second startled, looking shocked at the sight of him, as if he had seen a ghost or apparition. The man quickly tried to shake it off and headed to his side, starting to fiddle with the restraints on his hands and legs.

He thought he was finally getting some help until he noticed they were tightening them down, making it harder to move.

"Who are you? What's going on?" It came out louder than expected. He noticed he was having a difficult time controlling the volume of his voice.

Just as he was going to begin screaming for help, a third man walked into the room with a very calming yet utterly cold aura about him.

"Everything is going to be fine." His voice was icy, unsuccessfully trying to mimic concern.

He finished buttoning up his jacket while staring at him, "My name is Doctor Stintz. We are getting you ready for your procedure. Waking up a little early was unexpected but not out of the ordinary."

Procedure? He couldn't remember his name or his life before this moment, let alone the consent or knowledge of needing any sort of procedure. As he looked around, he took note of how empty the room was. It was a relatively big room but bare to the bones. There was nothing but him, the doctors, and some machine attached to his bed pumping gold fluid of God knows what into his arm.

His eyes went to Stintz after taking in the room, "What procedure? Why can't I seem to remember anything?"

"It's just an effect of the medications we have administered to you, nothing to worry about. We will have you back in perfect working order in due time." Stintz had his arms crossed waiting for the others to finish fiddling with his restraints.

"Can I at least know my name?"

Stintz sighed, "The less we talk about your personal life the better at this moment, I'm afraid. The more we delve in to that while you're still under the effects of the medication the more confused you will become." He nodded with a slight curved smile, "Not to worry though. Once all is said and done, we can start to take you off and things will come back to you over time".

Something was off. Every word out of Stintz's mouth seemed rehearsed, tired in a way like he had practiced them over and over again until he didn't even want to say the lines anymore. Or maybe just spoken to him every time he wakes up to keep him docile. Whatever the case was, something was off.

The lab assistants started to lower the table he was on to a horizontal position, unlocking the wheels and prepping for transport.

He tilted his head up to keep looking at Stintz, "What kind of procedure is this?"

Stintz closed his eyes for a few seconds and inhaled deeply, "It's really just a standard procedure, nothing to worry about"

They started rolling him through the double doors and out into a hallway. Everything was blindingly white. From the tile covering the whole wall, to the paint and lights on the ceiling. Even the lab coats, hats, and masks the doctors were wearing were stark white.

As they continued down the hallway at a slow pace, he noticed other double doors that looked exactly like the ones he had just exited from. Each with a single word and a number designation starting with subject four. As he rolled down the hallway, he took note of the numbers. Four. Five. Then Six. That means he must have been subject three.

Were there other patients just as confused and foggy as him? Just sitting in these rooms waiting to be whisked off to some procedure unbeknownst to them as well? What hospital labels their patients as subjects anyway?

The growing knowledge of Three's situation started to stick in his mind like a hot knife piercing through butter. This can't be for my benefit. Being lowered to the denomination of "subject" explains the doctor's unwillingness to provide any information on what is going on and the level of care he can expect moving forward.

I need to get out.

The thought started to consume his consciousness, flooding all parts of his brain in a wave of clarity.

They were arriving at the end of the hallway now, an immaculate looking freight elevator sat at the very end. A *ding* sounded off when Stintz pushed the button and Three could hear the elevator start moving down with a loud grumble.

They waited in silence for the elevator.

As it arrived, the large horizontal door started to open. They wheeled Three inside and waited for the door to close. More pure white awaited him.

What was this obsession with everything being blindingly white? It started to make him feel sick; he looked at his machine filled with golden fluid just to get a glimpse of something different.

"Level three?" The assistant looked to an unimpressed Stintz.

"That would be one floor up, like I told you earlier. Yes." Stintz's stare looked like it could pierce diamonds.

The assistant hit the button and the elevator began to rise. The grumble he'd heard waiting for it was more of a roar from inside the machine.

The more help he could get from the second floor, the better chances of leaving this place would be. Who knows what security looks like on floor one or, hell, even the layout and size of the building. Thoughts of escape rattled in his brain until the elevator stopped and the door started to open.

Unsurprisingly, the elevator opened to another hallway painted white. The assistants pushed Three down the hallway, passing more double doors on each side the whole way down, all labeled a variety of things this time. He tried to take note of them, but his head began to feel like it was splitting open again and his vision blurred. He caught a couple of them on the way down. One labeled *DNA Testing and Extraction* and another labeled *Special Projects*. As they reached the end of the hallway, they pushed him into the furthest double doors from the elevator. When he rolled in, he saw the label on his door.

Surgery

His heart picked up speed and his palms were sweating thinking of his "Standard Procedure" and what the doctor had in store for him.

"My assistants will prepare you as I prep for surgery. And they will do it exactly as I have instructed them to." Stintz was staring daggers at the shocked assistant from earlier.

"Of course, sir!" They replied in unison.

As Dr. Stintz walked out of the room, the two assistants relaxed a bit. One obviously more than the other, seeming like he was just coming off a live interview he was woefully unprepared for.

Three strained his cuffs and looked to the assistants, "So, is this where I'm getting my lobotomy?"

Their eyes shot at each other with a more worried look than he would have liked. They weren't actually going to lobotomize him, were they? His mind reeled at the thought of being made brain dead in a lab. He had no idea what he was in for, and a life he couldn't even remember. Even if he did escape, would his memories truly come back like the doctor had said, or was that just a lie to silence him for the time being?

One of them loosened up and shook his head, "No, nothing that morbid." He paused, "We are prepping you for a form of brain surgery, though. We woke you up because we need to have you awake and responsive to make sure we don't cut anything we're not supposed to. If you're still responding normally and answering our questions, we know we haven't done any irreparable damage."

Three's eyes widened.

What. The. Fuck.

"Standard procedure my ass." It slipped out, almost as if he couldn't hold it in.

One of the assistants chuckled. The other looked like he was struggling as much as Three was in this situation.

As fun as the thought of impending brain surgery in an unknown lab felt, he had to keep it together and focus on any way out he could. Just one slip could be enough of an opportunity to make a move. As his mind spiraled and struggled to focus, he worked his face to tell a different story of calm compliance.

"Now that you know the nature of the procedure, and your needed compliance in this situation, all that's left for us is to move you to the operating table." He pointed to a table next to Three.

With all the focus on the doctor and the assistants, Three hadn't even noticed the table next to him. As he turned his focus to his side, his face sunk. The table in question wasn't even a table in his eyes at all. It was a human molded box of steel with hinges connecting to a top cover with only a head hole visible. At the top was a clamp of sorts, presumably to hold his head and neck in one spot. A steel sarcophagus would be a better description than a table.

"Don't be afraid of the way it looks. It is simply to ensure you don't move around during the surgery. For your safety." Nothing they said sounded genuine, "Now, I am going to inject your IV with a serum that will help you relax so we can move you. Once the drugs take effect, my colleague here will start the transfer."

Three's mind started to unravel as the assistant walked over to a tray and picked up a needle filled with bright blue liquid. He panicked and struggled to think of a way out of this. His head was still pounding, making it hard to think straight. He struggled to keep focus through it all. The assistant reached his bedside. Slowly and precisely, he inserted the tip of the needle into the IV bag. The bag filled with the blue fluid, mixing with the gold, creating a sickly bright green color.

He pulled the needle out and capped it, "The drugs are relatively fast-acting, and you should start feeling the effects momentarily. After approximately ten minutes, they will have taken full effect. Unfortunately, we will have to keep a consistent flow for this specific drug to remain active. For part of the transfer procedure, we will have to relocate your IV from your arm to your neck so we can close the surgery table securely."

Fantastic, this just gets better and better. He could start to feel the green liquid pumping through his body; it had the sensation of soft embers traveling up his veins that unsettled him.

"As we wait for the drugs, I am going to help Stintz prepare for the upcoming surgery. My colleague," he nodded to the other assistant, "will keep an eye on you and finish prepping your transfer."

With that final statement, he turned around and quickly left the room, leaving Three and an obviously uncomfortable assistant alone. The burning of the drugs began to fade and was slowly turning to a lofty light feeling. It was making his motor functions start to slightly degrade, and his hope with it.

"Alright." The man was almost shaking, "I'm going to start loosening your restraints so we can get you into a movable position."

He slowly made his way to Three and put his hands on his leg restraints. As he loosened and removed them, Three's mind lit up like a Christmas tree.

This man's incompetence would be his saving grace. He could still feel some strength in his body that the drugs had not fully taken from him yet; he had to wait for the perfect moment. The worry of the drugs taking too much of an effect by the time he was free was the only thing he could think of.

The assistant moved from his legs to his arms, freeing one of them. He slowly moved to the other side, placing his hands on the last restraint, pausing for a second to make eye contact with Three.

"I'm sorry about all this." He muttered in a cracked voice.

With that, he released the last restraint, and Three looked over to match his gaze, "I'm sorry too."

The assistant's eyes grew wide at the words. He knew at that moment he had made a mistake, and there was no turning back.

Chapter 2

He shifted his body to face the assistant, swinging his arm like a club at the assistant's head and knocking him down. Three rolled off the table and crashed on the floor beside him, ripping the IV out in the process. His muscles felt like Jello, making it hard to get to his hands and knees. He was trying to pull himself together when he caught a glimpse of the assistant crawling back into a corner, horrified at what was taking place.

Three managed to get to his feet and started moving toward the door, paying little attention to the man cowering in the corner. Trying to stay upright took all of his focus; even the act of walking seemed like a challenge at first. He almost fell to the ground hobbling through the double doors leading to the hallway. The elevator was straight ahead at the other end. It looked miles away from him at this point. Three started the immense journey down the hall, feeling a tiny bit better and more stable with each passing step.

As he stumbled on, he wondered why he hadn't heard any alarms blaring. There was no security team, not even any other employees scurrying about the hall. What kind of hospital is this with no one here? Working his way down past the other doors, his head started splitting again, making it hard to keep focus.

Not now, not here. Not when he was so close and only a button push from a real chance at help or freedom. No matter how much he wished to will away his problem, his head worsened to a point of being almost unbearable. Three grabbed his head and lost balance, crashing to the ground. He laid on the floor, clutching his head just feet from the elevator as he began to scream. The pain had surpassed any manageable level and Three wondered if his brain was literally bursting out the back of his head, painting their perfect clean white walls with a dark red mess.

His scream must have alerted Dr. Stints and his other assistant. There was a door slam down the hall and muffled yells of anger and panic. He had to move but found even the thought almost too much to bear. Desperation gave him the surge of adrenaline he needed, mustering up the power to lurch forward the last few feet and slam his fist to call the elevator. Luckily, it was already on his floor, and the door started to grumble open. The manic footsteps of his captors coming back for him echoed through the hall. He managed to roll his body into the elevator and hit the first-floor button. The door closed just before they were able to get to him, and Three heard the panicked man slamming on the call button hoping for it to open, but it had already begun its slow descent.

Three thought about the other subjects and quickly, almost as if on instinct, pushed the button for level two. Thankfully, this was a slow elevator, and he managed to hit it before passing down to the first floor.

The door opened to the empty white hallway. Sluggishly crawling out of the elevator, he felt the pain starting to subside. He managed to make it back on his feet and noticed the lofty feeling from the drugs they had given him slowly but surely fading away. Three slammed the emergency stop button to ensure no one came down the elevator after him. The closest door wasn't far from the elevator. His head slammed along with the blaring pulse of the alarm. Standing in front of the door, he paused and looked at the label.

Subject Six

What monsters label people as subjects? Hopefully whoever was inside this door was in better shape than he was. He pushed the door open and walked inside, greeted by the horrific sight of what was left of a mangled man. The white empty room had the body on a vertical table in the middle hooked up to all sorts of machines. The top of his skull was opened and had mesh wires draped over it with pulsing glowing lights. An array of needles peppered his arms all the way from the bottom of his shoulders down to his wrists. One of his legs was removed at the knee and crudely stitched up, forming a ghastly wound.

Three collapsed backward in sheer shock and terror. He scooted back with his hands and feet, allowing the doors to fold close in front of him. What had he just walked in on? Was this the fate of all the subjects left to collect? Was this going to be his fate eventually if he didn't find a way out of here?

As terrifying as the thought was, he knew he had limited time. He pushed through his fear to the next door of subject number five. Subject six was forever burned in to his consciousness. He was holding back puke and didn't know if he could take another sight like that. Too much thought was making him lose his nerve. Ripping off the mental Band-Aid, he pushed through the door.

There was a sigh of relief when a fully put-together human being was on the table this time. In the center of this room was a woman, with an IV of the same golden fluid that Three had in his arm when he woke up. She twitched and shook her head a little bit as he walked in. Long brunette hair draped down from her head leading to her curvy figure. Her olive skin had patches of scars up and down her arms and legs, probably from needles and tests no doubt. She was clothed in the same white spandex shorts he had been issued, accompanied by a cut-off top of the same design.

As Three approached, she tensed up and started to raise her head. When she looked up and locked eyes with him, she was confused but more relaxed than a moment ago. He felt an uncanny wave of calm wash over him. Her eyes were green with a slight swirl of hazel and a stare that seemed to pierce right through him. This single moment of relief was cut off when he remembered he was on a very short ticking clock, at which point he noticed her mouth was scarred over. It looked as though the doctors had used some form of burning or chemicals to fuse her mouth shut in a crude way, leaving only a small hole open in the front.

"I'm sorry I have no time to explain, we need to go now." Three ran up and started to rip off her leg restraints, "We have a very short amount of time and no idea what the way out looks like. Can you walk?"

It appeared his words were falling on deaf ears when she only responded with a blank stare. It was unnerving and gave little hope of help if this woman couldn't even understand him.

The moment Three released her arm restraints, she pushed off the table and ripped out her IV in one fluid motion. She stood up, meeting Three's eyes again and then pointed to her mouth, making a mumbling sound.

He raised an eyebrow, "They burned your mouth shut?"

The woman seemed frustrated for pointing out her obvious condition. She made a motion of scissors cutting across her mouth with her fingers.

"I don't have anything to cut your mouth open with." He couldn't help but be a little disturbed at the fact she was willing to instantly take a knife to herself moments after gaining some freedom. "I'm sorry I can't help with that right now, but we need to get a move on. You look like you're in better shape than I was when I woke up, so we should try and get the other subjects moving."

There was a bit of confusion at first. Three gained some confidence when she gestured for him to follow and started for the door. When they got back into the hallway, she grabbed his arm and turned him toward her. She pointed down the hall and then put both of her hands up together, with one finger on each extended, separating them quickly.

"You want to separate? Check rooms individually?" A part of him longed to stay with her. To not be alone.

She nodded.

He clenched his teeth, "Ok, that's probably a better idea. Get everyone out faster."

She nodded again and turned down the hallway toward subject two. She couldn't talk, but Three was very glad she was able to completely understand him and not be at all foggy minded like he was. He faced the door and rushed in, feeling the pressure of time starting to weigh down on him.

It was blank. An empty white room with red stains on the floor by a drain near the center. He looked around confused for a few seconds before turning and leaving. The other woman was already back in the hallway walking in his direction. He had an eyebrow raised and lazily pointed to the room at the end of the hall she had checked. She shrugged and entered the next room closest to him.

He caught up to her through the doors and she was standing near the middle with her hands on her hips looking around at nothing, "I guess it was just the three of us then." She turned to face him with an eyebrow up.

A shiver ran up his spine, "Don't go in subject six's room. I'm not going to be able to shake that off for a long while."

She quickly walked past him through the doors. Three paused, realizing where she was off to and ran after her. The woman was already almost to the door when he popped out, forcing him to a sprint to catch up with her. He grabbed her arm before the door opened enough to see the body again and jerked her back. She smacked his arm off of her as fast as he was able to grab it with a fiery look in her eyes threatening to light him up.

Three put his hands up and took a step back, "Whoa, whoa there, I'm trying to help you! I get you're curious but that is not something you need to see. Trust me, It's not something you can unsee."

The woman stared at him, silent. She huffed and rolled her eyes, walking back down the hallway away from the elevator. Three trailed behind her, starting to feel his skin crawl at the time they were wasting not trying to find an exit. She pushed her way into the room he woke up in and was looking around for something.

"They took my table out when they rolled me to surgery, you're not going to find anything in here. We should get going before someone comes looking for us, if they already aren't." If he clenched his teeth any harder, he risked cracking them on the spot.

The woman paid no attention to him and blew out of the door and back to her original room. There wasn't any nook or cranny of her table that she wasn't meticulously searching through. Three kept looking back at the door with sweat starting to form on his forehead, "We need to go!" He pointed to the hallway almost screaming at her.

She grunted loudly and flipped the table over. Three recoiled while she turned around and smacked down the pole that was holding her IV bag. It split open and splattered the ground with gold. He was silently watching her breath as heavily as she could through her small mouth hole while looking at the mess drift to the drain.

He was shaking, nervous to say anything to her but couldn't help himself, "What are you looking for that's more important than getting the hell out of here?!"

She stomped over, putting her face only inches from his and pointed to her mouth while trying to say three words that he couldn't understand. Her intensity grabbed his attention enough to tamper down all of the anxiety he'd been feeling. He couldn't imagine what she had gone through up to this point, thanking his lucky stars that he didn't wake up with any intense changes like that.

"I'm sorry. I'm sorry you had this happen to you. I'm trying to get us out of here before they can do anything else to us."

Her face slightly softened and her eyes drifted to the ground. When she looked back up, he thought he could see tears being held behind her eyes. Her hand found his shoulder and she nodded while blinking slowly.

A tingling spark jolted through him from her touch. He wished nothing more than to be able to help her. If they weren't potentially being hunted, he would have savored the feeling as long as he could. She gestured her head to the door and pulled his arm with her.

Pulsing in his head matched the intermittent siren still coming from the elevator. He closed his eyes and let her guide him as long as she would before letting go of his arm. Light felt like it was piercing his eyes and reaching through his skull. The hallway began to vibrate and spin halfway down making him stumble and grasp the wall for balance.

The woman stopped when she noticed he wasn't following her anymore and was fully leaning against the wall with both hands extended out and eyes closed. When her hand touched his shoulder, he jerked it forward and shook his head. She stood back, not knowing what to do, looking to the elevator.

Three punched the wall and started sliding down to his knees, moaning in pain. There was a commotion behind one of the doors ahead of them. The woman threw his arm over her shoulder and dragged him as fast as she could in the direction of the elevator. He was waving his head and hardly standing on his own with his eyes closed.

What the fuck did they do to me? He thought. The pulsing in his head was dimming and he was trying to walk normally again but couldn't find his step. Lights were retreating back to their bulbs enough for him to open his eyes a crack intermittently. Glimpses of her face that made it through to him were stricken with worry. Her eyes were glued to something on the side of the wall that he couldn't turn to see instead of in front of her. He forced himself up and looked over at what was catching her eye. His head swung sideways and a door slammed open accompanied by angry shouting.

Chapter 3

Three spun around and was met with the brunt end of some sort of gun to his face. He flew from the woman's shoulder and slammed on the floor. The hit knocked his brain back in place for the time being and lined in his focus.

A man in all black padded armor shoved the woman against the wall with the length of his rifle contraption pressed sideways against her. Another guard wasn't far behind them in the stairwell, running down the steps. Three looked to the woman struggling to get free, then back to the open door. He used both his feet to kick the door as hard as he could from the ground as the second guard stepped in the doorframe. The force of the door slamming on him staggered him backward until he fell and hit the back of his helmet against the metal railing behind him.

Three gave it another kick to close it before pushing himself back to his feet. Processing what was happening was out of the picture and he was running on impulse, grabbing the guard who had the woman pinned down around the waist and ripping him off.

The guard dropped his weapon and threw an elbow at Three's head, landing it on his shoulder. He had no idea what to do and spun around trying to slam the guard against the other side of the hallway. Their balance shifted while they spun and the guard ripped Three's hands from around him on their way to the ground. The woman ran up and kicked his helmet off by the visor with his gun contraption in hand. Shock lit up his face for the split second before it was beaten off with the end of the gun.

She lifted it up and slammed it down on his head again and raised it up for a third strike. Three pushed himself up and grabbed it before she could start another swing, "Stop! He's out cold!"

Her muscles were tensed and eyes glazed over against her beat red skin while she stared down at the man bleeding from his nose, staining the perfectly white floor with a small puddle of red. When she looked back at Three, her body relaxed and fear painted her face.

"It's okay, it's done now." He slowly lowered the contraption from above her head and took the weight of it, almost losing his grip not expecting how heavy it was. The machine was at least a few feet long with a barrel that was bigger than any bullet he could think of. It had a long metal stock and what looked like a small arrow tip pointing out the front of the barrel. There were two triggers on it, one on top of the other. The jet-black color made it aggressively stand out against the white of everything else.

She nodded at him once more while her look drifted to the guard again.

Their silence was broken when the second one came bursting through the door trying to quickly put together what had happened. The moment he saw his companion on the ground he lifted his gun at them and pulled the trigger. The arrow shot out with a line attached back to the gun that was pulling out more as it flew.

Three lifted his gun just enough to block it, ricocheting it into the ceiling. When it stabbed in, there was the sound of metal scraping against each other. The guard pulled the second trigger, making the wire taught until it ripped a chunk of drywall out with it. He noticed the little arrow had two metal hooks that came out of the side after it had hit, dragging along the piece of ceiling across the ground.

The woman ran at him while she had the chance and tried to snatch the gun from his arms. Three went to take a step forward to help and immediately crumpled to the ground. If he didn't have the other gun underneath him, he would have thought he was shot through the back of the head.

He clutched his skull and shook his head violently, "Come on, not now!"

There was a slam and loud grunting from the scuffle ahead of him. It took almost all of his willpower to open his eyes and lift his head to see what was happening. The guard had the woman turned around with the wire line wrapped around her neck. She had one of her hands keeping it from completely strangling her in between the line and her skin.

His body waved back and forth struggling to keep him down while he fought to climb to his feet. The image of the two faded together and waved in his eyesight. He hoisted the gun, trying to aim down the sights the best he could with his blurry vision playing tricks on him.

If he hit her, he would never be able to forgive himself.

Three shook his head and was able to have a second of clarity. He pulled the trigger and stumbled backwards to the ground from the recoil. The hole in the ceiling was all he could focus on to try and not throw up, rocking back and forth on his back. There was a loud thud followed by complete silence. The woman's face entered his line of vision and blocked the hole. She kneeled down from behind his head with a look of concern, placing her hand softly on his forehead. Everything went too blurry for him to see so he closed his eyes. A deafening ringing blocked out everything else.

Was this the end? Blacked out on a hospital floor not knowing what was going on?

The room flashed back into view along with the elevator alarm when the woman slapped his cheek.

He moaned and rolled to his side, "What happened?"

She put her arms around his waist trying to help him up, making noises in an attempt speak that there was way to understand. When he was fully upright again, he turned his head to where he'd shot the gun. The woman cupped his cheeks with both hands and forced him to face her. She shook her head and eyed the stairwell through the door. A pit was forming in his stomach and an itch that he couldn't ignore in his mind. When she let go and stepped away from him, his jaw dropped, immediately looking at the scene.

His eyes caught the machine laying on the ground beside them first. They followed the slack wire down the hall. Black sludge pumped though him and everything lost color when he saw it. The spiked end of the line sticking straight up from the guard's eye. They were both motionless and he felt like he couldn't breathe.

It was only going to hurt him. Hurt him enough for the woman to escape. He couldn't have pulled the trigger if he had known any different. But this was different.

His legs took him closer without him wanting to until he was standing directly above the body. They buckled under him, bringing him to his knees. There was nothing more he wanted to do other than look away. His eyes were glued, his mind not wanting to process what had happened. A tear streamed down his face and his chin quivered. He would never not be a murderer from this point on. There was no going back.

The woman's hands found his shoulders and he shuddered to the touch. She knelt down beside him and wrapped her arms around him, pulling his face away and burying it in her shoulder. He allowed himself a few more tears before pushing off of her and standing back up, "Thank you." He looked down at the body one last time, noticing a key card dangling from the guard's belt that he yanked off with a *snap* and shoved in the band of his shorts. "We need to go, no more wasting time."

They left the body behind and walked down the hall, "We should take the stairs. First, I have an idea though." Three jogged to the elevator with the woman close behind. He pulled the emergency stop button out and the alarm ceased immediately, taking the pulsating sensation from Three's head with it. There were only four levels in the building. Three pushed the button for the fourth in hopes that it would send whoever else was looking for them to the top.

They went to the stairwell without waiting for the door to shut. The loud grumble of the elevator calmed his nerves enough for him to feel like he could take a full breath again. The woman slowly opened the door and peeked around at either set of stairs. It's bare unpainted concrete look with black metal railings was a shock to their eyes coming from the white hallway. She stopped him with a hand on his chest and looked around with her eyes slightly squinted.

"What is it?" Three followed her eyes, trying to find what she was looking at.

She looked at him with a hand on one ear tilted upward. He didn't hear anything or anyone moving around. The lack of security and personnel they had seen up to this point made him nervous, wondering what back-alley operation they were taken to.

They moved slowly, looking around the corners as they came. The woman stared at the door with a large red number one painted on it. She was frozen stiff on the bottom step. Three took the lead and cracked the door open, only sticking his head through. Another hallway, this one without any doors.

It couldn't lead to nowhere, could it?

He looked back to the woman and gave her a reassuring head nod to the hall. She took a heavy breath that shook her body and followed him through the door. Three was looking all around and feeling some parts of the wall for a secrete passageway or door that was blending in.

His body instinctively jerked back when they passed a short corridor that led to the elevator. The woman smiled and made a sound that he thought almost sounded like a giggle.

"Everything blends in here. Caught me off guard is all." He looked down the rest of the way trying to make out any other off shoot hallways there were. Stumbling out in the open around a corner without knowing it was the last thing he wanted to do.

As they walked the remainder of the way, he drug his hand along the wall slightly in front of him to make sure he wouldn't cross a corner on one side again. He peeked around the only other corner at the end of the hallway. A short section led to a much bigger open area with two sliding glass doors at the opposite end. Daylight shined through and painted the floor in front of them.

Three didn't realize how strong his longing for the outdoors was until it was in his grasp. Something other than the white abyss they'd traveled through. It was like looking at a painting that he could step into and be enveloped in.

The woman was tired of waiting on him and looked around the corner to the exit. Her eyes widened and body didn't skip a beat. She darted in a full-on sprint for the exit leaving him behind.

"Wait!" She dodged Three's attempt to reach out and grab her. He panicked and trailed behind her the best that he could. When they neared where the hallway opened up to the main lobby, he saw them. A guard on either side waiting to ambush whoever passed the threshold.

The woman was drunk on freedom and didn't notice, or didn't care enough to stop. One of the guards clotheslined her with a baton, sending her crashing to her back from a full sprint. Three changed course and slammed the second guard with his shoulder as hard as he could before he noticed him coming.

He grabbed the baton the guard dropped on his way down and turned to the first one. The other guard was already halfway through a swing at his head by the time he was in his vision. Three threw an arm up to take the hit and was knocked down to his knees.

He could now barely hold up the baton in his right hand, swinging wildly at anything he could damage. A loud groan came from the guard as his knee buckled from the hit. The woman grabbed around his waist and threw him to the ground on the other side of her. She snatched the baton from Three and batted the guard in the head before he could fully try to get back up.

The other guard was up and punched Three in the back of the head while his eyes were trained on the woman. The blow had him on his stomach, propped up by his elbows with speckled stars clouding his vision. There was a scuffle behind him that was looping in and out of his hearing. He wasn't able to rid himself of the stars the first few head shakes, pulsing them brighter with anxiety. The moment his knees found the strength to prop up his lower half, he was kicked to his back from the side.

The guard got on top on him and wrapped his hands around his throat, "You still feel strong, tough guy?"

Three gasped for air, frantically darting his eyes around as much of the room as he could to find some hope of survival.

"That is quite enough." He felt Stintz's voice force its way into his ears like an uninvited guest barging through the front door. The guard's grip loosened without fully letting go. "If you have forgotten, we need both of them alive."

The guard was staring down into Three's eyes, "You said you could do it with one."

Stintz quietly clicked his tongue a few times, "You don't seem to understand the word, *can*. I *can* do it, like I *can* have you and your team removed from this detail and placed on street surveillance. Much like that though, it would make my life harder than it needs to be."

He grunted and released Three, standing back up and taking a few paces back. Stintz hovered over with his hands behind his back, "Gave us quite the scare, didn't you?" Three was still trying to catch his breath while Stintz's almost black eyes examined him up and down. "Get them both up."

The two guards drug them to their feet and stood in front of them waiting for orders. Stintz leaned his head in towards Three, examining his face, looking for something, "Where would you have run to, I wonder."

The doctor lingered for a few seconds. Three didn't know if he was expecting an actual answer or if he reveled in making people uncomfortable. He gave up and turned to walk down the hall to the elevator.

Three shared a look with the woman. Her eyes dotted to the glass doors and he nodded slightly. He kicked his guard in the crotch, toppling him to the ground. Almost in unison, the woman punched the guard in front of her in the throat. Three grabbed the card from his shorts and made a break for the door. A beeping sound chirped when he placed the card on the reader and the doors slid open. Fresh air hit him for the first time since he woke up and filled his body with hope. The woman passed him out the doors and he broke into a sprint trying to catch up to her.

Black pavement carved up the bottom of his bare feet. A tree line was on the other end of the large parking lot that the woman was headed for. Nothing could break his pure joy in this moment. Feeling the sun on his skin and the breeze through his hair took his mind off of the fact that they were still running for their lives.

He didn't care. They'd made it.

He reached the halfway point when a sharp pain surged from his upper back. He yelled out and felt something yank him off his feet. From the ground, he looked back and saw the guard from the second floor that the woman had bashed with the weapon. His nose and mouth were still dripping blood but he had a smile on his face. The weapons line draped over the hot pavement and connected straight to Three's back.

He reached back and felt the hook buried in his skin.

The woman stopped and whipped her head around to see what was going on. When they locked eyes, the wire tightened and began dragging him across the pavement at a torturously slow pace.

Chapter 4

Three yelped helplessly. His hands were flailing back and forth in a hopeless attempt to grab the wire like it would make a difference. Increasing pain surged from his stretching skin and overthrew his senses.

The woman froze as he was being dragged off. Her mind ping ponged back and forth from breaking for the woods and trying to help him. Another scream from Three getting stuck on a parking curb broke her division and moved her legs for her. She shoved him from the curb to stop the barb from ripping the better part of his upper back off.

The man holding the other end of the machine was struggling to keep it in his hands and started shifting sideways to a column that held up the outside entryway. The woman looked at Three sliding away from her and then back to the man who was starting to wind the cord around the column.

She wasn't going to get the barb out. There was no way to sever the metal cable. Only one option came to her before it would be too late.

The guard was halfway to a full loop around the column by the time she had gotten between him and Three. Her hands wrapped around the cable and feet dug in the pavement as she yanked with everything she had. The guard flopped to the ground while the machine swung from his grip and arced around the column. The two other guards jumped and scrambled to get their hands on it.

"Get up! Now!" She pulled the machine far enough away from their grip to feel the slightest bit of safety and slung the limp cord over her shoulder.

Three no longer felt in control of his movements. Everything blurred together. His body carried him up and was running beside the woman with the machine skidding across the lot behind them before he could process anything that was happening.

Two of the three guards were tripping over themselves in an attempt to catch up to the tumbling heap of metal. It bounced off another parking curb and knocked something loose enough on the second hit back down to break free from the cable.

The woman stumbled and almost fell over from the lost weight. When she recomposed herself, she easily passed Three and took the front. The two guards stopped at the broken machine, picking it up and glaring at the two, giving up on the increasing distance between them.

Three focused on Stintz for a second before he turned back toward the woods. The doctor didn't look phased or even mad at what was taking place. He just glanced across at the guards bringing back the broken machine for a moment before he turned his eyes to meet Three's. With a crooked smile that sent shudders up his spine, the doctor slowly waved goodbye. Almost as if saying farewell to an old friend who had just come over for a visit. Someone he was planning on seeing again. Maybe he was.

They continued running and as the intensity of the situation started to decrease, he noticed how cut up his feet were getting from running bare foot on pavement. The sting of his eye reminded him of the damage he sustained getting to this point. A slight ringing through his head was surfacing, followed by the almost migraine level headache. They needed to get somewhere safe that he could rest before long, the fading adrenaline could not keep him going forever.

The soft cool feel of the grass was more than welcoming as they left the hard hot pavement behind. Even though sticks and pebbles berated his feet with almost every step, it was still an upgrade from the parking lot.

They ran deeper and deeper into the woods. No direction, no sense of where they were going or how far civilization was. It felt like they had been running for an hour and Three was about to collapse from exhaustion. He tried to push on, fearful that the woman would leave him behind. He couldn't handle the thought of being alone right now. He was terrified of slipping into madness or collapsing in his turmoil without someone there beside him. Regardless of his fears, it wasn't enough to keep him going.

"I can't," was all he could muster out as he slowed to a stop, slamming his hands on his knees. He started gasping heavily, unable to catch his breath.

To his joy, the woman stopped as well. She fell to her knees with both of her hands on a nearby tree, almost whistling as she tried to breathe through the small parting she had in her lips. Three started to catch his breath and he noticed the woman still wheezing heavily through her nose as her body started to shake slightly.

She fell to the ground and rolled on her back, clutching her neck. Three ran up to her and put his hand under her head, hovering over her on his knees. The panic in her face was translated through her piercing stare and he immediately understood the problem.

"Just try and focus your breathing through your nose. I know it may feel like you're going to suffocate, but I promise you that I won't let that happen." He didn't know what he would be able to do to keep that promise.

Reassurance seemed to calm her, if only a little bit, and help her focus on controlling her breathing.

He was relieved when she started falling into a rhythm. He had said the words with no plan and was thankful he didn't need to pull one out of thin air. Would he have ripped her mouth open? That might help her breathing but create a whole new slew of problems. What he would give to have grabbed a loose scalpel from somewhere on his way out.

He was unconsciously stroking her hair as she started to calm down and return to normal breathing. Almost like muscle memory had taken over for a moment, or his subconscious thought it was a good decision without informing him.

She pushed his hand off her head gently as she finally began to breathe normally enough to sit up. Her back lay against the tree as she tiredly gave him a weak thumbs up.

Three laid down in the grass, taking in this moment of minor relaxation. He looked up to the sky but could only make out bits and pieces of it through the tree canopy. Grass tickled his skin and gave him a feeling he could only describe as faint familiarity. Had he spent all his time outside in the past? Or maybe he just vacationed in the woods and was welcoming a happy association that had prevailed through the cocktail of drugs.

He sat up and looked at the woman who was staring blankly further into the woods. He didn't know what it was, but there was a soft warm feeling that enveloped him while he looked at her. She did save his life back there a few times. Her head turned his way with a concerned look. He broke their eye contact, realizing how long he was just staring.

"I'm sorry, I wasn't staring at you. I mean I was, but I wasn't staring at you like that you know?" He stumbled over his words getting flustered.

Her look seemed to change from concern to embarrassment.

"Not that I wouldn't want to look at you like that, but I was just zoning out in that direction. I mean, I don't mean that in a weird way I just." Three could feel the panicked rush of how weird this all had to be sounding to her. What was wrong with him? They had just survived through a string of horrible events, and he couldn't even speak like a normal person to her? He must not have been any sort of Casanova in his previous life.

He looked down with his tail tucked between his legs, "I'm sorry"

The woman chuckled and gave him a slight small smile while rolling her eyes.

At least she didn't think he made this moment as painfully awkward as he did. He wished he had started out their first conversation any other way. They should be forming some sort of survival strategy instead of laughing at his inability to talk.

She walked the few paces to him on her knees and waved her finger in a circle for him to turn around. Her hands gently pushed on his skin around the rod jetting from his back. There was a real concern that his teeth were going to break from how hard he was clenching trying to let her do whatever it was she needed to do.

The woman got up and grabbed a stick and wrote "Pain" in the dirt in front of him with it. She handed it to him and he looked at her puzzled. She sighed and snatched the stick back and opened his mouth, shoving it in sideways for him to bite down on. Sweat formed on his head in anticipation. She positioned herself back behind him and tapped his shoulder a couple times.

The pain surged, harder than when he'd been stuck with it the first time. He couldn't tell what she was doing but it wasn't gentle. Clenching snapped the stick in his mouth on either side and he tried his best to channel his screaming into to quieter grunts. There was a hard yank and he could feel it slide out of his back.

He was leaned over and shaking, spiting what was left of the stick on the ground. The woman sat him up and showed him the small metal rod that now had two hooks jetting out of either side. She pushed on them to show how they telescoped back in, almost looking intrigued before tossing it aside and leaning back against the tree.

He caught his breath and managed to sit back up, "Do you remember your name?"

She looked puzzled for a moment, as if searching the memory banks of her brain, then shook her head while her eyes slowly fell to the ground.

"I don't either." He swallowed a hard lump in his throat, "In fact, I don't remember anything before waking up on that table just a few hours ago. They took everything from me, and I don't even know why. Or what they took."

His voice started to shake as he filled up with a mixture of loss and grief about his lost time. He hoped this was just a nightmare that he would eventually wake up from, lying in a warm bed under some thick comfy blankets. A house to himself to welcome the morning, or maybe even a family.

Family. The thought had not crossed his mind until now. What if he did have a family that was still out there, waiting for him to come home from some errand he was abducted during? Maybe trying to find him or fighting their way to the lab he had just ran from. The thoughts were enough to steam his brain and make him start sweating again. He desperately pushed everything down and tried to focus on something, anything else, before he was pushed over the edge.

He looked back to the woman, who was staring at a small patch of sky where the branches parted, "Well, I need to be able to call you something if we're going to be in this same boat for a while." There was a pause, "What do you want your name to be? We get to choose whatever we want now. Anything you want to be called."

"Hmmmm" she mumbled with a blank stare.

After a few minutes, she picked up a nearby stick and started writing something in the dirt. She looked at him and pointed down at it.

Three crawled over on his hands and knees to see her new name, very curious as to what she thought of and if it would give any insight to the person she really was. He looked in the dirt and said it out loud, "Dahlia. I like it. How did you come up with that?"

She pointed to a nearby dandelion with a small smile.

"It's a type of flower?"

Dahlia nodded. He wondered if she was a gardener or a florist before all of this and how much she could remember about the world. The image of her tending to flowers inside a small shop in the middle of a bustling town made him smile.

Dahlia pointed to Three, indicating his turn for a new name. He thought about what he knew or facts he'd learned in his short time to give him any indication of the man he was. The thoughts all swirled together in one big melting pot of diluted information, making it impossible for him to discern one from another. The more he thought, the more his headache pounded. He quickly gave up trying to force his memories back, noticing the increase in pain.

He pushed around a stick in the dirt aimlessly, "I want my name to be me, but I can't think of anything me is."

Dahlia reached over and stuck her finger out, placing it on his forehead. She looked at him and shook her head, moving her finger to his heart and staring at him, hoping he could make sense of what she was attempting to say.

"I'm thinking too hard about this, aren't I?"

She formed a smile and started nodding her head.

What did he feel was right? With all the horrible feelings he had been plagued with, he had not even considered using his emotions to give him an indication of what was normal. He decided to try and calm his head as much as possible and just be open to what would come.

"Reed." It left his mouth before he could even think as to why. The moment he spoke the word, a foggy memory pushed its way through to the top of his mind. A vision of a pond with large reeds protruding out of the water's surface on a bright sunny day. He wanted nothing more than for the memory to continue, like a movie he was seeing for the first time, but a flash was all he was given.

Dahlia stared at him for a moment with an inquisitive look on her face that quickly turned into a small smile as she extended her hand out. He took the invitation and grabbed her hand shaking it up and down in a calm fashion.

"I remembered something." He smiled, "A pond came to mind, full of reeds on a nice day. It seemed very peaceful. I don't know if it was a memory, or just something nice that popped into my head. Whichever one, I'd like to go there someday."

Dahlia nodded in agreement, sustaining the smile from earlier for another moment. She let go of his hand and looked at the woods with a determination. She Pointed at her wrist as if to an imaginary watch, and then pointed deeper into the woods. Reed nodded as they both gathered their strength and rose to their feet.

Reed put a hand on her arm, "I think we should walk now. I haven't heard any noise of vehicles or people starting to chase us and I don't want you to have to worry about struggling to breathe."

Dahlia led the way, giving him a reluctant nod as they started to walk. Reed knew she couldn't know where she was going any more than he did, but he trusted her for some reason. There was something about her that he couldn't place. It was as if there was a warming aura around her that made him feel a little bit safe.

After a couple hours of walking through the woods in complete silence, Reed saw something he couldn't explain. A black figure shot out from behind one tree to another, concealing itself again. He stopped dead in his tracks, shock taking over his body.

"What the fuck was that?" his voice was soft and quiet.

Dahlia looked back at him with concern and then over to the tree he was staring at.

"I saw something." He motioned his head to the tree, "It was like a tall black figure, it was so fast I couldn't tell exactly."

Dahlia looked more confused than frightened and moved toward the tree in question. Before he could beckon her to stop, she had reached it and whipped around the trunk. She shrugged and gave Reed an inquisitive yet slightly angry look.

There was something, he was sure of it. He saw it clear as day shoot from one tree to another right in front of his face. He couldn't have imagined it, could he? It seemed so real; although he couldn't even make out what *it* was. The very real suggestion that his mind was slipping was a hard pill to swallow. If he couldn't trust his own brain, then how could he possibly trust anything else? Or even worse, how could Dahlia trust him. Back at the lab they were forced on each other. No choice or time to think about the matter of trusting this total stranger. But now. Now she could leave him at any moment. At any point if she thought he was unstable or wouldn't be worth the trouble, she could just leave.

He needed her. He knew it. She was in much better condition than he was and showed no signs of slipping. His own body was just a stone's throw from being a wreck at this moment, and everything ached. With all this in mind, he decided he needed to hide any further cracks from her, unless he was certain it was real. He dreaded his condition getting worse.

"Never mind." He shook his head, "I must just be exhausted, my mind playing tricks on me."

His words sounded unconvincing, and it seemed as though Dhalia thought the same. She rested her arms by her side and gave him a doubtful look as she turned to keep walking.

For the next few hours, they continued in silence. Reed's head was aching, and his emotions were trying to bubble up to find any escape route out. He was struggling to keep it together. It seemed that the more time he had inside his own head the more it felt like a prison. Vicious images of the guard he had killed in the lab kept flashing through his consciousness, bringing mountains of guilt and horror crashing through him. He kept everything locked in. A straight face looking forward.

It started to get dark, and hunger was beginning to find them. Reed could hear Dahlias stomach growling over the rustling of the trees. His own stomach had been feeling empty for quite some time. His mouth felt like a desert with the lack of water he'd had. He feared they may have escaped just to die in the woods, having helped no one in the process.

They were climbing a small hill as he was thinking about this. In the low light of twilight, Dahlia tripped over something at the crest of the hill. She grabbed Reed's arm for balance but merely dragged him with her. They tumbled down the slight hill on the other side and came crashing to a halt in a small ditch.

Reed stood up and helped Dahlia to her feet, they looked around to see where they had landed and were filled with a mixture of joy and fear as they looked at paved road stretching on for miles.

Chapter 5

The joy of finding a way out of the woods was quickly out done with all the "what-if's" pilling in his head.

"Get back in the woods!" He yelled as he started to climb back up the steep hill behind him.

Dahlia grabbed his arm and yanked him back into the ditch. He fell onto his butt and looked up at her, worried about someone passing by. She held his arm tight and pointed down the road.

He tugged away from her, unable to escape her grip, "What if someone from the lab drives down and spots us? What if a random person decides to report two half naked people dirty and beaten to the authorities? What if they take us back? I can't risk that!"

She gave the back of his head a good smack and pointed down the road again with an angry look.

He squeezed her arm with his free hand and looked in her eyes, "I know we need to find some sort of civilization, but I just think it's too dangerous."

Dahlia rolled her eyes and released his arm. She started walking down the road leaving Reed in the ditch.

He stared blankly at her; she's really not going to listen to me. There's got to be some way we can meet in the middle.

"The tree line!" he blurted out. Dahlia stopped and turned around with one eyebrow arched.

"We can walk along the road like you want, just please, let's do it in the tree line out of direct sight, just in case."

Dahlia looked frustrated at the inconvenience and stared at him for a moment in silence.

He was sitting on his legs looking up to her, "Please, I can't imagine having anything happen to either of us. At least until we find somewhere to lay low for a while."

She sighed and motioned her arms, beckoning for him to start up the hill.

Back in the tree line, they started their walk, hopefully toward some civilization. Preferably some civilization with a burger place. Reed could not take his mind off the thought something to eat. As visions of food flooded his brain, he started to notice something. Even though he could think of a vast array of different foods he thought he knew he liked; he couldn't remember how any of them tasted. A cruel joke while his stomach churned in empty pain.

I suppose I'll have to try all the food again. There are worse tasks in the world to have. Like walking bare foot in the woods for who knows how long.

As time passed on, the light started to completely fade away with the last remnants of the sunset leaving the sky. Just as it got to the point of complete darkness, Reed noticed the road. The street lines lit up as if there were lightbulbs built into the paint. It created enough light to illuminate the whole road and brighten up the forest so they could see where they were walking.

The complete lack of traffic on the road got Reed wondering about things. They had been walking for quite some time now and not a single car had passed them, or even been heard in the distance. Was this just a very unused road that only led to the lab? Even if that were the case, where was the lab security team? Had they just given up and let us go live our lives? The more time passed the more puzzled Reed was by it all, it didn't seem to make any sense.

His thoughts were interrupted when he heard a high pitched, excited sound coming from Dahlia as she grabbed his arm and pointed ahead. Reed spent so much of the walk looking downward, lost in thought, he did not notice the glow of lights that appeared in the distance.

At first sight, his mind raced, jumping to the conclusion of a car headed their way. He saw the lights weren't moving and were placed higher in the air upon further inspection. It had to be some sort of billboard or lit up sign stretched high up for everyone to see.

"A town, finally." His tone was weary, but excited. "Still a few more miles but I'm sure they have food and water"

Dahlia was nodding her head furiously while holding a smile that lit up her whole face. She started to pick up the pace with the thought of something to eat and maybe even a place to rest on the horizon. Reed was struggling to keep up, his body felt heavier as time moved on. The swelling on his face was reaching a high point and his head was still throbbing on and off. He barely managed to keep his emotions in check and started to lose track of what he was even feeling anymore. The only thought that kept him going through all of this was the fact that he couldn't let Dahlia see how fragile he was.

Dahlia was moving faster the closer they got to the town, almost jogging at times. Reed did his best to follow along, but she was starting to lose him in her excitement. She turned back and saw the large gap that emerged between them and came to an immediate stop. Reed slowly caught up and fell to his knees when he reached her. He was ashamed he couldn't keep up.

Dahlia crouched on one knee in front of him and put her hand on his shoulder while he struggled to catch his breath. The moment she touched him he could feel her calming presence start to deteriorate his worries. Maybe she did care enough about him that she wouldn't leave him behind. He could feel his connection to her growing, which worried him a bit. A part of him wanted to keep her at arm's length just in case something changed. It was too strong and too fast. They'd barely spoken to each other, technically she hadn't even said a word!

Reed was catching his breath and looked up to her. She stared directly into his eyes, just a foot from his face. It was the look of a concerned friend, which set his mind at ease.

"I'm okay." He muttered through labored breaths. "I just need a few seconds to catch my breath and I'll be fine."

His words did little to change Dahlia's concern.

Reed stood back up before returning to a normal breathing rate, determined to push on. Dahlia took her hand off his shoulder and gave him a thumbs up with a questioning look.

"I'm good," He nodded, "we're almost there and then we can find some food and water."

They continued their walk, only now he noticed that dahlia had returned to a much slower pace. The gesture warmed Reed's heart but did little to tamper his guilt.

It took a couple more hours of walking at their reduced pace to reach the town. They were greeted by what looked more like an oversized road stop than an actual town. There was a small gas station with neon lights rimming the outlines of the pumps. They glowed with a bright blue shimmer that was the same color as the paint. The roof that dawned over the pumps was painted shiny red with more neon lining its rims. A few vending machines with matching blue lights filled the spaces between pumps. The large sign the two had seen in the distance was extended high above the roof and lit up like a tv screen. It had bold black lettering saying "LAST GAS UNTIL HARRION" centered in the screen atop a vibrant blue backdrop.

Two stores lined the road down from the pumps. They both looked like they were covered in the same bright red paint job as the roof of the station. Every corner and edge of the buildings were rounded out. Large windows encompassed by chrome tubes took up most of the wall, the brightness of the store lights shining outward. Reed was delighted by the fact that the only neon he could see on those buildings was a lonely "open" sign above one of the doors.

An unsettling silence shrouded the whole station, only the buzz of the neon lights and the slight rustling of trees could be heard. The forest lined the entire station and continued as far as their eyes could see, following the road. A very distinct line in the grass cut the woods a few feet short of the buildings and road line, separating it from the short, manicured grass on the other side. The perfectly shaped buildings and lawn seemed so unnatural against the backdrop of unkempt, wild woods.

The two slowly walked out the woods and past the gas pumps, making their way to the storefront. Reed took the lead and put his hand out behind him just before reaching the first set of windows, signaling dahlia to stop. He peered his face over the windows edge enough for one of his eyes to see inside. To his surprise, there was not a single person in the store. Not even one employee managing the front. The isles upon isles of food immediately drew his attention away and melted his curiosity about it.

Tall Shelves filled with packages and snacks perfectly aligned and in place took up three quarters of the store. The remaining shelves had small trinkets next to household amenities and car supplies from top to bottom. A small clothing section could be seen over the shelves in the opposite corner. In the back of the store, he could see rows of coolers filled with all sorts of drinks of every color. Large bottles of water on the bottom rack of the cooler drew his attention. The dryness in his mouth immediately felt much more intense at the sight of them.

He removed his head from the window and turned back to Dahlia, who was waiting in excited anticipation.

"It's weird," He looked around slowly, "I don't see anybody in the store. In fact, the whole place looks completely abandoned yet still clean and kept up."

Dahlia looked unconcerned about how many people there were, her stomach still growling loudly. She pointed to it with her expression changing to frustration.

"We don't have any money." He shrugged, "We can't risk getting in trouble or bringing attention to ourselves. I'm as hungry as you but we need to think of a smarter way about this."

Reed's hunger was starting to drown out his own words. He wasn't a thief, at least he didn't think he was. What other choice did he have? Was his position to starve to death in the woods or abandon all his morals?

The guard from the lab clawed his way back into the front of his thoughts. He had killed a man earlier that day to escape but wouldn't steal to survive? No, he told himself that was self-defense and that's how he needed it to stay. If he had not done what he did then both of them would have been harmed, or even killed. He was a good man put in a bad situation. Or was he a bad man desperately trying to convince himself the opposite? He was trapped in this tug of war of morals.

He could feel his anxieties starting to rise, the hard squeezing around his heart. He started to heat up, sweat forming on his head. The struggle to keep himself calm in front of Dahlia was slipping. This entire time his eyes were fixated on the ground. He was sure she was staring at him, judging him. He knew this silent struggle he was tormented by had gone on long enough to create a lingering awkward silence. He had to say something to her. He pulled his head up, masking his emotions as much as possible. He was shocked seeing that Dahlia wasn't even standing next to him anymore.

She had become tired of waiting for a plan apparently. Reed stood silently, wondering what she was up to as she walked toward the vending machines. Did she know some sort of trick to override them and get food out?

Dahlia approached the machine and stared at the snacks and drinks, only a pane of glass separating them. She looked around the machine before grabbing one of the pump handles, removing it from the pump. Before Reed could make sense of anything, Dahlia slammed the nozzle in a jabbing motion against the glass sending large cracks throughout.

Reed's eyes widened. He screamed without meaning to, "What are you doing?!"

Dahlia paid no attention to Reed and continued to slam the glass over and over again, cracking it a little more with each blow. Reed rushed to her, his heart in physical pain from worry. Dahlia secured her footing to give one last heavy blow and thrusted the nozzle into the glass with all her force, shattering it into hundreds of small shards. She tossed the pump nozzle aside and started frantically grabbing anything she could carry.

Reed impulsively followed her lead and grabbed drinks and snacks when he reached the machine as well. With arms full of plastic bags and bottles, she started running back to the woods. Without much choice, Reed followed behind her. They ran through the forest a few hundred feet before stopping. Dahlia dropped all she had on the ground and fell to her knees, struggling to breathe through her nose again.

Reed dropped everything except for a bottle of some bright green drink. The label was impossible to read with the dark of the night now fully upon them. He untwisted the bottle cap and took a large gulp. An intense fruity taste mixed with strong hints of lime assaulted his taste buds. The unexpected carbonation that hit the back of his throat was an unwelcome surprise. He immediately started coughing and spilling the drink everywhere.

Reed struggled to catch his breath, dropping the bottle entirely and grabbing his knees with both hands. He could feel the stress of not being able to breathe building on his already high anxiety. He slowly started to get a few strong breaths but felt a weird tingling feeling throughout his skin. The feeling grew along with white rims around his vision. Panic rose and the feeling of pins and needles spread throughout his brain. He quickly felt woozy and lost his balance. His legs gave out and he crashed to the ground, slamming his head on the root of a tree. As the white around his eyesight started to close in, the feeling in his body was phasing out. It quickly consumed his entire vision until he saw nothing but the white glow as his body surrendered and drifted off.

Chapter 6

Reed woke up in a haze, the glow of the sun coming over the horizon caressed his face. His vision was still a little blurry and body was taking its time to wake up. He noticed his head was resting on something soft and smooth. He rolled it over to the other side and saw that Dahlia was leaning against a tree with his head on her lap. A brief, unexpected moment of warmth after his collapse the night before.

His comfort was cut short at the sight of blood stains littering the pure white of Dahlias top.

"What happened?" Reed blurted loudly, struggling to get upright

Dahlia shot awake, wide eyed and frazzled, "What? What? Oh. I was hungry."

Her voice was soft and a bit hoarse, but it brought the same calming presence to him as when they touched. He was shocked to hear her speak. His sight recentered and he saw what she was forced to do to rid herself of hunger. A large red stained shard of glass was sitting in the grass next to her. Her mouth was scabbed up from top to bottom, puffy and swollen. Empty bags of various chips and candy bars were strewn all over where they had laid for the night. Two water bottles were at her side, one unopened and one with only a sip left.

"Don't worry, it only hurts way more than it looks." She smiled weakly.

"I'm sorry you had to do that." He examined it more without getting closer, "It looks horrible."

Her smile faded, "Thanks, you're too kind."

"I mean, it looks painful is all. Not that you look horrible. I think you pull it off great." Reed wondered why he apparently couldn't say anything resembling normal.

She nodded and raised her eyebrows at him for a second, "I'm sure."

She grabbed the unopened water bottle and extended it out to him, "Might do you better than that Lime Captain Fizz you tried to chug down last night."

Reed grabbed the bottle and twisted the top off without question. He started chugging it and instantly felt hugely reinvigorated. He tilted it back down and wiped his mouth, "Is there any food left?"

"Course, you wouldn't think I'd eat it all would you?" Dahlia handed him a bag of chips from her other side, "What happened to you last night anyway?"

Reed grabbed the bag of chips and started shoving handfuls into his mouth thinking about what he could tell her. He choked down a wad of chips large enough to hurt his throat on the way down, "I don't really know. I must have just been completely exhausted, or maybe some drugs they gave me at the lab were still making their way through." He looked down before stuffing his face with more snacks, "Thanks for not abandoning me"

"You saved me, it wouldn't be right to toss you aside at the first sign of trouble." She paused for a moment, "Plus, it got a little chilly last night and your fever was a decent blanket."

Reed chuckled and was appreciative of her no matter what the reason.

"No one came last night either." she looked in the direction of the station, "After I broke into the vending machine I mean. At least I didn't hear anything or see any lights."

He thought for sure there would be some sort of authorities that showed up after that fiasco. Where was everyone? Were they just that far in the middle of nowhere that people didn't even bother to check on things? "I guess that's a blessing for us."

"Yeah, I was thinking we should get some new clothes from that little store before we try to head anywhere else." The lack of response apparently giving her the green light for more criminal activity, "If we do see some people, it'll be pretty hard to blend in half naked, covered in blood and dirt."

"As much as I don't want to, I think you're right." Reed swallowed hard, "Some food for the road too if we're going to be taking things anyway."

Dahlia stared through him, "Hey, we're taking from some corporation to survive. Not robbing people in the streets. I don't think they'll miss the profits off some pants and a little food."

"I know, I know." He threw his hands up, "I just don't know who I am right now, and I want to convince myself I was a good person."

Dahlia's demeanor changed, reverting to a more comforting state, "It doesn't matter who you were, or who either of us were. Once we find a way to disappear permanently, we can be whoever we want to be. But first, we have to survive long enough to figure that out."

He understood what she was trying to tell him and was comforted by the way she seemed to imply them sticking together through all of this, but he couldn't force himself to stop caring about what his past could have been. What he could have done, either of them could have done, to deserve to end up in that lab. He took a minute to choke down the rest of the bag of chips and polish off his water while thinking about it.

"I guess let's do this." He got to his feet and extended a hand out to Dahlia.

She let him help her up, "You're sure you are going to be alright?" She dusted off the loose dirt from her legs.

He took a hefty lung full of air, "Yeah, I feel a lot better after getting some rest."

They left for the edge of the woods again. Right before Reed was about to cross the threshold onto the manicured grass, they heard a truck coming from down the road.

Reed froze in his tracks and extended his arm out, blocking Dahlia from continuing.

"Shhh! get down, quickly!" Reed whispered loudly.

They both took a step back and laid on their stomachs in the tall grass.

A large vehicle puffing out exhaust fumes with huge circular brushes attached to the bottom drove up quickly to a couple feet before the first store. It stopped and made a loud mechanical sound of shifting gears and moving parts as the brushes touched down to the street. The scrapping of the brushes on the pavement were accompanied by a loudspeaker which started to blare out advertisements for various things they couldn't quite make out yet while the truck slowly made its way down the road. When it reached the edge of the first store, two huge hose nozzles stuck out of the side. Soap and water blasted the storefront in a sweeping motion from top to bottom as it continued.

Reed nudged Dahlia, "I don't see any spot for a driver on that thing, do you?"

"Not unless they're hiding in the back."

They both hopped up and cautiously crossed the forest line. They stood there for a few minutes as the truck trundled down the small gas stop, waiting for it to be done with its route. The entire time, it continued blaring random advertisements.

"Come to Best Cut Barber Shop for the cleanest cut in Harrion, guaranteed satisfaction or your money back! Located on the corner of Fourth Avenue and Dane street"

"Karies Custards is the number one place for doughnuts in all of Harrion, delicious treats for the whole family! Located on Tenth Ave, just between Bodel and Pickard street. Come get yours today!"

The cleaning vehicle reached the gas pumps and continued to douse everything with the soap and water spray, paying no attention to the broken vending machine. The water stream was so powerful that it ripped apart the bags and bottles of snacks that they'd left. Once it reached the end of the station it stopped again to retract its sweepers back up and sped off down the road.

Reed watched it shrink in the distance, picking up speed away from them, "Well, this place obviously isn't monitored if it's just going to blast a crime scene with water, so I think we're good to go."

They started their walk to the store, his nerves still chiming in with anticipation as they approached. With the sun shining down now, he noticed the second store's windows were covered up with plywood and the door was chained shut. He hadn't seen that in the darkness of twilight from the night before and it gave him an eerie feeling.

They reached the door and as Reed pushed open the chrome handle, a speaker perked up with a staticky sounding woman's voice, *"Welcome to the last gas!"*

He couldn't imagine how annoying that would get if the store ever got busy, after just one time he wanted to rip the speakers down. Once inside they were immediately in front of a large silver archway with counters on both sides starting at the entrance, corralling them to go through. Cautiously, Reed and Dahlia stepped through the archway and onto the store floor. The moment they did they heard the speaker kick back on with the same crackling tone as before.

"Facial scans show no link to any known bank in the Last Gas family of banks. Please exit the store and come back when you have opened an account within the Last Gas approved list of banks. Any attempt at leaving the store with unauthorized purchases will lead to notifying the authorities."

The static faded as the voice cut out, leaving them in dead silence, blankly staring at each other. Before Reed could start spouting his feelings of caution, Dhalia spoke up, cutting him off quickly, "I know that's a little concerning but think about it. I smashed through a glass vending machine, and no one showed up. I don't think anyone is coming for a few missing items, and even if they do, we can be gone into the woods before they could possibly get here."

Reed's whole being was telling him not to chance it. He wanted to run out of that store as fast as he could and head down the road to wherever the next town or city was and figure out something from there. He also wanted to trust her. For her to know that he trusted her. He knew that trust was a choice he had to make and that they wouldn't get anywhere without it.

"Let's just get what we need and get out of here." Reed walked down the aisle of home goods and trinkets while Dahlia walked down the one with food. Most of what he saw at first was a random assortment of chemicals and cleaners beside rows of different types of motor oil and coolant. He spotted some mild pain relievers on the bottom row of the shelf. His head and face were still aching. The box was ripped open revealing a white bottle inside before he could think twice about it. Twisting off the top, he popped four into his mouth and choked them down hoping for some relief to kick in soon. He continued to shuffle through the shelves finding some small tubes of antibiotic cream and a couple of one-use ice packs.

Dahlia hadn't made a peep since he'd been shuffling through and he figured he should probably check on her. He peered over the aisles looking for any indication but didn't see anything.

"Dahlia?" Reed called loudly enough to be heard throughout the store.

"I'm back here, just one minute."

Her voice came from the back corner by where the clothes section was. Reed walked over and saw two dressing rooms, one with the red occupied indicator flipped over. He saw some blue jeans sitting on a shelf that looked about his size and started to put them on over his white spandex shorts. Without much to choose from he grabbed a plane bright green shirt with no logos or writing on it and a pair of blue sneakers with orange laces that were slightly too big for his feet.

The lock on the fitting room clicked and Dahlia walked out. A bright purple fitted dress was wrapped around her with small ruffles on the bottom and an oversized purple bow on a strap crossing her waist. Without many other options, she had on a black pair of sneakers that stood out against her more elegant looking dress.

Reed was stunned at the difference one dress could make. He thought she was absolutely stunning as she stepped out. Her new look had his nerves running and he could feel his stomach becoming warm and uneasy just at the sight of her.

"You look amazing." His mouth was hanging open and eyes locked on to her.

She blushed and looked down with a shy smile, "Aww, thank you." She took a step his way, "I know this isn't practical and I can't leave here in it, but I just wanted to see how I would look if we were just going for a trip on the town instead of running for our lives."

Reed just continued to look at her for a period to soak up every last second of her beauty.

She looked at the ground, "It's stupid, I know. I'll change."

He shook his head and stepped closer to her, "No, no. It's not stupid, I get it. If I looked even half as good as you, I would want to flaunt it for at least a minute myself."

Her smile perked back up, "You're not so bad yourself." She looked up at him, "I might have even considered talking to you if we happened to bump into each other before all this."

Reed chuckled and held up the supplies in his hand, "I found some antibiotic ointment. I figured you could use it for your lips, might help them heal a little faster."

She paused and touched her lips gently like she had forgotten about their puffy scabbed up condition. "Thank you, that's very thoughtful." Her eyes dropped, a little ashamed.

She swiped a pair of jeans off the shelf and grabbed a purple short sleeve shirt with a matching purple jacket on her way back to the changing room. Reed felt like he had done something wrong reminding her about her lips. He didn't care about them at all. He hardly even noticed them when he looked at her. Her face was brand new to him still, perfect in its own flawed way.

Reed started rummaging through the drink and food aisle, tearing into some jerky and water while he waited. A rack of reusable bags with the "Last Gas Stop" logo striped across the side caught his eye as he wandered through. He Grabbed a bag off the rack and started filling it with chips, jerky, water, and other assorted snacks.

A slight, high pitched, ringing noise was chiming in his ear. He looked up above the aisle to quickly scan the room but saw nothing. The noise sounded like it was coming from outside. Reed began walking toward the front of the store to look out the windows. He swept the road with his eyes and didn't notice anything out of the ordinary, calming his nerves.

Just as he went to turn away from the window, he spotted a man in the same guard uniform from the lab staring straight at him with blood running from his eye socket. He let out an audible gasp and fell to the floor, flinging snacks everywhere. He struggled in a mixture of trying to get back to his feet and shuffling backwards away from the window. When he peered over the windowsill back to the street the guard had vanished. The ringing in his ear intensified while his skin started crawling.

Dahlia came rushing out of the changing room, hearing the commotion, "What is it?! Are you okay?" She called loudly, half-panicked.

"Yeah, yeah. No, I'm okay. I just slipped and fell. It caught me off guard." Reed forced himself from the window. For once, he was actually able to calm himself down before going over the edge.

She took a deep breath in, "You scared the shit out of me. I thought you fainted again or something."

"No, like I said, that was a one-time thing. I was just exhausted from everything that happened yesterday. I'm fine"

The conversation started to ground him, and the ringing was dampening down. Although not entirely true, he did feel much more capable today. He felt like he was trying to convince himself it was a one-time thing as well as her.

He was picking up and tossing all the supplies strung around back into his bag, "You ready to go?"

"Sure. It feels good to be somewhere normal, but we should slip back into the woods and figure out our next move."

The two walked along the counter leading to the door, feeling better about their chances with some food and clothes. They reached the sliver archway, and just as Reed's foot crossed the threshold the speaker blared on, much louder than before.

"*Unpaid merchandise detected. Theft protocol engaged.*"

Steel bars shot up through the windowsills and from under the door, closing off all exits from the building.

"*Please sit tight as the authorities are notified. Have a nice day!*"

Chapter 7

Dahlia ran up to the door and grabbed the bars, shaking them violently.

"Fuuuuuuck!" she screamed, "Now what are we going do?!"

She turned toward Reed, looking for some explanation or plan. He stared at her, trying to remain calm enough to have a chance at thinking clearly, "Obviously were not getting through those steel bars."

"No shit." She snapped back at him. She shook her head, "I'm sorry, we just need to think of something fast."

Reed shrugged, "Unless there's another exit then I think all we can do is hide until someone shows up and unlocks the bars. Maybe slip out as they come in or something."

Dahlia glowered at him, "Yeah, if they only send like one guy then maybe. Somehow, I don't see that happening."

"I don't know, think about it. For that entire lab they only had four guards. At least that we saw. And nobody has passed through this town the entire time we've been here." He spun around, taking in his surroundings, "We're missing something, something we're not remembering."

"That was a lab in the middle of nowhere. These guys are probably coming from the nearby city." She raised her eyebrows at him, "That's a little different in population."

Reed grabbed at his neck and scratched his chin, "Maybe. If that's the case though, slipping through or fighting our way out probably won't be an option."

"So, what's left then?"

He shrugged again and looked at her, "You don't happen to know how to bend steel with convenience store supplies do you?"

"Seriously? Now's not the time for jokes." Dahlia turned her back on him and walked out of the entrance area.

Reed could tell she was starting to have her own struggles, her own panic to deal with. He ran to the back of the store where he spotted a smaller window to check if they would have better luck with it. The bars were just as tightly packed and the same thickness as everywhere else. His head was spinning, his panic was morphing into anger at Dahlia for suggesting they rob the store. Why did he listen to her in the first place?

He stopped himself before getting too deep in his thoughts and inhaled deeply through his nose and then out of his mouth. That's when it hit him, so simple, "I bet they don't have bars through the wall."

She walked up behind him, "What are you talking about?"

"The walls should just be dry wall and insulation, right?" He walked up and smacked the wall a couple times with the side of his fist, "I bet if we found some blunt objects we could dig through this back wall and get out before someone gets here."

"That's better than anything I can think of. Let's get moving."

They went in separate directions to scan through the store in search of something useful. Reed's emotions were running high and the longer it took to find something the more images of the lab started to creep in his thoughts. It felt like he could feel them physically pulling him back to that horrible place. He went up and down aisles wishing someone thought an axe or a crowbar was a good thing to place in a convenience store.

The racks! The thought exploded into his mind. He ran over to the clothing corner where Dahlia had grabbed a dress from a small rolling rack. He started manically throwing all the dresses and shirts behind him.

Dahlia dodged a flying pair of overalls, "What are you doing?"

"Come over and help me!" Yelled Reed, as he flipped the rack upside down. "These racks are pretty thin, I bet we can bend these legs off the connecting top part. A big metal pole should be good enough to bust through."

Dahlia grabbed the other side of the rack to balance it as Reed bent it over. He was only able to bend it a little bit at first, but it was enough to start the process. With all his strength, he started to bend it back and forth until it eventually could bend almost all the way to the floor. The metal began to fray and crack near the joint.

With every tug Reed could feel his anticipation and stress growing, waiting for it to weaken enough to sheer off. The seconds started to feel like minutes, and the minutes like hours. An inexplicable rage was snaking its way through his body, growing more the longer it took to snap off the metal leg. Seconds before he felt like the rage was going to boil over in an explosion of curse words, the metal from the top portion sheared off, sending him flying backwards.

He fell to the floor on his butt, with the freshly sheared off metal pole in his hands. The gnarled twisted metal at the end of the pole had broken off in a way that made it look almost like a miniature scythe. It was a better result than he had hoped for.

Reed jumped back to his feet, "Here, take this one while I start on the other leg." he tossed her the pole, "Start about a foot away from the window. That should be pretty close to the middle of a stud bay."

"Got it." Dahlia jogged to the wall and started in on it.

Reed was spouting out the directions without even thinking about it. While he started to work on busting the other leg off, he wondered where this information was even coming from. He couldn't remember a shred of his life, but he had acquired this information from somewhere. Perhaps he'd been a carpenter, or a handyman? This made him wonder what the people from the lab would want with such a commoner like himself?

It took a few minutes to break off the second leg of the clothing rack. Once it was free, he quickly hurried over to where Dahla was smashing in the wall. They each stood on opposite sides of it, swinging their makeshift clubs into the drywall. Every swing closer to freedom. Every minute closer to capture.

Drywall was chipping off bit by bit with tuffs of insulation peeking through the cracks. Once there was a sizeable hole made, Reed stuck his hand up toward Dahlia signaling her to stop. He thought they were taking too long and lunged toward the hole, ripping it apart with his bare hands. Large chunks of drywall were flung everywhere with him furiously tearing at it like a back ally cat in a scuffle. Once the drywall was sufficiently torn away between the studs, he wasted no time in ripping the insulation out.

Reed stood back and caught his breath for a moment staring into the empty stud bay.

Dahlia nodded at him, "Feel better?"

He glared at her, "I'll feel better once we're on the other side."

He felt bad for being so abrasive, but there was no time for pleasant distractions. His mind, which was usually a disarray of sporadic thoughts and emotions swirling in an unending whirlpool, was laser focused on getting through this wall and back into the woods.

Reed took a second to stare at the wall, realizing that getting through the drywall and insulation had been the easy part. Behind the insulation was plywood sheeting, and then the thin metal siding past that. Although his mind was set on his goal, he started to feel doubt creep back into his sights. He knew they were on the outskirts of the city, but how long did they really have? Especially after all the time they had already spent. He felt like his efforts were becoming pointless. But he couldn't stop, for Dahlias sake if nothing else.

"Let me handle this for a minute while you take a break." She handed him a bottle of water.

He didn't want to take a break. He wanted to burst through the wall like a wrecking ball, but he reluctantly took her advice.

Dahlia swung her pole at the plywood, chipping away tiny little pieces with each hit. Hers was much better when it came to tearing at wood with the twisted metal end digging in quite nicely. After only a few good swings, Reed wanted to push her aside and take point again. He couldn't stand sitting there watching as the clock ticked down. Without the swinging taking up his energy, it lifted his anxieties back into the fold.

A squeaking sound caught his attention from across the store that had him wondering if his mind was playing tricks on him again. The wretched degradation of his mind had him starting to question anything out of the ordinary. He decided to check it out and walked over to the front of the store. Nothing could be seen straight out of the windows when he approached, making him think his mind was indeed trying to fool him again.

He grabbed the bars and pressed his face against them when he reached the windows to get a better look at the surrounding area. On the right side of the store, he spotted it. An SUV painted black as the night sky with all the windows tinted the same, making it impossible to see how many sat inside.

Reed shook his head and looked away for a moment to make sure he was really seeing this. Turning his sights back to the car, it was still there.

This was the one time Reed invited the thought of a delusion, but they were out of time. The door opened slowly and a pair of black boots laced up tight all the way to the top landed on the ground. The person took a step back and closed the door, showing off a full combat uniform as if they were headed to war.

His whole uniform was colored in a black and dark green mixture of squares in a pattern looking like it was supposed to imitate camouflage. Leather gloves covered his hands, which were both at his hips as he looked toward the store. A utility belt was strapped around his waist with a handgun holstered on the side and some other weird looking gadgets that Reed couldn't make out. A black mask, seemingly made from the same material as his shirt, was pulled over his head with black tinted shades built in over his eyes.

It only took one second for Reed to decide he was not waiting to see what that person had in store for them. The supposed officer started to grab something from his car as Reed turned his head. He ran back to the other side of the store yelling for Dahlia.

"They're here!" He cried out, "We're out of time! We need to be through!"

Dahlia's head turned and face sank as his words set in.

"Let's go!" He yelled, picking up his pole and starting to ferociously swing at the plywood.

Reed and Dahlia were both frantically hammering away now, taking off only little chunks at a time. A good portion of the wall was starting to get very thin, but not enough to satisfy Reed's panic.

They heard the speaker flicker on with the staticky background and a deep booming voice filling the room, "This is officer twelve tuning into the intercoms. I'm sitting outside of the storefront. Every exit is barred tight so there is no escape."

Every exit was barred, but they were making their own exit now. Nothing he said could make him stop. He wasn't going down in here.

"I'm going to start my approach toward the door now. When I release the bars and enter, do not resist. I am armed and will shoot at any sight of retaliation or harm to myself."

Reed's stress and panic took him over, filling his very being to the brink. He threw his pole to the ground and flung his body into the wall at the weakest looking spot. His shoulder rammed into it, shooting pain throughout his arm. He was no longer controlling his actions, slamming into it again and again with no amount of pain able to slow him down. The wall cracked and push outward, bending the thin metal siding on the other end.

The intercom chimed on, *"Theft containment system override engaged, releasing door"*

This was it, now or never. He backed away, wanting to get some better momentum. With a running start this time, he threw his body into the wall with all he had in him. The thin metal of the siding ripped apart enough for him to fall through to the outside. The jagged metal cut the exposed portion of his arm. He laid on the ground unable to move, bleeding on the dirt, exhausted.

Dahlia crawled through the broken wall and grabbed him, "We need to move!" She was trying to pull Reed to his feet, "The bars were retracting as I came through!"

Reed clamored to his feet. His heart was pounding and with every pulse he could see different specks of his vision blurring in and out.

"What the hell?" They heard the officer shout.

The two started running into the woods without regard for the man. They heard a burst of metal as the cop slammed through the hole they made. The man landed on his feet in a crouched position, he quickly rose back upright and started to chase them down. Obviously trained and more equipped than the two of them were, Reed did not like their chances, "Stop! You're only making this harder on yourselves!"

Just keep running. Just keep running. This was the only thought that Reed could focus on, everything else melted away as he centered on it, his vision still pulsing with blurry spots. The more he ran the faster his heart pumped, and the more his heart pumped the more frantically the blurriness faded in and out.

Dahlia was right behind him, starting to catch up. She began to pass Reed and a small gap was growing between them.

Only one officer. At best one of them was going down. Reed began to hate the fact she was faster than him. He started to spiral at the thought.

I break us out of the store and I'm the one who's going to go down. This isn't fair, nothing has been fair since we left that damn laboratory. If this is it, then he wasn't going down without a fight. He could at least give Dahlia enough time to get away and go live her life somewhere better.

It all hit Reed like a sack of bricks to the head, but at the same time filled him with a feeling of absolution.

He heard a loud bang, followed by a *whooshing* sound that quickly caught up to him. His hair was grazed by a black ball that zoomed past, hitting a tree not far in front of him. When it hit the tree, the ball cracked open and two thick black straps wrapped around it, connecting on the other side. His eyes were glued to it until he passed.

What the fuck was that.

Another bang ensued, followed by the now familiar *Whoosh* sound. The black ball flew past him and hit Dahlia square in the back. Just like with the tree, the ball opened and sent straps flying around her, clenching her arms to her side. She screamed and slammed on the ground, all the momentum from running sending her rolling violently until coming to a stop.

Nothing could have prepared him for the shock of her going down. He turned to look back at her, fearful of her condition. Her body was quivering in pain in the dirt. The sight was haunting to him, instantly stamping itself into his mind. Before he could think of his next move, he slammed full force into a tree.

Reed momentarily blacked out, waking up on the ground. His vision was foggy, it looked like the forest was spinning around him. He could hear heavy footsteps trudging through the brush next to him. Reed pushed his body to climb back to his hands and knees, barely being able to hold up the weight of himself.

"You put up a good fight, I'll give you that."

Up close, the officer's voice was gravely and deep. Reed could feel his defeat in his bones, but he couldn't let this man get away with hurting Dahlia like that. He grabbed the cop's ankle and tried to pull, not even knowing what he was attempting to accomplish.

The officer chuckled, "You've got heart, I admire that."

He kicked Reed back down to the floor on his back and loomed over him, a large rifle pointed down at his chest, "It'almost makes me feel bad about this. Almost"

He pulled the trigger, blasting Reed in the chest with one of those black projectiles. It felt like a boulder being thrown down on him as the straps tightened and lock around his torso.

He was caught.

Chapter 8

The officer pulled a strap from his belt and dropped it onto Reeds legs. It automatically wrapped around them the moment it touched him.

"Now you just sit tight while I go check on your partner over there." The officer nodded to Dahlia.

Reed felt helpless and afraid of all the unknowns, the same feeling he had when he awoke in that lab. Who knows what their treatment was going to look like, or if they're going to be handed right back to the lab. Fear took over and he started to feel nauseous and lightheaded. He began to struggle and squirm on the ground hoping for something to break loose.

The straps slowly tightened the more he struggled. They clamped his arms so harshly he could feel the blood flow slowing down. Bones in his legs were mashing together, shooting pain through his lower half.

The officer glanced back at Reed, "If you want to keep breathing regularly then I suggest you cut out the squirming or it's only going to get worse for you."

Reed knew he wasn't lying. It was already getting harder for him to get full breaths of air. Would this contraption tighten until he suffocated? He stopped writhing around, not wanting to test it. Reed looked to Dahlia to see what the officer was doing to her.

Once he reached her, the officer gently pushed her onto her back with his foot. He stared at her for a moment, then dropped a strap to secure her legs as well. He reached down and sat her up, kneeling in front of her, "That was quite the tumble you took, can you breathe?"

Dahlia quietly nodded her head.

"That's good, let's get you in the car." The officer picked up Dahlia and threw her over his shoulder. She showed no signs of struggle, her body draping limply over him.

"I'll come back for you. Don't sneak off while I'm gone now?" He said with a slight chuckle in his voice.

Reed laid in his confinement as he watched the officer walk off with Dahlia. The way he was talking to her almost seemed like he still had some compassion for them. Was it compassion or some tactic to get them less guarded? Would he attack them full force, then act like a caretaker to win them back over? Why would he need to win them back over? They're not spies or criminal masterminds. As far as he knows, they just tried to rob a convenience store and that's it. What was his angle in this? Reed couldn't shut his mind off or dam up the floodgate of questions. It seemed like an eternity had passed with one paranoid delusion bleeding into the next.

He heard plants rustling in the distance, like something or someone was running around near him. The steps were too small and close together to be the officer. They were getting closer, almost like a whisper he could hear darting around him. Reed looked around as best he could, trying to catch a glimpse of what was going on. The footsteps sped up, faster and faster the closer they got to him. He could feel something about to pounce on him, helpless and alone in the woods.

Just as it sounded like the steps were right at his head, they disappeared. Unintelligible whispers invaded his ears, swirling around him, coming from all angles. Most of them sounded like a soft woman's voice tickling his eardrums. Without warning, loud furious screams pushed through the whispers.

"You're not real. You're not real. You're not real." Reed quietly chanted to himself, trying to claw his way back.

"I can tell you with full certainty that I am very real." The officer's voice cut through the screams and instantly snapped Reed back into the moment. He reached down and started to rummage through Reeds pockets, rolling him on his side to check the back ones, "Your girlfriend over there didn't have anything on her either."

Reed couldn't help but feel a slight ping of joy from the mention of Dahlia being his girlfriend through all the bleakness.

He returned Reed to his back, "No IDs, no phones, no wallets, no nothin." The oversized shiny black eye coverings stared down on him, "Even raiders usually have a radio or something. Where are you guys from?"

Reed coughed up a small amount of blood, "We came from a town nearby. We got lost in the woods when we stumbled upon the store."

"Mmmhm." The officer walked around to his other side, his eyes never leaving Reed's, "Now, that wouldn't be the worst lie I've ever heard, had your partner told me the same thing. She seems to think you two came from the city and apparently just had some banking problems. Neither story explains why you felt so strongly about me that you had to dig through a wall to avoid a conversation."

Of course he asked Dahlia the same question. Why wouldn't he separate them to try and figure things out. Reed felt stupid assuming he could outsmart this man so easily.

"I'm going to ask you one more time before I take you in, and I want you to think really hard about it this time. Where are you from?" His tone grew sharp and precise when he asked. Reed no longer felt any concern coming his way. He feared what his answer's reaction would get, but decided lying was getting him nowhere.

"I don't know." Reed said coldly.

The officer continued to stare at him for what seemed like minutes, the black tint of his glasses taunting him, "Is that your final answer?"

Reed's head went limp, "It's the truth."

He grunted, "If that's how you want to play it." The officer's tone made it clear that he obviously did not believe him. He pulled Reed to an upright sitting position, "I don't know what you two are playing at, but we're going to find out." He threw Reed over his shoulder with little effort.

What could he say that wouldn't make him look like a lunatic? Saying the full truth would likely make him look more like a liar than his previous story.

The officer opened the car door and plopped Reed in the back, sitting him up next to Dahlia. He strapped them in with seatbelts and pulled them tight, "Wouldn't want anything to happen to you." He threw the door closed and hopped into the front seat.

The inside of the car was completely black, matching the outside. A solid metal mesh separated the back of the vehicle from the driver's seat. The windows on either side of Reed and Dahlia were blacked out on the inside as well, making it impossible to see the surrounding area. Reed could barely see through the front passenger side window with how shaded it was, and the driver's side matched the total blackout of the others. Only the windshield was clearly visible to look through. He noticed that the more forward he leaned the less shaded the passenger side window became. Still hardly being able make out vague shapes leaning completely forward. The engine revved up and the car was rolling. They pulled out onto the street headed down the road opposite the lab.

Reed was ecstatic that they were at least traveling further away. Anywhere would be better than back there. Even if he were to be thrown into a jail cell to rot, it would still be a small step up. He looked over to check on Dahlia.

Her arms were covered with small cuts and scrapes with only a few on her face. A bruise was starting to form and well up a little bit on her forehead where she must have taken most of the force from the fall. Her eyes were glued downward, silently staring at the floor.

The more injuries she got the more it hurt Reed to look at her. He wanted her to be free and safe as much as he wanted it for himself. His mouth almost opened wanting to promise her that everything would be okay and they would be safe, but closed, realizing how empty that promise would be. It was eating him up how powerless he was.

A thick green canopy of trees was the only view that accompanied them as they drove, the branches touched one another from either side of the road forming a tall lush tunnel. The sun could barely reach them through the trees, covering the road in shadows with only small strips of sunlight breaking them up.

After about a half hour of silent driving, the trees started to slowly thin out, giving way to the bright blue sky.

"We're coming up on Harrion soon, only about five more minutes to the checkpoint." The officer adjusted the rearview mirror to see them better, "Once we get through, it'll be about another ten to the station."

When they started to approach the check point, Reed looked out intently to try and survey the area. The checkpoint looked like it was repurposed from an old toll booth plaza. There were five lanes in total with all but one of them blocked off by cement block barriers. Where the lanes ended, a giant cement wall began, jetting up out of the ground at least thirty feet and encompassing the entire city. Only one officer stood guard at the open booth, wearing the same fully concealing outfit as the one that captured them. A spike strip pointed toward the outside roads was imbedded into the ground and fully upright. Past the checkpoint were buildings of all different shapes and colors. Skyscrapers packed tightly in were at the center of the city, being the tallest buildings in sight. The further out the buildings were from the center the shorter they were, forming a dome shape that made up the city. Every one of them had a different brightly vibrant color, assaulting the senses and making it almost hard to look at for too long. As if the colors weren't enough, many had their own neon light design coursing around them, giving the entire city a soft glow. Large screens and billboards littered the walls throughout, three quarters of them not turned on anymore or showing a static blue background.

The sight both astounded and repulsed Reed. He thought about his time before, and if he had spent much of it there, or possibly even lived in one of the glowing monstrosities. If he did live there before, whatever they did to him in the lab made him shudder at the possibility. The calm of the trees canopying over them as they drove felt like a much more inviting place.

The car reached the checkpoint and the officer rolled his window down.

The officer manning the entrance walked over and put a hand on the window, "Facial ID."

The driving officer pulled his mask up to reveal his face. Reed couldn't make out anything from where he was sitting except for his dark skin tone. A scanner of sorts was pointed at him that shot out a red glow with lines darting in all directions covering his face. The light turned green along with a small high-pitched beep and he pulled it back, "Have fun in there, Jack."

Jack pushed the button to roll up his window, "Will do, don't drop of heat stroke out here."

The road spikes lowered and allowed them passage into the city. As they began to drive, Reed noticed that there was a severe lack of people. Dirt and debris covered the majority of the street level shops and sidewalks. The places that weren't open anymore had their windows boarded up and their doors chained shut. The couple of places that still stood open were so brightly colored and cleaned that they were visible for miles down the road against the depressing backdrop of everything else.

"What happened here?" Reed couldn't take his eyes off of any and every building passing by.

Jack's black lenses looked into the rearview, "What do you mean?"

Reed's head recoiled, "I mean everything's shut down and I've only seen a few people since we got here."

"Either you're on some strong drugs, or you're trying to be funny. Either way, shut it until we've arrived."

Apparently, all was well to the officer, there was not a thing wrong with how run-down things looked. His reaction put a knot in Reed's stomach. Maybe he was better off not remembering what was going on. He shook his head, willing something to shake loose that would clue him in. He figured they must have these memory drugs down to a science; Which would make sense, seeing as they're scientists.

The car pulled onto a ramp leading into an underground parking garage. Jack stopped it right in front of a closed gate. The officer pulled something off his belt that looked like a remote control with just one black button on it. He pointed it at the gate and pressed it gently, opening it.

On the other side of the rollup gate was a square dimly lit concrete tunnel. Down the path it opened up into a large open area with a few other cars that looked just like the one they arrived in all parked together. The officer started to back the car up to a metal wall, pointing the remote at it as he did. When he pressed the button this time, the metal wall opened from the center starting at the ground, pushing outward in all directions forming a round hole. He backed the car halfway into the hole and pushed the button again. The wall closed down tight to the car between the front and rear doors, separating them from the officer.

"I'm releasing your ties now and opening the doors. Step out of the vehicle and move into the next room." He clicked the remote back on his belt and pushed a second button near the same area.

The doors opened and the restraints immediately gave way, falling to the floor. Reed felt a huge relief as the blood could flow freely through his arms again. He was beginning to worry if they were going to fall off; they felt like jelly for a few seconds before the feeling started to return. He and Dahlia stepped out of the car on either side into a small box room fully made of cement from floor to ceiling. The only thing that wasn't concrete was a solid metal door on the opposite end from the car.

They passed through the door into a room where a large transparent wall separated the prisoners from where the officers would sit. The only thing that let them know there even were walls present was how much dirt was caked over them. There was a metal bench and a small cot that was attached to the back concrete wall. The door creaked closed behind them and made an audible locking sound.

Dahlia wrapped her arms around Reed and squeezed him tightly. They hugged in silence. Reed took in every second of her warmth that he could.

"I'm sorry." Her voice was resisting cracking, "If I didn't get hit, we wouldn't be in this situation. I should have-"

"No, no, no." Reed cut her off. "It was us verses a well-trained officer with a rifle, our chances weren't great anyway. If he didn't get you first, then it would have been me. Don't blame yourself for any of this."

A few quiet tears rolled down her cheeks. Reed held her tightly feeling bad that she took any of the blame. No matter what happened or who did what, they both were in it together until the end.

An officer walked into the room on the other side of the transparent wall. Reed assumed it was Jack, but it was impossible to tell with their uniforms. He had one of those scanners in his hand like the man at the checkpoint.

"It's time to figure out what's really going on here."

Chapter 9

Reed could tell from his voice that they were talking to the same man that had ran them down. Dahlia and Reed broke their hold of each other and turned toward the wall. Reed wanted to figure out what was going on as badly as Jack did.

"You're going to walk up to the wall and stand closely while I scan your faces. It'll only take a few seconds and then I'll run them through the system to see what I can find on you two." He waved his scanner slightly to usher them over.

They walked up slowly and stood by the wall with their faces almost pressed against it.

"Ladies first." Jack put the scanner up to Dahlia. The red lights scanned across her face just as they did to Jack at the checkpoint. A click sounded off as well, but no green light showed this time at the end of the scan. Unaffected by the difference, he moved on to Reed. The lights weren't nearly as bright as he thought they would be staring right into them, but it still gave his eyes some discomfort. He squinted and blinked after just a couple seconds making the officer chuckle. The scanner beeped off and Jack turned away to head out the door.

"This will only take a couple minutes, sit tight." He told them as he walked out of the room.

Reed took a seat on the bench with Dahlia following close behind him. Even though it was in a cell with no way to escape, Reed welcomed the moment of rest. He let his muscles relax, not realizing how sore his body was. He hoped that the last couple days would be the extent of his new injuries. His body couldn't keep taking this kind of punishment for days on end.

Dahlia looked to Reed, "At least we'll find out our names now."

The thought surprised him. He had taken such a liking to his new name that he almost forgot it wasn't real. Hopefully his parents hadn't named him something ridiculous or hard to spell. He thought about it and decided he could keep his name if he didn't like the one Jack came back with.

Reed looked back to her, "Yeah.... Although Dahlia does suit you well. It's very pretty."

Dahlia slightly blushed as a small smile crested her lips, "I don't know about that in this condition. Maybe after a few days of good rest and recovery you can try to tell me that again."

"What I would give to have a long sleep in a comfortable bed." He tried to change the subject before he put his foot in his mouth again.

"Yeah, but right here isn't so bad either." She slid over to rest her head on his shoulder.

A mixture of anxiety and excitement flowed through him at her touch. A childlike giddiness made him forget about everything else that was going on, allowing him to fully live her for the moment. Wherever he was before, he hoped he had known Dahlia. They both sat there and silently enjoyed every morsal of time until the officer came back into the room.

The officer rolled a chair through the door and took a seat near the transparent wall, "Your facial scans don't match anything in our database."

Reed shrugged, "Maybe we're not from around here."

He shook his head, "You don't get it. Everyone is in that database. Every person born in the past eight generations in the world is in that database."

Dahlia squeezed Reed's hand, "What does that mean then exactly?"

Jack sighed heavily, "It means that either you two look very good for your age, or someone deleted you from existence." He leaned forward with his elbows on his knees, "Do you know anyone who would want to do that to you?"

Reed was torn at this point. Other than their capture, Jack had been nice enough to them and seemed like he wanted to help more than discipline them. He wanted to tell him their whole story about breaking free from the lab but was still fear stricken at the possibility of being shipped right back.

He looked to Dahlia, who had returned to sitting upright, to see if he could get some sort of unspoken confirmation from her. She had a serious look like she knew exactly what he was thinking. Neither of them wanted to make the move that could possibly end their freedom.

"You have to give me something, you're not going anywhere until we figure this out."

Dahlia bit her swollen lower lip, "How do we know we can trust you, Jack?"

"You don't. But you don't have any other options either."

Reed couldn't contain himself anymore, "We're from the lab."

Dahlia glowered at him.

"The lab?" He scratched his cheek, "You mean the one in the repurposed building way down that road in the woods?"

"Yes, we were being experimented on and were able to escape. The people that run that lab probably erased us." The words were coming out of Reeds mouth almost faster than he could string them together.

The officer sat back in his chair and stared at them, absorbing what he had just heard. He grabbed the bottom of his mask and pulled it off, tossing it on the floor beside him. He was an older dark-skinned man with some deep scaring on his cheek and forehead. There was concern in his look and his stare dropped to the ground. Most of Reeds fear of the man melted away without the lifeless black mask on.

"I heard some rumors that they were doing some terrible stuff down there. But it's all government funded so I didn't think it could have been all that bad." It was clear that Jack was unsettled. He looked back at them, wanting more answers, "Earlier, when I thought you were being a smart ass, and you said you didn't know what happened. You weren't lying, were you?"

Reed nodded, "I remember random bits of how things work or what things are, but it's more like I just know some facts more than remembering anything. I don't know who I am or what's going on with anything."

Jack looked at Dahlia, "I'm assuming it's the same for you?"

She nodded as well, "Yeah. Whatever they did, it was effective."

Jack sat back in his chair, "So, you guys have no idea about the population problem?"

Reed jerked his head back and raised an eyebrow, "Population problem?"

"Oh lord." He rolled his eyes, "I hate to break it to you, but we're a little fucked"

Dahlia tensed up, "What do you mean?"

Jack shook his head, "I don't know the ins and outs of it, but people aren't having kids anymore. For whatever reason, people slowly stopped being able to get pregnant. I heard at first it was gradual, and then it really started to plumet after a few generations. Everyone blames everyone else for why, and the higher ups just keep on trying to sell us everything they can and pretending nothing is happening." He looked at the wall, "Schools started to go downhill as they lowered the working age so that whatever kids were popping out could fill in the work force. It wasn't long before things began to really fall apart. Most people don't even know that much about it anymore, the only reason I do is because you get a small education in things when you enter the militia."

Reed piped in, "The militia?"

"We're what protects the city from the outside world. We keep scavengers and raiders out while trying to keep some form of law and order in the city and some surrounding areas. Our numbers are severely dwindling as time goes on though. Believe it or not, I'm one of the younger ones on the force."

"Are there still some people who can have kids?" Dahlia asked.

"Well, they were doing something to people in the hospitals for a while which seemed to work. The TVs regularly have commercials telling us that all is fine, and they are on the forefront of a solution, but I haven't heard of a new birth in a long time personally."

Was this why they wanted us in that lab? Were they taking people from the streets to be lab rats in search of a solution? The more Jack told them the more Reeds heart sank. He never thought not knowing would be more comforting. The information filled his head to bursting and almost made the room start to swirl.

Dahlia appeared unfazed, "What do you know about the lab?"

Jack shrugged, "Nothing really. Just word around the water cooler is that some pretty high-class confidential stuff is going on there. They didn't even have us run security for it, brought in some other mercenary types is what I heard. From the story you two told me, they probably don't want us interfering with anything."

Reed felt a glimmer of hope, "Now that you know, can you do something?"

He smiled solemnly, "I'd like to help, especially if there are more people like you. But we're already spread so thin that they wouldn't want to spare the manpower to check it out. That's even if I could convince the captain to investigate it, and there's a fat chance of that. He'll take bribes from the government and any officials he can. I'm sure if they don't want us there then he was already being paid to look the other way."

His heart dropped, "So, what happens to us now?"

Jack looked at him, pondering the question, "Well technically, you don't exist. So, I can't charge you for shoplifting and destruction of property. I'll have to keep you overnight at least, while I think about it. I feel for your situation, but I need to think about my own well-being too."

"A night of rest actually sounds rather inviting right about now." Dahlia leaned back against the wall.

"I'll get you some food before long, it's still jail food so it's not the best. For what it's worth, I'm sorry you guys are in this mess. I don't think anyone should have to go through something like that." He stood up and pushed the chair to the side, heading for the door.

Reed found his words comforting, even with the lack of action, "Thank you, for believing us."

Jack stopped in the doorway placing his hand on the frame, "You seem like good people, and no one in a fair situation would have their scans wiped from the server." He left the room and shut the door behind him.

"Everything keeps getting worse," Dahlia whispered.

"Well, everything was already shitty. We just didn't know about it." Reed tried to muster up a small smile to comfort her.

"I suppose." She looked down, "I just want to forget about everything for a while and get some rest."

"You can take the cot." He nodded to it, "I'll sleep on the bench when I get tired."

"Thank you, I'm just going to lie down and rest my eyes for a little while." She walked over and curled up on the cot.

Reed laid on the bench and spent the next hour staring at the ceiling, thinking about the world they now lived in. He wondered how it got so bad and how people's bodies could randomly not be able to bear children. He refused to believe that it was mere chance, and that the human race decided to give up and die out of nowhere. His money would be on the same people that paid for the lab being the ones who messed everything up. It had to be the government, the higher ups stinging bad decisions together like they didn't know any other way. He noticed when the thought came up that he felt a strong connection to it. It made him wonder if in the past he'd disliked the government, and the feeling was still embedded in him.

Jack opened the door after a while with a couple of trays that had brown blocks on them and a paper cup of water. He placed them inside a glass box that locked from both sides near the corner of the wall. When the small glass door closed on his side, it popped the door open on the cell side.

"I know how they look, and they don't taste much better. They're actually full of all the nutrients you need. It's just very concentrated."

Reed thanked him and Jack left them to their dinner. Dahlia woke up and quickly scarfed her loaf down before retreating back to the cot. Reed poked at it for a few minutes before taking a bite. When he chomped into it, he could feel his tastebuds retracting. It was somehow completely bland, yet utterly vile at the same time. He didn't know how Dahlia choked hers down without even flinching. He reluctantly finished his loaf and downed his water as fast as possible. Although he had to try, there wasn't much chance of getting comfortable enough to sleep on the cold metal bench.

His body and mind craved rest more than ever right now, but he couldn't sleep. Not with his mind racing around trying to connect dots that weren't even there. A little while passed and the lights in the cell turned down to a soft glow, making it almost impossible to see more than a foot in front of you.

After a couple more hours of rolling around on the uncomfortable bench, he heard Dahlia shifting in her sleep. "Will you come sleep with me?" She was soft and quiet.

Reed jumped at the chance and moseyed on over to the cot. He climbed in behind her and she pulled his arm over her side, cradling it in her hands. Reed felt the instant comfort of being with her wash over him as he slowly drifted off. His mind was finally focused on one thing while it shut down for the night.

Chapter 10

They were abruptly awoken by the door slamming. Jack quickly entered the room and knocked on the wall wildly, "Wake up!"

Reed and Dahlia stumbled out of bed and saw how panicky Jacked looked.

Reed rubbed his eyes and swayed his head back and forth trying to wake up, "What's going on?"

"I got a call from the captain. Apparently, someone high up on the food chain wants to see you two. He told me after they arrived and spoke to you that I would need to allow them access to our cell's loading bay.

Every inch of Reed tensed up and his heart was pounding out of his chest. There was nowhere for them to run or hide this time. If Dr. Stintz had come to collect, then they were fish in a barrel.

"You can't let them take us!" Reed yelled, "There's no way that isn't the doctor on his way!"

tears streamed down Dahlia's face.

Jack paced rapidly, muttering something unintelligible to himself.

Reed started out at a normal volume, raising his voice with every word, "Please, I can tell you're a good man. You need to do something!"

Jack was conflicted about the situation. Reed could see it in his eyes, wanting to help but fearing the consequences. "What am I supposed to do?" He flung his hands up, "If I let you go then I'll definitely get fired, maybe even wind up in jail."

Reed pressed his hands against the glass, "And if you don't, then you're condemning both of us to be lab rats until they decide it's time for us to die."

He hated trying to manipulate Jack. He was just a man trying his best to do his job and remain a decent person. Reed knew he didn't have choice though. Jack was their only ticket out of this place that didn't involve an endless sea of pain and confusion.

Dahlia realized what Reed was up to and joined in on the conversation, "Look at my lips." She pointed to the scaring on her mouth. "They burned my mouth shut at some point, leaving nothing but a hole barely big enough to breathe out of. I had to cut it open with a piece of glass just to eat something. This is who they are over there. Monsters dressed in white."

Jacks face sunk and started to lose color, he looked disgusted and distraught with his eyes puffing up, "I..." His voice trailed off with his eyes.

"Don't let fear win. I know it's hard, one of the most difficult things you can do. But if you let it win, then we all lose. Not just you." Reed hoped that would be the last hit he had to give Jack. Every dig at him made Reed feel lower.

Jack clenched his teeth and closed his eyes, "Okay, okay. Enough. The only way in or out is through that tunnel and you need a remote to activate it."

"You don't have a spare one laying around I'm guessing?" Reed looked around the mostly empty room behind Jack.

He shook his head, opening his eyes, "No. We each get issued one when we enroll. Even losing it comes with huge disciplinary action. I can't just open all the doors and give you my remote, I'll most likely get exiled."

Of course it wasn't going to be that simple, Reed looked around the room hoping for some inspiration. A part of him wanted Jack to do just that and let them run out of here, sacrificing his own life for them. It made him feel dirty, not just wanting it but wishing for it. He didn't know if he could live with it if he did. He feared being consumed by the guilt of taking advantage of a man caught in the middle.

"If you want my help then we have to think of something quickly, they're already on their way." Jack sat in his chair and rubbed his bald head.

The room felt like it was closing in on him. His breaths shortened and he couldn't get a full breath of air. He was no tactician. How could he plan an escape from a jail with only one entrance?

Dahlia's head snapped to Jack, "We'll overpower you. It's the only way you could try to act innocent in this while we escape. You had to come in the cell for some reason and we overpowered you."

Reed finally got a full breath, loving Dahlia's brilliance taking the pressure off of him.

"Say we got into a fight. You had to come in or we would have killed each other." Dahlia started pacing, "You made a mistake in the heat of the moment and didn't take off your belt before coming in here."

"It makes me look like an idiot." Jack face relaxed and he reclined back, "But I guess that's better than an accomplice."

"What about those?" Reed looked to the corner of the room where a camera was fixed on the cell.

Jack looked over, "The captain took those offline a long time ago so there were less eyes on him. I don't know why, and frankly I don't want to know."

"So how do we play this out?" Reed's eyes jumped between the two.

"Well, first things first. Plausible deniability." Jack pulled out a retractable baton from his back pocket.

"One of you are going to have to smack me around a bit to make this believable. No way am I getting overpowered without a scratch on me."

"You can't do it yourself?" Reed wanted to keep his hands as clean as possible through this.

"No. There will be an investigation into this and a hit from myself will be distinguishable from a hit someone else gave me. I could never get the right angle to fake it." Jack looked at his club, "After I get in the cell and we take care of that, you take my remote and run for it."

"If we're going full throttle on this then I think we would steal the car." Dahlia almost sounded excited with the suggestion.

Jack exhaustedly chuckled, "Every militia car is tracked. They would find you in minutes. You need to go on foot, and we need to do this now." He paused, "Before I change my mind."

Jack turned around and rushed through the door. Reed thanked the universe that they were arrested by a man with a heart. Had he been a mercenary type with no qualms about their situation they would be right back where they started, having gained only a couple days of freedom.

The metal wall opened with a low screech in the other room, the flanges scraping against each other. The door popped open and Jack walked in. He was shaky and looking at the baton in his hands from the doorway. Reed thought he was going to back out while they waited for him to take a deep breath that puffed his chest out as far as it could stretch. Jack looked up at the two and took a step into the cell, "Who wants to do the honors?"

Dahlia and Reed looked at each other, neither wanting to do him any harm. Although he knew that he would be racked with guilt about it, Reed reached out for the club. As much as he did not want to do this, he wanted to save Dahlia from those feelings. He couldn't actually take any of her pain away, but he could at least prevent her from having more.

He tried to minimize the situation, thinking it would spare him pain in the long run. What's one more trauma added to his list anyway? He had already killed a man, so this shouldn't even compare.

Reed squeezed the handle, "Are you ready?"

Jack locked eyes with him, "I don't think you're ever ready to take a club to the face. Just make it worth it."

Unable to keep himself from trembling, Reed cocked his arm back. Jack closed his eyes preparing for the hit. Right before Reed built up the courage to swing, car brakes screeched to a stop from the parking lot outside the door.

"Fuck." Jack turned his head to the sound, "They're here."

Before he could even think, Reed swung with all his might and pounded Jack in the face with the club. Jack spun sideways and fell to the floor, slamming down on the hard concrete. Reed grabbed the remote from his belt without hesitation and headed for the door. Hearing the brakes of the car, knowing that the people from the lab were so close, had Reed shifting into an almost animalistic state. All his anxieties and morals holding him back had been suspended.

They walked through the metal door to the loading bay where Jack thankfully left the retracting metal wall open for them. Dahlia grabbed Reed and pulled him against the outside wall.

"*Shhhh*! They're still getting out of the car." Dahlia whispered.

Reed poked his head out just far enough to catch a glimpse of it. There were two vans identical to one another parked by Jacks car along with a sedan. Both the vans had sliding side doors with no visible handles. All three were pure shiny white, catapulting Reed's mind back to the lab, making him feel like he never left.

Two guards exited the first van, walking toward the front and pausing to let the other men catch up. Out of the second van came another guard and someone in a lab coat. Reed recognized him as the assistant who had released his restraints early allowing him to break free. The two grouped up with the other guards as they all faced the sedan. The car door clicked open, followed by the footsteps of someone walking up to the group. Turning the corner around the front of the vans was Dr. Stintz.

The sight of that sadistic monster froze Reed's blood in his veins. His presence broke whatever spell was holding all of Reeds feelings at bay and turned his brain to mush.

Dahlia grabbed his arm, "The second they get through that door, we run like hell."

Reed nodded and they waited for their chance.

Dr. Stintz was giving a talk to the group before they entered. Reed couldn't make out what he was saying, but he looked extremely serious about it. After a minute of directions, the group walked into the building behind the Doctors lead.

Reed and Dahlia started sprinting up through the tunnel toward the gate. In the car it had only seemed like a small way down; on foot was another story. The dimly lit tunnel looked a half mile long to him and it felt like his skin was tightening around him.

They were almost halfway to the top when they heard a commotion coming from behind them. Reed turned his head to look back at what was coming. The guards were running around in a frenzy searching while Jack was yelling and pointing them away from the tunnel. Dr. Stintz walked out of the loading bay cell with his icy calm demeanor intact and watched everyone else run around. Almost immediately, he looked up and made eye contact with Reed.

He could make out a smile forming on the doctor's face as he pointed up to them. He called to his people, and they all turned their heads to the tunnel.

"They've spotted us!" Reed yelled out to Dahlia who was a few paces ahead of him as usual.

The guards all scrambled to their vehicles and revved them up trying to flip around quickly. In their panicked state they were bumping into each other and blocking one another off, giving the two just a few extra scraps of time.

Reed pulled out the remote and pressed the button aiming it at the gate, but it didn't budge. They were only a small way away from it at this point, but Reed assumed he had to be closer for it to work.

They reached the gate and Reed was furiously pressing the button to no avail.

Dahlia's eyes were wide open, "Come on!"

"It's not working!" Reed worried he would break the remote if he pressed it any faster or harder.

The vans were just shy of halfway and closing in fast. He couldn't think of anything to fix the situation. Stress and fear warped his mind into something completely useless and they were going to die because of it.

Dahlia snatched the remote out of his hand and pointed it at the top of the gate where a small black box sat while pushing the button. The gate slowly began to open as the lab's cavalry was closing in. They only let it lift enough to fit their bodies though before cramming themselves under it.

Chapter 11

Dahlia snapped back around and mashed the remote once they were on the outside. The gate shuddered to a stop and rolled itself back down.

"Let's move!" Dahlia had already started sprinting up the ramp before she saw the gate start closing.

Reed's muscles ached and he had to force himself to keep up. The gate was only closed for half a minute when he heard the clinking of it opening behind them.

He pointed to a small space between two of the buildings across from the top of the ramp, "Through that ally!" No traffic or people blocked their way through the street. They booked it through, fearing the sound of the cars catching up to them.

The buildings in the city were so close together that the alleys were nearly impossible to fit in. Reed squeezed in first, having to turn his body sideways to even begin try. Dahlia was right behind him as they pushed their bodies further into the space. The farther into the ally they went, the more Reed noticed it was shrinking. Halfway through, they were only able to inch forward one small push at a time.

The lab convoy rolled out of the tunnel, both vans in front with Stintz bringing up the rear. One van immediately pulled to the right and peeled out down the road. The second turned left out of the rampway before screeching to a halt.

Reed looked back and could barely see the guards jumping out of the van past Dahlia. They had spotted the two and rushed toward the ally. Once they reached the entrance, one of the guards raised his harpoon gun and aimed it down the small space.

"Don't shoot them you imbeciles!" Dr. Stintz pushed his gun down by the barrel, "I told you, we can't risk killing them!"

Dahlia and Reed were only a few steps from the end of the alleyway and Reed was having a hard time moving himself further. An unknown claustrophobia set in, he felt like he couldn't breathe and would die wedged between these two walls. He struggled furiously trying to force his body through the final stretch without much progress.

The guards hurried back to the van, chucking their heavy harpoon guns into the side door. They rummaged through the back until they emerged with a smaller rifle of the same make as the officers.

Unable to move much herself, Dahlia tried her best to push Reed through to the finish line. He managed to fully wrap his arm around the backside of the building and was attempting to tear his body through. Once his hips were more than halfway out, the rest of his body came flying to the ground. He immediately jumped up and grabbed Dahlias hand, pulling with all his might.

The guards had resumed their position at the other end and took aim. That familiar *Bang*, and *Whoosh* sound assaulted Reed's eardrums once again as they fired toward the two. The black ball flew down the alley until about halfway where it clipped the wall and cracked open prematurely. With nothing to wrap around, the straps continued careening through, bouncing back and forth between the walls. They made it to the end and flew out into the opening, just barley skipping over Dahlias head.

Dahlia, being a little bit thicker than Reeds slim stature, was still jammed in tightly right at the very end. Reed was pulling as hard as he could with nothing to show for it. His hand slipped off and he crashed back to the floor.

"Just go!" Dahlia screamed at him.

The words did not even register in Reed's mind. He would walk right into the doctor's car himself rather than think about leaving her behind. He got back to his feet and grabbed hold of her again with both hands this time. He left the ground with his feet against the wall hoping he wasn't going to rip her arm out in the process.

A second *Bang* and *Whoosh* came screaming down the alley as he pulled. The second ball got much further down before hitting the side of the building. It crashed open and sent the straps flinging out.

Dahlia was able to get her free hand over her head to wrap her fingers around the buildings corner. Giving one final pull with their combined strength, she finally slipped out and slammed down on top of Reed. The straps whipped her in the back on the way down, bouncing off and jetting past them.

The back of Reeds head hit the ground hard, immediately rattling him back in a fog. Dahlia jumped up, expecting Reed to quickly follow. Her body locked up when he stayed down, disoriented by the fall. She grabbed his hand and yanked him up, throwing his arm around her shoulder. They ran down the road, completely lost in the maze of the city. Reed couldn't bear to slow her down and tried to run on his own. He was wobbly and confused but was able to make do enough to not completely drag her down.

"We need to get off the streets." Everything was chained shut and boarded up. Even the thought of squeezing through another alleyway was enough to make his heart tense up.

"Where?!" Her eyes were darting back and forth to either side of street.

Reed looked around and spotted an open shop at the bottom of a tall building a couple blocks in front of them. "Maybe there's some stairs to the upper floors in that store."

The two dumped the rest of their energy out keeping up their full sprint to the store. There was a sign on the outside of the store that read *Cheese Please!* They slammed it open and ran inside without giving anything a second glance.

The walls of the store were painted vibrant yellow with giant pictures of cartoon style cheeses randomly splashed throughout. A row of windows at the front of the store were the only parts spared from the design. Large white tiles with black grout spanned the entirety of the floor, making each one stand out on its own. The ceiling matched the wall's yellow color with fake, oversized, blocks of cheese hanging from wires over tables. Each one was round with multi-tiered shelves on top, each taller and slightly smaller than the last, filled to the brim with the cheese that matched the wedges hanging above them. Just like the storefront in the woods, there was no cashier or employees of any kind. Instead, jetting out of a wall in the back of the store, there were large cameras on long mechanical arms that locked on to Reed and Dahlia as they entered. Just past the cameras Reed saw a back hallway with a few doors slapped with labels that he couldn't read from where he was standing.

Reed nodded to the back, "That's our best bet."

A noise came from outside. Dahlia moved closer to the window to check out, "They're starting to patrol with the vans I think." Her eyes were above the window sill only enough to barely see over, "One's coming this way, get down!" She ducked under the window. Reed dropped to the floor and quickly army crawled the short distance over to her.

The van slowly cruised in front of the store. He was safely under the view of the window but couldn't help feeling like they could see him anyway. His heart was pounding so hard he worried they would hear it. Every one of his breaths sounded like a hurricane to him.

They didn't stop to check out the store and continued down the street. Reed let out a huge sigh of relief trying to get his heartrate under control. Dahlia lifted her head enough to peek through the window, "They should be far enough down now that we can move."

The two stood up and walked toward the back rooms, the cameras following them as they did. When they approached, Reed stuck his hand out like he was going to give the camera a high five. It zoomed at his arm, making high pitched electrical noises with every move. He waved his hand back and forth in a large arching motion, the camera following it closely. The way it moved and mimicked him made him chuckle while he messed with it.

She glared at him, "What are you doing? Is this really the time for that?"

"Sorry." He laughed again, "I couldn't help myself."

He was about to leave the camera alone and move on when something caught his eye. It looked like red liquid was forming behind the lens. The camera was suddenly dripping red from multiple points on its mechanical arm. Drips quickly changed to streams and formed pools of dark red on the floor. Reed heard a loud screeching noise coming from it as it began to squirm like it was in pain. The screeching was a human voice crying out in agony, filling every crevice of Reeds head.

He quickly turned to Dahlia who was unaffected by all the commotion, not breaking her stride to the back hallway. He covered his ears and closed his eyes, shaking his head profusely in hopes that what he was seeing would stop. He knew in the back of his mind that it was all fake, but it consumed him anyway.

A hand on his shoulder steadied him. Dahlia's voice almost couldn't be heard behind all of the screeching, "Are you okay?" It sounded like a muffled whisper.

"Aghhhhh! Stop it!" The screeching scrambled his brain, making it impossible to think clearly.

He lost control and swung his fist at the camera, catching it right on the lens, then grabbed it and tried to rip it off the mechanical arm in a frenzy. Dahlia hugged him around the waist and ripped him from the camera to the ground. When he landed, everything stopped and went quiet. The pools of red disappeared, and the screeching had vanished.

Dahlia stood over him, "What the fuck is going on?!"

Before he could reply they heard a voice chirp out of the speakers, "*Property damage detected, alarm sounding and video evidence being reported.*"

A high-pitched alarm blared out the sound system.

"I'll explain later." He pulled himself up with her help, "We need to move, they're sure to hear that."

They ran to the back. A faint engine could be heard in the distance, getting louder by the second. Two doors labeled bathroom were on the left of the hallway with a door labeled stairs at the end. They ran through the door into a dimly lit stairwell, rushing higher into the building.

The stairs seemed endless when Reed looked upward at the ceiling. Just the mere thought of climbing them all the way to the top exhausted him. After they had raised three floors, Dahlia began to check if any doors were unlocked. The next two levels were inaccessible and Reed was getting nervous.

The door on the first floor burst open and the guards found their way in. "Go, go, go!" He heard one of them yelling at the others. He was talking to the other guards, but his words sunk right into Reed's head. The pace he thought was fast already, picked up the second the guard yelled. They were met with another locked door every floor they passed. The few seconds it took Dahlia to check the handle each time let the guards catch up a little bit more. They must have gone up ten floors to with no end in sight.

Still a few floors ahead of the guards, they ran by a door that was barely wedged open with a piece of wood. Dahlia burst through with Reed close behind into a long bleak hallway. She turned to the right and ran, hoping not to meet a dead end. It was completely stripped of all life until they turned the corner and saw a half-dozen blank brown wooden doors, all on one side of the hall. Dahlia pushed through the one in the middle and, to her surprise, it opened with no problem.

Endless cubicles and cleared out desks in disarray covered the room, only leaving small walkways between them and the wall to get through. Parts of the concrete walls and ceiling were chipping off in blocks, eroding with the slowly deteriorating building over the years. Dahlia kept running to the back of the office. There were big windows taking up the entire wall, looking directly into the next building about six feet away.

She grabbed Reed's arm and yanked him down into a cubicle. They scurried under an abandoned desk and tried to keep quiet. The two struggled to keep their labored breathing down, unable to catch their breath.

They heard the guards running through the hallway scrambling to find them until they stopped just a few doors down. One of them was yelling at all the others in a loud commanding voice, "We know they're in here somewhere. We're going to fan out and start searching room by room. You're going to guard the door to the stairwell so they don't slip past us."

An impending fight with the guards allowing them a desperate attempt at escape didn't feel like it was in the cards for Reed. Surely the two of them could take on one guard, but even if they did that the others would hear them and then they would be finished. The only small comfort he could think of was the fact that they were now under direct orders not to be killed. Although being killed might be a better outcome than going back to the lab at this point. Either way, he did not like their chances in the situation.

"Got any ideas besides trying to fight our way out?" Reed whispered.

Dahlia had a determined look on her face that gave him some hope. She looked around the cubicle for anything helpful and reached for a large chunk of concrete with a piece of rebar sticking out like a handle.

"I guess not then." He picked up the next largest chunk and prepared for the worst.

She looked out the window, "I have an idea, but it might be more suicidal than a fight."

a guard kicked in the door to their room, slamming it open. He slowly entered and scanned the area for them. It sounded like he started his search in the opposite direction of the path they took.

Dahlia looked at Reed and gently grabbed his hand, lacing their fingers together, "Do you trust me?" she whispered so low it was barely audible.

Reed stared into her eyes, wondering what she was about to attempt. There was no question that he trusted her with his life. He nodded and waited for her signal.

The second there was confirmation, she stood up and faced the wall of windows. Cocking her arm back and throwing with all her might, she lobbed the concrete chunk at them. It connected with the glass and shattered the entire panel, flying through the outside and into the adjacent building. The piece had dropped after it flew through the first window and broke a window one floor down on the other building.

The guard was shocked and preemptively shot his gun before being able to aim anywhere close to them. The black ball projectile flew outward and hit a desk a few cubicles away, the straps wrapping around it and tightening down.

"That's your plan?!" Reed was terrified she was going to do what he thought she was going to do.

"No choice now!" She got a running start in the direction of the window and jumped out of the building landing successfully onto the floor of the other, slamming down into a roll when she did. Reed was petrified at the sight. He didn't think he could force his body to do that.

His timid movements allowed the guard to shoot another ball at him when his head peeked over the edge of the cubicle. He immediately dropped down. The projectile flew over his head and smacked into the ridge of the cubicle, shattering open and sending the straps flying. The other guards were stomping through the hallway to the room.

The fear of imminent capture suddenly overtook his fear of the jump. Without question he stumbled back up into a half run toward the opening. He looked over and saw the guard aiming the gun right at his chest. Reed dove out the window face first in an attempt to doge the blast. The guard shot and missed again watching Reed fly out of the building.

Unlike Dahlia, Reed had not gotten as much of a running start and only managed to get the front half of his body through the next broken window. Before he hit the ground, he managed to wrap his arm around the inside edge of the nearest windowpane. The moment his body connected to the concrete floor he latched his arm as tight as he could around the inside, just barley keeping himself from being flung back out from the impact. Dahlia was already right there tightly grabbing his arm. She managed to quickly drag his body back in and started to pull him away from the edge, out of sight of the guards. Once they were out of the opening, she flipped him over onto his back with his head in her lap.

Reed looked up at her feeling like his ribs were cracked in half, "You're fucking crazy."

She smiled back at him, "You're welcome."

Chapter 12

Reed cherished this moment of rest with Dahlia, taking in the little joys even though they could hear the guards gathering at the window looking across the buildings.

The same man who was giving orders before was yelling at the rest, "Jump down there and get them! We'll meet you at the bottom!"

"With all due respect sir. No way I'm jumping that; the money isn't worth my life."

"Yeah, I'm out."

"I'm with them."

The leader grunted loud enough for them to hear from the other building, "Fine! We'll go down and cut them off at the bottom then, you bunch of whinners. Move out!"

Their stomping footsteps slowly faded out of earshot. The tightness in Reed's chest gave him a break and his muscles relaxed. He knew the chase wasn't over but he felt like he could survive anything as long as Dahlia was by his side, "Where to now?"

She looked around the room, "I think it's your turn to save us, isn't it?"

Reed chuckled, pondering the possibilities. He supposed they could smash through another window. Getting caught sounded like a better alternative than risking that again.

Once was more than enough for this lifetime. Fighting their way out was still out of the question as well, even if they could find some weapon-like debris. He was out of good ideas and decided to throw out whatever he could think of, "Well, if they're going down to cut us off. Then I guess we go up?"

Dahlia's faced scrunched, "Up to where? The roof?"

"I suppose so." He looked up at her, "Maybe go up there and then think of our next move?"

"I guess it will give us a little more time at least." She gave the room one last look around and shrugged, "I don't have any better ideas so let's do it."

Reed started to get back to his feet, feeling every inch of the hit his body took from the fall. He winced in pain and thought he heard a crackling in his back when he straightened out his spine. Not as bad as he thought it would be, but still it hurt to move.

He took in the space and was surprised how much of it resembled the building they had just left. More abandoned cubicles and desks. The lights in this one were hanging down at odd angles, their supports giving out without maintenance. The gray of the office spaces was in high contrast to the bright vibrant colors of the building's exterior. Even if it was in its functional state, Reed thought it looked like such a depressing place to be.

The two walked out of the door and into a hallway that was also a replica of the one they had been in before. It gave Reed an eerie feeling knowing where to go to get to the stairs.

"A water fountain!" Dhalia pointed to one attached to the wall at the end of the hallway.

She rushed over to it and pushed on the wide gray piece to make the water come out. Overwhelming joy took her when she saw the clear liquid streaming upward forming an arc. She immediately started gulping up water as fast as she could, coughing between sporadic mouthfuls. Reed waited for her, amazed that the thing still worked. She lapped it up until her stomach couldn't hold any more.

She wiped her mouth and hit her chest until she could stop coughing after getting more water in her lungs, "Here, sorry, I was just so thirsty."

Reed filled up as much as he could, not knowing the next time they would get the chance. They left for the stair entrance after he felt like he was going to burst open and had to stop himself from drinking. Reed looked up at the mountain of stairs they were about to climb. There had to be at least another ten to fifteen floors left for them before reaching the top.

Reed already regretted filling himself up so much at the top of the first set. The water sloshing back and forth in his stomach was making him queasy. They were moving much slower than when they were being chased up the other side, feeling more confident in their lead.

Reed was using his arms to pull him up by the railing more than his legs already, "You think they're just going to wait at the bottom for us, or start coming in?"

"Hopefully they just wait down there forever and we can find a different way out."

Their options were concerning him the higher they rose. He knew it was his idea, but now that he had some time to think about it, what could possibly be waiting up there for them? It's not like a fully fueled private helicopter was going to be up there. Even if there was something like that, he would probably have a higher chance of killing them taking off then taking on the guards.

It was a long tedious walk to the top floor. Even the less than brisk pace they stayed in took it out of Reed. He attempted to mask his fatigue by slowing his breath to copy Dahlias. Matching her pace and breath made his lungs tighten up not getting the oxygen they needed. No matter how many times she showed him she was going to be there for him, he couldn't allow himself to look weak to her. No matter what she said, he was scared of her leaving him for it.

Sunlight blinded them when she opened the door to the roof. They walked out to the flat rooftop and tried to make out their surrounding while their eyes struggled to adjust.

The roof was an open square with pea gravel lining the ground. There was a waist high ridge around the entire perimeter with a black membrane lining. A few large mechanical structures were randomly spaced around, presumably controlling some sort of systems in the building. The lackluster number of options it gave him made his heart sink a little bit.

Dahlia immediately closed the door behind them and removed her jacket. She laced one of the sleeves through the handle of the door and tied it to a piece of exposed rebar around the corner of the stairwell enclosure.

"Hopefully that helps." She pulled the knot with both hands as tight as she could.

"Better than nothing."

"Come on, I've got something to show you." She walked toward one of the mechanical structures. Reed followed her over and she plopped down in the shade of the structure, beckoning him to join her. He sat down close to her, thankful for the time together. Dahlia rummaged through her pockets and pulled out some folded up paper with cheese inside, "I swiped it right before you tried to box a camera."

She split the large piece of cheese in half and handed him some. Reed devoured it without a second thought. The strong sweet yet sharp flavor blasted his taste buds like a fire hose, giving him a peculiar expression he couldn't hold back.

She giggled, "That good huh?"

He tried to scrape his mouth with his tongue like a squeegee to clean off his taste buds, "It's way too sweet for how I thought cheese tasted. Like it was infused with a block of sugar or something. It just took me by surprise is all."

She fiddled with her half in the paper for a second, her expression losing all of its lightheartedness. Her eyes shot downward and Reed could feel that she had something heavy on her mind.

"Now that we have a moment, can I ask you what happened down there?"

It dawned on him that was the first time he hadn't been capable of hiding his struggles from her in some way. There was no lying his way out of this conversation even if he wanted to. The truth terrified him. Blood deserted his face, making him light headed and foggy. He knew she would figure it out eventually.

He spoke slowly, "Since I woke up. I've been having some fractured moments. Sometimes it's not so bad; hearing things, seeing something briefly. But sometimes...." His voice sank, "Sometimes it's more real. Seeing and hearing things together. It seems random when it strikes, and I have almost no control of myself when it happens. I start out knowing it's all in my head, but the longer it goes on or the more intense it is..." He paused, holding back tears, "I start to get lost."

The more he explained his situation the more he felt all of the emotions he had been shoving away start to bubble up. The mixture of everything he had been holding onto was overloading his senses to the point he couldn't even tell what he was feeling anymore. He wiped away a single tear and sniffled, "I'm terrified it's going to keep getting worse."

Without saying a word, Dahlia grabbed him and wrapped her arms around him. The dam broke and he started bawling, burring himself in her.

"I'm so sorry you've been dealing with this." She rubbed his back, "You don't have to do it alone though, I'm here for you. We're in this together, okay?"

Her words were like a sedative, strong enough to calm him down and put a cork on his crying.

"Well that's embarrassing." He muttered out between sniffles.

She pushed him back and looked in his eyes, "You have nothing to be embarrassed about alright? You had your mind messed with by some psychotic doctor and have had to see and do some terrible things to escape. If that's not a time to cry, then I don't know when is. I mean, it sounds like a fictional story!" She smiled, hoping to infect him with a small amount of joy.

Reed chuckled through his labored breathing, feeling a lot better after letting her in on his problem. The two separated and leaned back against the structure. Dahlia slowly nibbled on her block of cheese, savoring what little food they had, "Thank you, for not leaving me behind by the way. Even after I yelled at you to go."

"Of course." He grinned, "No way I was going to leave you behind, no matter what you told me."

"I'm happy to hear it." She pressed a hand to her chest, "Even if it did feel like my boob was almost ripped off being pulled through that last portion."

He laughed. The way she could bring him back to joking around astounded and impressed him. He'd almost forgotten that they were trapped on a rooftop with no clear way down. This feeling of joy felt suspended in time, and he basked in every second of it, "Sorry about that, I bet it was better than getting blasted by one of those guns again though."

She looked at him from the side of her eye, "Just barely."

They sat in silence for a few minutes and enjoyed the view of the clear sky from the rooftop while Dahlia slowly ate her cheese.

He was grateful she had thought to grab anything to eat in the shuffle of it all but could still feel his stomach churning, begging for more food. They couldn't stay up on the roof forever and going down was a death sentence. How much time would they even allow to pass before they came barging through the door to get them? Reed's survival mode was switching back on and taking him out of their peaceful bubble. He wished he could stay and drown in it, forgetting about everything else.

"We should probably take a look around, start to think of a game plan."

"Yeah, you're probably right. Fun time is over I guess." She cracked her neck and crumpled up the paper.

Reed stood up and started to walk to the side of the building that they had entered on the first floor, Dahlia following close behind him. He reached the edge and immediately looked downward at the street. All the lab vehicles were parked right in front of the new building they were in. None of the people could be seen, so they had to be either inside the building or waiting in their cars. Reed was getting nervous at the thought of them running up the stairs at this very second. Before he could get too wrapped up in himself, Dahlia interrupted his train of thought.

"What a view." She looked out at the area surrounding the city.

Reed was so busy looking at the street he hadn't even noticed how far they could see outward from the roof. It was a breathtaking view of the land. More than half of the area was open to them. The buildings closer to the center blocked their view of anything else. The way the rooftops descended in height the further they got from theirs gave them an almost stair like look.

The forest they were first lost in drew his attention. It looked so much smaller from where he was. It was short in width compared to the land around it, making up for it by going on so far that he couldn't see where it ended. The gas station sign was the only thing that could be spotted poking up through the thick ocean of treetops. They thinned out to nothing at least a mile from the city entrance. The entire surrounding area was mostly green flatlands with various sporadic buildings littering the grounds far away from one another. A portion had large square areas of land that were cut out in equally sized chunks. Some looked green with an abundance of plant life, while others were a tan lifeless dirt patch. They could only see three major roads from their view, two of them jetting out on opposite ends of the city from one another while the one that led to the forest was a quarter of the city from either of them.

He leaned with his hands on the outer ridge, "It is pretty amazing from up here"

"I know we need to think of a way down, but just imagine owning a little piece of that land out there. I feel like I could just walk down the building tops and take a piece of my own." She reached out and grabbed the air.

Her words sparked an idea. He ran over to the adjacent ledge of the building and looked down at the rooftops, eyeballing the height difference.

She tried to figure out what he was looking at, "What is it?"

"You're a genius is what it is."

"How's that?"

"We're going to do exactly as you said." He pointed to the next rooftop over, "We're going to jump down the building tops, all the way to the edge."

Chapter 13

She leaned against the perimeter wall looking over the city, "That's your big plan?"

"We already jumped from one building to another through the windows, why not roof to roof?" He looked her way, "It only looks like one story drops from building to building, so we should be fine to just keep jumping across until we reach the end."

She couldn't take her eyes off the next rooftop, "What if we slip, or some of the buildings are farther apart down the road from here?"

"Well, if the buildings get too far apart to jump then we will have to cross that bridge when it comes. As for slipping, I guess it would be a faster way to go then the lab."

"You better not slip up then, I don't want to have to do this alone." She looked past the buildings at the open fields.

He brushed some dust off of the ridge like it would be the deciding factor in his success, "Get a running start, leap to the ridge and then catapult ourselves over. Easy peasy."

"Didn't you call me fucking crazy for the whole idea of jumping through the windows just an hour or so ago?" She raised an eyebrow.

He smiled, "I was distressed. And It's not, *not* crazy. It's the only way I see us getting out of here without trying to take on a squad of armed guards though."

She gestured with an opened hand to the next roof, "So, are you going to take the first leap then?"

"I was thinking ladies first, but if you insist then I guess I'll go first." His nerves were perking up and his skin felt like it could be vibrating.

Reed walked a good distance away from the edge of the building to get a running start. He was thankful for the fact that he couldn't see down until after there was already no turning back this time. He faced the ledge, anxiety radiating from his heart and sweat forming on his forehead. Even with his view blocked he could see the fall to the street clear as day in his mind. His feet were like stones holding him in place. Subject six flashed through his mind out of nowhere. The vision of that poor guy and the knowledge that the people responsible for him were possibly on their way up lightened his body.

Reed began to run to the ledge, progressing into a full sprint before he came up on it. He made a small awkward leap onto the ridge and sprung himself forward with everything he had. While he flew over the empty space leading to the street his mind went blissfully blank. He landed hard on the next roof, unable to catch himself and rolling to the ground.

"Six out of ten! You botched the landing!" Dahlia yelled at him.

He knew she was joking but the pain from how he landed had him hoping for a minute that she would crash and burn as well. Guilt about the thought quickly replaced the feeling.

He got back to his feet and looked back at the building where she was still staring at him, "Your turn!"

Her head quickly disappeared out of sight. Reed backed up a little bit to not get in the way of her landing. He waited for a few minutes before wondering if she was going to get cold feet about the whole jumping part of the plan. She'd be all alone when the guards came and he couldn't bear that thought.

Before his doubts could grow to large, she came flying through the air in his direction. Her jump was far more majestic than he imagined his looked. Her legs buckled and she rolled until she came to a stop on her back. Reed extended a hand, which she quickly took, and helped her back to her feet, "I'll give you an eight out of ten. Flawless jump, but you didn't stick the landing either."

She brushed the dirt off her pants and arms, "And you want to do that, like, fifteen more times now?"

He shook his head, "I don't want to be doing any of this. I just don't want to go back to the lab more."

"Maybe we do a few more jumps and then see if they have moved at all. If they're still casing the same building, then maybe we can go down the stairs and slip by them." She looked longingly at the stairwell door to the roof they were on.

Reed wanted to jump the whole way down, thinking it was the safest route to take, but didn't know if his legs could take it. They already hurt after the one jump they accomplished.

He bit the inside of his lip and looked around, "Yeah, as much as I don't want to, you're right. My legs would probably shatter before making it all the way down to the lowest building. A few more and we should be far enough away I hope."

The two geared up for their next jump and landed about as gracefully as the first time. With each one their legs and body got a few more bruises and pains until they decided they shouldn't go anymore for fear of getting too injured. The two had made it a good four buildings further before deciding to stop.

The rooftops all looked almost exactly the same as one another, the mechanical structures differing in location being the only noticeable difference. Reed wondered if every building in the city was the same inside, with a shopping storefront on the first floor and the rest of the building just filled to brim with lifeless cubicles.

Reed was sitting down rubbing one of his shins, "Should we make our way down?"

She wiped some blood from a scrape on her arm, "I thought you'd never ask."

They walked over to the stairwell and thanked the heavens that it was unlocked. Their pace descending through the building was a much slower and easier walk than when they had been climbing up the other one. Walking at their own pace was so rare up to this point that it felt like a luxury. Once they approached the bottom of the stairwell Dahlia stopped and lowered her voice to a whisper, "We should still be extremely cautious when we walk through that door into whatever's on the first floor."

"Of course."

Dahlia gently pushed the door open just enough to peek through the crack. Reed couldn't see anything from behind her while she surveyed the room.

"I think we're good." She continued to whisper, "It looks completely abandoned. The windows are even boarded up."

She pushed the door open to a dark room that was only lit up by the many cracks between plywood sheets covering the windows allowing the sun to shine through. The room was filled with small tables and chairs only fitting for two people at a time. Right in front of the stairwell door was a long counter with some broken-down equipment bolted to it resembling the face scanner that the officer had used to try and identify them. Some left behind machines were sitting on another counter against the wall behind the first. Reed couldn't tell what they were but thought that they looked mostly like something to make a sort of beverage. Everything was covered with a thick layer of dust and large mold spores were growing out of various parts of the machines.

Their steps were slow and cautious as if the place was layered in boobytraps.

"I wonder how long this place has been closed. It's weird they left all the furniture and equipment behind."

"A long, long time it seems." Reed brushed his finger against a table, picking up a large amount of dust, "They must have left in a hurry or didn't care enough to empty the place."

"I wish I could have come here in its prime. I can just imagine stepping in here for my morning coffee on my way to work or something." A sly smile curled her lips, "Maybe running into a cute guy as I rushed to get my order."

"Er, uh, yeah. I would definitely try to talk you up." He shook his head at himself in disbelief. What the hell was that.

Dahlia laughed, "I'm sure you would, you're just oozing with flirtation."

Reed became flushed in the face and hoped that this awkwardness was just a side effect from the lab experiments and not how he was beforehand.

"I'm only teasing."

He tried to take an offramp, "Do you think we should try to go out the front door?"

She sighed, "I don't know. We could try it, but it looked like all the abandoned buildings were chained shut from the outside."

Reed walked to the front door and gently pushed on it until it cracked open, letting the sun beam in on his face. There was a chain and lock dangling from the handles on the outside. That detail had slipped his mind when they decided to try and sneak by instead of jumping their way down. He slowly closed the door back up, trying to make as little sound as possible, "Well, we can try to take a board down and break through the glass, or we can climb back to the top and continue our jumping plan until our legs break off. Not the best sounding options so far."

"What about the second floor?"

"What about it?"

"I figure if we're going to have to smash and run then maybe it would be better done jumping down from a second-floor window that's not facing the street. If we leave from the side then they still won't know exactly what building we left from."

It was a good idea strategically, but he loathed the thought of jumping down from another height. His knees were ready to explode from all the impacts they've taken. "I guess that makes sense, yeah."

"We run like hell the second our feet hit the ground."

"We should try to make it outside the city. Less places to hide, but also less places to get trapped in." He yearned for soft dirt and grass to replace the cold concrete they were surrounded by.

"I'd like to leave this place behind too." She placed a finder on her chin and looked at him, "Where would we go from there?"

"I don't know. Do we ever know where we're going though? We're just blindly running from place to place. At least out there we're not like rats in a maze."

She hesitated, "I guess we just keep making it up as we go along then."

They left the store and headed back up the stairs to the second floor. Luckily, the door popped right open, and they walked into another eerily similar hallway to all the other ones they had visited. They entered one of the office spaces around the corner. The same old decrepit cubicle filled sight awaited them.

Out of the wall of windows was a view of the other building's brick wall painted neon vomit green about six feet away. Dahlia looked around for something to break through the window, slowly weaving in and out of the cubicles. Reed was doing the same in the opposite direction with no luck. Unlike the last buildings, the walls and concrete ceiling were still fully intact for the most part, with only small pebble sized pieces flaking off. Nothing was a good enough size to smash through a window.

Dahlia called to Reed across the room, "I'm done looking for rubble. I'll be right back."

She walked out of the room and left Reed by himself to wait. He looked out the window down to the street, visualizing all the things that could potentially go wrong. If there was ever a time he was going to break an ankle from a jump, he thought this would be the time it would happen. Or worse, if Dahlia was injured in the fall. He knew he couldn't carry her and escape at the same time, especially being exposed by all the noise they were about to make. She would beg him to leave her behind again and he knew he wouldn't be able to.

Dahlia reentered the room, breaking Reed from his thoughts. She had a chair in hand and did break her stride to the window, "Hope you're ready!"

The chair connected with the window and bounced off flying from her hand. It took her off guard and she stumbled back, almost falling. She only managed to leave a large crack in the glass instead of shattering through it.

"They probably heard that." Reed quickly picked the chair up and prepared a swing. The window was still intact, only cracking a little bit more. He got frustrated and continued to strike it over and over. After four more good hits he finally managed to break through and shatter it.

Reed threw the chair and made the jump out first, falling onto the hard concrete and catching himself from collapsing completely with his hands on the ground. Dahlia landed next to him before he could regain his composure. When she landed, she slipped off her feet and smashed her hip on some shards of glass, "Fuck!"

Reed pulled her back up to her feet, "You okay?"

"I'm fine, let's go" She kept one hand held to her hip.

They ran down the alley away from the street where they had last seen the vehicles. They approached the other end and Reed fearfully slowed down his pace before running out to the street. Dahlia quickly passed him and crossed out of the alley.

The moment her body passed the building corner he heard a blasting noise slightly different from the familiar gun sound. A strap launched off the wall from the street side and wrapped around Dahlias legs, collapsing her to the ground.

"Dahlia!" He ran up to her position and looked around the corner. There was some sort of black block that had been attached to the wall with an invisible light pointed straight across the alley entrance.

The bastards set traps.

Chapter 14

Dahlia tried to squirm around and push the straps off with her hands, but they only kept getting tighter. She instantly flipped into panic mode and couldn't stop even though nothing was happening.

Reed's mind swirled as he tried to think of a way out of the situation. *How could they have possibly figured out which building we were in? It didn't matter, they had figured it out and would be there any moment to collect if he didn't do something.*

He grabbed Dahlias arms and turned her around, dragging her back into the alley out of sight.

"I'll be right back." He attempted to sound calm for her sake.

Reed ran down the alley to where they had jumped through the window and grabbed the largest chunk of glass he could find. He smacked it against the wall on its side to break it into a thinner piece that was easier to hold like a knife. By the time he was running back he heard the sound of engines roaring down the road.

"Shhh!" He whispered to Dahlia as he passed. He ran up to the edge of the alley, flattening his back on the side of the building the vans were approaching from.

They came screeching to a halt before reaching the alley and Reed heard the doors all sliding open and slamming shut at the same time. The guard's footsteps stopped before getting too close to the opening.

Reed tightened his grip on the shard of glass until it was almost cutting through his skin. The pain hardly registered while he waited for the guard's next move. He knew he couldn't take on all of them at once with just a piece of glass, but his instincts had taken over. If Dahlia was going down, then he was going down with her.

He heard one last car door click open and slowly shut in a calm manner. Slow light footsteps joined the group and no one else moved a muscle.

"They can't be far. Probably waiting around the corner as I speak." Doctor Stintz could have been browsing for a new book or hunting down people and you would never know the difference in his tone.

The immediate knowledge of his whereabouts sent a shiver up Reed's spine. The guards he could maybe outsmart at some point, but not the doctor.

"Stand back and sweep the alley, blast anyone in sight. They're not getting away this time or none of you are seeing a cent for any of the time you've already put in."

"Yes sir." The group said in unison.

He had a split second to decide his next move or it was going to be made for him with a blast to the chest. Everything went blank, a plan to stay free left the train. Without a thought, his body took over, running out toward the one guard that was slightly separated from the group about to do the sweep. He put his arm down in a stabbing stance with his shard while rushing him.

The guard was taken aback and shot off his gun at Reed, missing him slightly and blasting the wall behind him. Reed made it to him and tried to stab the glass shard into his torso. The guard quickly smacked Reed's arm down with the side of his gun. He managed to hold onto the shard, slicing the guard's stomach all the way down.

Two blasts interrupted the scuffle and Reed was wrapped around his torso and legs. The glass flew from his hand while he tumbled to the ground. He remembered how the straps had tightened on him last time and didn't struggle. Instead, he looked up at the clear blue sky and took in as much of it as he could before it was gone forever.

"Son of a..." The guard that Reed had attacked shouted while raising his foot to stomp down on his face.

"Don't you dare!" Dr. Stintz shouted at the guard.

The guard stomped his foot down right beside Reed's head, "The bastard cut me!"

Stintz immediately recomposed himself and walked over to Reed, "Occupational hazard. I need him in as good of a condition as possible."

He stood over him, looking right into his eyes. Reed felt like all the joy in the world was being sucked out of him through his two black holes. He was like fear incarnate to Reed, filling his entire body up with only a glance.

"You gave me quite a scare there." Stintz looked him over, "I thought I might have lost you for good jumping through that window."

Reed's voice was void of emotion, "What do you care if I died?"

"Oh, I care a great deal about you." He smiled, "You'll come to realize that. In time." Stintz looked at the alley, "Go get the girl. Put them in separate vans and prepare them for transport. I'm going to go ahead and get the lab ready to receive them." Even his footsteps looked too neat and composed, like nothing he did hadn't been thought of ahead of time. He got in his car and pulled down the road.

One of the guard's pushed Reed's head to the side with his foot, "Let's get the girl first."

Reed watched helplessly while three guards grabbed Dahlia by the arms and dragged her down the concrete into one of the vans. He couldn't help but struggle at the sight and the straps tightened around him. The blame was on him. He wasn't fast enough to save her.

A softer tone came out from one of the vans. The assistant they were traveling with stepped out looking displeased, "Come on guys."

The guards dropped Dahlias arms to the ground like they were nothing, "What?"

"They're human beings. Have a little decency." He walked over to Dahlia and crouched down to look her in the eyes, "I want to do this more humanely than these guys would. For that to happen I need your help." He paused, waiting for any semblance of a response, "Are you able to do that?"

Dahlia stared at him for a few seconds before answering, "I can do that."

"Okay," he clapped and rubbed his hands together, "I'm going to release your leg restraints and let you stand up. If you try anything funny then I won't be able to keep these men from treating you however they see fit."

She nodded silently. The assistant grabbed a remote out of his pocket and pressed a button, releasing the restraints. Dahlia slowly pushed up to her feet and looked over at Reed.

Reed's eyes were glued to her the entire time and she could tell he wanted her to run or distract them and get away somehow. She knew it would be a mistake to try.

The assistant looked to one of the guards, "Give me your cuffs."

The guard pulled out a small metal square with an indent on the top from his pocket and handed it over to him.

"Hold out your hands please."

She listened and he placed the square between her held out hands. With a push of the indent, two straps flew out and around Dahlias wrists, tightening them down together.

"Now, if you would calmly walk over to the van, the guards will help you into the back." He motioned his hand to the vehicle.

She continued without a fuss and walked over with two guards to the first van. The assistant continued to Reed and crouched next to him. He couldn't keep eye contact with Reed for more than a second and switched from staring at the ground to the building behind him, "You've shown much more hostility than she has. Can I trust you to come without a fight?"

"I know when I'm caught." Reed exhaled deeply and looked to the sky again.

"I'm going to choose to trust you." He grabbed the remote from his pocket, "Please don't do anything stupid like at the lab."

Reed wanted nothing more than to do exactly what he did at the lab and bust him over the head. There was no element of surprise this time and everything was different now, he knew that. The best he could think of was to play along and hope some opportunity would show itself soon enough.

The assistant released his restraints and Reed got back to his feet. He put his arms out for cuffing while trying to force the assistant to meet his eyeline. His presence made the man nervous, or at least uneasy. The assistant grabbed another cuff from one of the guards and wrapped his wrists with it.

He nudged Reed forward with his hand on his upper back, "I'll be supervising your transport due to the lack of guards after the incident at the lab."

The other two men had Dahila already loaded up. One stayed in the back with her while the other drove. Reed walked with the assistant to the open sliding door on the second van. The last guard hopped into the driver's seat as the assistant beckoned Reed in. Reed pulled himself up into the enclosed steel box separating them from the front. It was completely empty besides two benches on either side and a small light attached to the roof. A door that led to the front of the van was closed beside him by the entrance. He took a seat on one of the benches. The assistant closed the door behind him and sat on the bench opposite him. Reed could feel the van start up and bump along beginning their trip back.

Reed stared at the ground with his elbows on his knees, contemplating all the horrible things he might be subjected to when they returned. The doctor didn't seem like he was someone who would have any second thoughts about taking some form of revenge. He looked at the assistant with one question that had been stuck in his head the entire time he could remember.

"Did you release me on purpose?"

The assistant looked shocked at the question, darting his look over to match his in an instant. He averted his eyes down after a small time passed with an ashamed look over his face.

"I didn't mean to." His voice was shaky, "I wasn't thinking when I released you too early, I was just so shocked at...." He cut himself off.

Reed was surprised, not only by how honest his answer was, but also by the pain he could hear in his voice, "Shocked at what? Me? What about me was so shocking?"

"Nothing, never mind." He shook his head, "I shouldn't have said that."

Reed was determined to get him to talk. He would have felt worse about trying to break down the man for information if he hadn't been part of a human experimentation facility that he was intimately familiar with, "Your secret would be safe with me. I'm likely going to forget everything or be dead soon enough anyway."

Every mention of something the lab did made the man almost wince. He didn't look like he approved of what they were doing even though he was part of it. There was a deep sigh before he looked directly at Reed, "It was the first time I had ever seen one of the subjects."

Reed was puzzled and instantly filled with anger being called a subject again, "You mean people."

"Errr. Uhh. Yes. People." The assistant stuttered out. "I haven't been out of school for very long and was assigned to the lab. I learned a lot from books. It didn't prepare me for..."

Reed cut him off, "Human experimentation?"

His eyes closed and neck twitched looking to the ground.

Reed raised his brows and tilted his head, "Is that what you learned in school?"

His face scrunched and voice got louder, "No, no, not exactly."

"But it's what you were training for right? To take my life for your own benefit?" Reed got louder with every sentence as well.

"No. I didn't. I mean..." The assistant struggled to get anything cohesive to come from his mouth.

"I don't even know who I am! You took everything from me!" Reed half yelled.

The assistant screamed, "I DIDN'T ASK FOR ANY OF THIS!"

His outburst put Reed's temper back in place, the response intrigued him, "What do you mean you didn't want any of this?"

Tears dropped down from the assistant's face, "I mean what I say." Heavy breaths separated his words, "I didn't want to be a part of this."

"A part of what?"

"A part of The Solution team. That's what they call the people at the lab."

"The Solution? Solution to what? The population thing?"

The assistant's head shot up at the mention of the population.

Reed smirked, "Yeah, I've learned a few things. Not much about it though, just that people stopped having kids for some reason."

"Yeah, well it's a little more than that. We did this to ourselves." He looked at Reed for a short time with a new feeling of comradery after their outbursts, like they had some mutual understanding of one another now.

"The food." He told Reed, "As the population rose up, we had to find new and improved ways to grow food at an accelerated pace. On top of that, all the major food companies started to mess with their recipes to make everything sweeter and more addictive. Over generations of time, all those factors mixed together started to physically change our DNA through pregnancies."

"What did pregnancies have to do with it? I thought the problem was that people couldn't get pregnant?" Reed struggled to put the complete picture together.

The assistant sighed and rolled his eyes, "Put more simply, we shoved too much altered food full of chemicals into pregnant people. It affected the children throughout the gestation process. It began with small birth defects and an increase in sickness, with only a small number becoming infertile. It didn't take long for infertility to become the main birth defect though. The food companies were at record profits, and with brand loyalty at an all-time high they wouldn't stop. It became impossible for people to eat a clean fresh diet, even if they wanted to."

The dump of information was hard for him to process. He knew the world wasn't doing well. He had hoped it wasn't this dire, "So why us then?"

"That is unfortunately information above my paygrade. I don't even want to know at this point. They are looking for a solution to quickly reverse the damage to our bodies at any cost now. I just never wanted to be a part of it. No matter what the stakes are, I can't get behind what he does there." One of his fists was clenched tight.

"Then what are you doing here?" He looked around the van and then pointed at him, "You even came to retrieve us with the doctor. That doesn't paint the picture of someone who isn't on their side."

The assistant extended his arms out sideways, "You think I want to be here? I'm here on Dr. Stintz's orders as punishment. I'm the reason all of this happened, so I needed to go out and help clean things up. He also wants to break me, I think. To be like his other assistant who has no care left in him, like he does. I believe that's why he required me to be in the back of the transport with you. There's also the small fact that he has another back up plan if getting you didn't work out because of me anyway. They might be too young yet though, and it would set him back for who knows how long."

The doctor would really stoop to experimenting on *children*? Reed wanted to ask about it but knew he needed to keep the conversation going in a more positive direction, "You didn't even get to pick where you wanted to work after your schooling was done?"

He shook his head, "Dr. Stintz is my uncle. I've been groomed for this from the day I was born. I'm one of the last few children born out of successful implantation. My generation is the last time any person has been able to successfully be inseminated or carry full term." A bitterness draped over his voice, "Since my family is so high up and respected in the science community, my parents were able to buy a child from the last batch."

"I'm sorry." He genuinely felt bad for the guy, still needing to push on his morals. He didn't have a choice in what happened to him just as Reed didn't, "I know a little bit about not having a choice in your life. I've only had to deal with it for a couple days now, you've had your whole life to be forced into something you don't want. It's the worst feeling in the world, having no control."

The assistant managed an empathetic grunt with a small smile, "I'm sorry too. For your situation..."

"Reed," he interrupted. "My names Reed, and hers is Dahlia."

"I'm sorry Reed. For both of you."

"What's your name?"

He paused for a moment, as if to contemplate if it was a bad idea to tell him, "Isaac."

"I'd say nice to meet you Isaac, but it honestly hasn't been a very nice introduction."

Isaac chuckled, remaining silent.

"So, you probably lived in a nice place in the city your whole life then huh?" Reed wanted to keep him talking, wanted to dig something up that could help him.

His back straightened up in confidence, "It's nice yeah. Top floor in the center of the city nice, just on the corner of Burley and Nelson." He deflated and slightly shook his head, "Sorry, I forgot you wouldn't know where that is for a second."

Reed had to restrain his eyes from rolling into the back of his head, "It sounds nice. You know what sounds nice to me?"

"What's that?"

"A house out on some land somewhere, open areas with plenty of places to roam and explore. None of this concrete shit everywhere I look." Reed looked at the back of the van where a window would usually be, "It's too bad I'll never get to experience that." his eyes fell between his legs, placing his head in his hands.

Isaac swallowed hard and his voice dropped, "Again, I really am sorry. I wish I could help you."

Reed looked up at him, "You can. You're the only one who can." He stuck out his banded wrists, "Just release me. Take off my cuffs and I'll jump out the side door. You can say I overpowered you."

"What happens to me then? What happens when I'm the reason you escaped a second time?"

"Doing the right thing isn't always easy. If you don't help me, then my blood will be on your hands. By ignoring this opportunity," He pointed hard at Isaac's chest, "you become the reason I die in that lab."

Isaac teared up again, pushed to the brink. He slammed his fist back against the wall, catching Reed off guard. "Fine." He closed his eyes, "I'll loosen your ties so you can jump out. If you don't get away or if you get caught again, I can't help you though."

Reed nodded, "I understand... You're a good man."

Isaac reached into his pocket and pulled out the remote. He tapped the tip of it to the indented center piece and the straps gave way, falling off Reeds arms to the floor. Reed rubbed his hands over his wrists, which were turning a shade of pink from the pressure. He considered doing as he said and jumping out the side of the van and making a run for it. It would likely be his best chance of escape, albeit not a great one. In his heart he knew that if he was making it, then so was Dahlia.

"Alright, go on. Get out of here." Isaac thew his hand at the door for him to leave, "We're probably not far from the lab already."

Reed looked at him and hated that Isaac would be caught in the crossfire. He was a good man in the wrong place at the wrong time. He gritted his teeth before he spoke, "I can't do that."

Isaac raised his voice, "What do you mean? Why spend all that time convincing me to set you free then?"

"I can't leave without her, I'm sorry for this."

Before Isaac could get out his next question, Reed bolted to the front of the van and opened the door to the cab.

Chapter 15

Isaac stood up, "What are you doing?!"

Reed ignored his question and shoved his front half into the cab with the guard. The guard snapped his head to him with shock pouring from his face, "What the..."

Before he could finish his sentence, Reed grabbed the seatbelt and wrapped it around his neck. The guard frantically tried to pull the belt off of him with one hand while attempting to steer with the other. The van started to swing violently from side to side as the guard struggled to keep it on the road.

"WHAT ARE YOU DOING?" Isaac repeated louder.

"It's the only way I'm going to get Dahlia! This has to be done!" Reed yelled back at him. The guard's face was turning a slight shade of blue and the van's swaying became increasingly more erratic. Reed pulled one hand off the belt to grab the steering wheel, attempting to straighten things out. The guard was able to get enough slack for a slight gasp of air.

The moment Reed's hand touched the steering wheel, the guard let go and flung his elbow back at him. He connected with the top of Reed's forehead, his elbow sliding over the top. The glancing blow was enough to knock Reed back a few inches and tear his grip from the seatbelt and steering wheel. The guard quickly grabbed the steering wheel again and turned it hard to the left. The momentum, on top of the hit, flung Reed into the passenger seat almost upside-down. The guard was unable to get a grip on his gun that was sliding back and forth across the dashboard, frantically reaching for it.

Reed quickly regained his composure and punched the guard square in the jaw. The punch hardly seemed to faze him which caught Reed off guard and made his stomach churn. The guard swung his free hand wildly, trying to do any damage he could. Reed grabbed it, wrapped the guard's arm in both of his, and flung himself backward through the door leading into the back of the van. The guard's elbow hit the edge of the doorframe and bent backward with the force. There was a loud crack before the he started to howl in pain. The guard flung his arm back in the front, waiving it like a limp noodle.

Reed quickly jumped back to the cab side of the van and unbuckled the seatbelt. The van was swaying side to side so much that it was barely staying on the road. In one swift movement Reed reached over and pulled the handle to the door open while trying to shove the guard's lower body out with his free arm. He grabbed the steering wheel, barely keeping the van from crashing into the ditch, continuing to push on the guard. The door swung fully open and the guard grabbed the top of the frame desperately pushing himself back in the vehicle.

Isaac popped up behind him and grabbed the steering wheel attempting to straighten the van out. When Reed noticed him, he completely let go and focused all his strength on shoving the guard's legs out of the van. Reed put his feet onto the passenger seat and used it to push off of while he tried to scoop the guard's body out of the driver's seat. Even with only his one remaining arm he was putting up a good fight to keep his bottom half as far in the van as possible. Reed began to throw punches down on his abdomen in an attempt to weaken his core. He gave one large shove off the passenger seat with his legs after a few of them and flung the guards bottom half out.

The guard was hopelessly clinging to the door frame with his feet and knees skipping off the pavement careening down the road. Reed plopped himself in the driver's seat and shooed off Isaac from the steering wheel.

"PLEASE!" The guard shouted at them.

Reed ignored him and instead swung the van right and then left in long hard turns. The intense sway slammed the door closed on the guard's fingers and he finally let go, tumbling and rolling down on the pavement.

Isaac sat back in the passenger seat, talking through labored breathing, "What's your plan now?"

Reed's eyes were glued to the road, "To save Dahlia."

They were just getting into the thickness of the tree line. The second van was far enough ahead that their taillights looked like small red dots. He slammed down on the gas, determined to push the van to its limits.

"How do you even know how to drive?" Isaac clicked in his seatbelt, "In your paperwork it stated that they had already initiated the memory wiping process."

"I don't know. I didn't think about it; it's just feels like muscle memory or something." He was afraid that if he did think about the why then he would lose it, "I guess the key word there was that they only *initiated* the memory wipe. Believe me, they still took enough."

The adrenaline pumping through Reed's body made him feel like he could take a bull head on. His mind felt truly focused for the first time since they escaped with only one thing on repeat coursing through. No matter what he had to do, he was getting her free.

They were slowly catching up to the second van, only about five car lengths behind. Reed saw the convenient store ahead on their left and knew he was quickly running out of time. Closing in on them, he wondered what the best way would be to try and get the van to stop without harming her.

They were only a few feet from the bumper as they zoomed past the store. Reed moved into the oncoming lane and attempted to overtake the van. He got three quarters of the way up the side of it when they suddenly turned into him, pushing his left tires slightly into the ditch. He knew they weren't going to gently come to a stop now. Whatever was going to happen would happen and Dahlia would have to find a way to forgive him.

Reed turned out of the trench and slammed into the side of the other van, sending them deep into the ditch on the other side. The driver quickly popped the van out of it, hardly losing any speed. Reed pumped the brakes, bringing the front of his van slightly ahead of the others bumper. He turned into it and the opposing van's tail slid out while the driver tried to correct them before it was too late. Their van swung completely sideways in front of Reeds.

The driver in the sideways van had a mixture of terror and confusion in his face when he caught a look at Reed in the driver's seat. Reed gingerly turned his wheel to the right in an attempt to steer the other van into the ditch while slowing them down.

The two moved over with the turn until the back of the sideways van's tires fell into the ditch. The tires dug in the dirt, lifting the bottom up off the ground. Before Reed could react, the momentum of his van flipped the other onto its side, spinning out before crashing to a halt on the side of the road.

Reed slammed on the breaks, bringing the van to a screeching halt. He silently stared out of the window at the crash, wondering if he had just killed the only other person he cared about in this world.

"Oh my god." Isaac put a hand over his mouth, "What did you *do*?"

Reed couldn't think straight, paralyzing him to the moment. His mind and body were at odds, one wanting to run out and find her while the other couldn't budge. The twenty seconds he sat there and stared felt like an eternity had passed him by with his worst fear lying sideways in front of him.

He finally was able to pull himself together enough to open the door and jump out. His feet felt like they were concrete blocks when they hit the pavement. His body and mind shaky from the incident making it hard to stand up straight. Lifting one foot and placing it in front of him felt like an enormous task with every step.

Pushing himself forward, he made it to the van. There was no noise in the air other than the twisting metal sounds from pieces of the frame that hadn't quite settled yet. He climbed on top of the vehicle and looked downward into the driver's side window. The guard that had been driving was hanging in the seat by his seat belt, blood dripping from the forehead of his unmoving body. The airbag had deployed but didn't seem to help wherever this poor man slammed his head into.

Reed opened the door and dropped down into the cab, his feet landing on the broken passenger window. He rummaged through the hanging man's pockets until he pulled out one of those black remotes with one button that seemed to control all of the restraints. He slid it into his pocket and looked at the door leading into the back. His heart sank with the possibility of what he could be walking into. If the guard in front was in a seatbelt and unresponsive then what were the chances that she was alright in the steel box with no protection?

Before he could get too in his head about it, he grabbed the handle and pushed open the door. It fell into the back making a loud smacking noise when it hit the other side. Reed peered in and saw Dahlia kneeling on the back of the other guard with her cuffs wrapped around his neck. She was still pulling intensely even though the guard's body was completely still.

She looked over and made eye contact with Reed, releasing her pull when she did. Reed climbed in the back with her as she pulled her restraints out from under the guard's neck. He leapt forward and wrapped his arms around her.

"Hell of an escape plan." She whispered.

"I'm sorry, I didn't expect it to go this way. Are you okay?" He tried to contain himself and not squeeze her too hard.

"I think so. Pretty banged up but I landed on the guard who took most of the impact. He was still out of it when I came to, so I took advantage of the opportunity."

Reed pushed her back a bit to quickly check for any injuries. There were a few drops of blood that were coming from her ear and some bruising that was starting to form on top of her forehead but nothing extremely serious.

She smiled weakly, "I'm okay."

Reed grabbed the remote from his pocket and released her cuffs.

"Thank you." She grabbed her wrists, "How did you ever get control of the van?"

"Convinced the scientist to let me go. He was expecting me to jump and run but I couldn't leave you behind."

She leaned into him, "The next lifesaving plan is on me."

"Let's get you out of here before we start to think about that." Reed was thankful that the crash hadn't crumpled her sense of humor. He reached up and pulled the sliding door open above them, "Think you can walk?"

"Of course." She struggled to get upright.

Reed knelt down and cupped his hands together to give her a boost, "Here, let me help you."

She put one foot in his hands and he hoisted her up through the door. She bent the top half of her body over on the outside and struggled to fling her legs up out of the van. Once she managed to climb out, Reed heard the thud of her feet hitting the pavement outside. Reed grabbed the door and pulled himself up out of the back. He sat down on the side and pushed himself to the pavement, landing next to Dahlia.

"We can take this van to wherever we want to go." Reed pointed at it.

"Let's go somewhere far away then." She struggled not to limp taking her first couple steps, obviously in pain. Reed grabbed her arm and wrapped it over his shoulder.

Isaac finally got out of the van when they approached, "Is anyone else alive in there?"

Reed looked up to meet his eyeline, "One of them might just be knocked out, hanging in the driver's seat. It doesn't look good though."

He nodded while staring at the crash, "I see."

"You can come with us if you like." Dahlia told him.

"No, I can't. I have to call this in or I'll be hunted down just like they're hunting you, only they don't need me alive." He turned his head their way without looking at them, "Take the van and go. Don't come back."

"Don't plan on it." Reed opened the passenger door and helped Dahlia into the seat. She sat back and melted into it, closing her eyes instantly. Reed closed her in and turned to Isaac, "Thank you again." He put his hand on Isaacs shoulder, "For what it's worth, I'm sorry that I lied to you."

Isaac brushed off his shoulder, seemingly still in shock from the chase and crash, "At least you got them all. No one to dispute my story."

"You're a good man and you did a brave thing today, don't forget that." Reed gave Isaac's back a small pat before turning away from him and leaving him to the crash, walking around to the driver's side door. He opened the door and hopped into the van, pulling the seat belt over his chest and clicking it in, thinking about how he had just used the same belt to try and strangle a man. Dahlia was already dozing off and Reed thought it best to let her sleep.

He started up the van and turned it around, driving down the road back in the direction of the city. Their destination was unknown at this point, but Reed felt freer than ever now. He would be fine with driving until there was nowhere left to go as long as it was still in the opposite direction of that lab.

Chapter 16

They drove down the long road surrounded by trees, wondering which way they should go when it ends. Dahlia was drifting in and out of sleep on their way through the dark wild archways. No matter how strong he knew she was, he worried about her injuries. The small amount of bleeding from her ear had stopped after only a few drops, the blood crusting and flaking off. He couldn't believe his luck that they were still together through everything that had happened.

Reed saw something in the road a little way ahead of them. As he drove closer, he realized that it was the first guard he had thrown from the moving vehicle, still lying motionless in the road. He gently swerved around him as they passed, feeling tremendous guilt forming in his head from the trail of destruction he left behind.

Was their treatment in the lab worth all of this? The longer time went on the harder it was for him to keep justifying their life's worth over the things he had to do. Especially with the new fact that they might be needed in some way to help solve this catastrophe. Was he accelerating the worlds slow death without giving up his life to them?

Since his escape, Reed wanted to try to keep his moral high ground intact as much as possible. With every passing hour it seemed like the world was trying its hardest to beat it out of him and make him just as bad as the people he was running from.

His thoughts were flying in from all angles. There's nothing he could do that would put him on the same level as those monsters. They took people from their homes and played with their lives and minds to try and make up for their own mistakes. Dahlia and him weren't fixing their own mistakes. They were surviving everyone else's. The guards made their choice to work for the bad guys and treat them like untamed animals. It wasn't their fault for what they were forced to do to them to keep their freedom. That was their fault, and they were going to have to live or die with that dirt on their hands.

The trees were thinning out on their way to end of the road and the city came in to view. Reed slowed down at the sight, contemplating what their next move should be. The officer blocking the checkpoint would presumably still be waiting for them there. He didn't even want to go back into the city for any reason anyway, however the road only led one way. the van rolled to a complete stop while he was unable to decide.

He reached over and gave Dahlia a gentle shake to wake her up. Her chest raised slightly in short breaths without movement from her eyes. He jumped to conclusions and shook her more frantically the second time. Her eyes shot open and Reed could feel her anger, "As loving as it is to be violently shaken awake, I'm not a fan."

"Sorry." He rubbed the back of his neck, "I tried to be gentle, but you wouldn't wake up, so I panicked there for a second."

"What's going on? Why are we stopped?" She straightened up and took in her surroundings.

"Where do you want to go?" Reed looked to her, "The one road leads into the city, and I could go a whole lifetime without stepping foot in there again."

"Hmmm, well I guess we can test this van's off-road capabilities. There was a few large, almost factory looking buildings I could see when we were on the rooftops." She pointed across the field next to them, "Maybe we should look for one of those and see if there's any food left around."

"Doubt there's any food still edible in those buildings. I suppose it's worth a try ."

Reed revved up the engine and turned the van off the road to the left. The two were thrown around a bit as they ran through the sizeable ditch and onto the grassy field. The van struggled cutting through the tall waist high grass. Everything out of the strict road line was completely unkempt and overgrown. Reed could feel and hear rocks getting thrown up at the underside of the van from the wheels. Although flat, driving through the field felt particularly bumpy and vibrated the cab the entire time.

After about ten minutes of aimless driving, they came up on their first structure in the distance. Reed thought of the view from the building top and how everything seemed so close together. He was surprised how large the field felt from ground, thinking they would have been able see almost everything from wherever they were.

When they got closer, they saw that it was some sort of old manufacturing building with one large concrete stack protruding out of the back of the roof. Windows were laid out in a gridded fashion covering most of the side of the building.

Some were boarded up, while most of the rest were broken or missing entirely. Siding was falling off the walls in every direction and was stained by the weather, giving the whole building a coating of dust and grime over the faded yellow paint. Two large shut garage doors took up a small portion of the wall in the back. There was an entrance of double doors with a massive glass overhang that protruded from the front of the building facing the city.

Reed changed course to the entrance. When he started to pull up on it, they noticed that there was a parking lot tucked to the side. The lot didn't have more than one square foot of it that wasn't cracked with weeds and grass poking up. It had been sitting out unused for so long that nature had begun to take back its landscape. The road leading up to the lot suffered the same fate and was almost completely unnoticeable less than a mile down the road.

Reed pulled up and parked to the side of the glass overhang, "Are you good to walk?"

"I'm fine, feel a lot better after that small nap." Her hand was still clutched to her side.

He wasn't convinced, even the best nap in the world wasn't fixing the damage from being in a flipped van, "You know, we really don't need both of us to go searching for scraps. It would also be a good idea for someone to stay with the van, just in case ya know?"

"Mmhm. Just in case of what exactly?" She raised an eyebrow.

Reed shrugged, "I don't know. The officer said there were scavengers out here. Don't want one of them waltzing in and taking it." He struggled to make up an excuse for her to stay in the van and rest. He didn't want to make her feel useless while also wanting her to stay put.

She winced from swallowing and leaned her head back, "So, let me get this straight. You want to leave me here by myself in case any scavengers come out looking to take advantage of us? Am I getting that right?"

"Uhhh. Well, when you put It that way it doesn't sound very good."

"Can you say it in a way that does sound good?"

"Well. Uhh. You see..." He was almost amazed at how deep of a hole he could dig himself into in a matter of seconds.

Dahlia interrupted his stumbling, "I'm just messing with you." she smiled, "I don't like not helping but I probably should sit this one out. So have fun rummaging and don't worry about me, I'll be here."

Reed took a deep breath out; thankful she agreed to rest and that he wouldn't have to try and make up any more excuses because apparently, he was very bad at it. He took the keys out of the ignition and handed them over to Dahlia, "Keep the doors locked while I'm gone, please. I'm going to worry the whole time if you don't."

She gave him a weak smile while slowly turning her head to meet eye to eye with him, "If it'll make you feel better then of course I will. It's cute how much you worry over little ol' me."

Reed blushed and broke eye contact with her, the intimacy making him feel awkward. He wondered why his first reaction was to push away from something that he knew he wanted. Something in him wanted to reject the warm feeling of becoming close to another person. He felt like the two halves of his brain were at odds with each other, one wanting to run, and the other desperately wanting to embrace it.

"Of course I do." He spat out before too much time had passed, "I'll try not to be too long, hopefully there's some packaged food left that's not too old."

"I hope so, I can feel my stomach trying to eat itself." she raised her head toward the building, "Good luck in there."

Reed opened the van door and jumped out into the waist high grass. He closed the door behind him and waited a few seconds to make sure he heard the click of the doors locking. Dahlia had given him another open invitation of flirting and he was already kicking himself for letting it slip by. All he had to do was think about it for his hands to get clammy and his heart rate to spike.

He shook his head in an attempt to free himself of the missed opportunity and walked toward the door. The double doors were made of glass and cracked so badly that you couldn't see through them, yet they still stood standing. He approached and pulled on one of the handles needing to use a lot more force than he expected. The door was heavy and the rust on the hinges wasn't helping either. He only pried it open enough to walk through and enter the building.

Inside the first room there were a few chairs scattered around and an empty desk in the shape of a half circle connected to the wall. A broken television was hanging by its wires in the corner. Another set of double doors lay directly across from where he was standing.

There was an uncomfortable silence in the building. He could only hear the light wind whistling through the broken windows of the next area. It put Reed on edge and had him tuning his ears to every slightly different creak.

He made his way through the next set of doors into a room that opened to the rest of the facility. The ceiling had to be more than fifty feet up with skylights every ten feet across the entire way. Most of them were so covered with filth that you couldn't see through them anymore. The rest were busted out, being the only source of light in the dim area.

Massive machines attached to a spanning conveyer belt system connected to each other and ran the entire length of the building. At first glance, everything that used to run through this plant had been wiped clean. Even a lot of the control boxes on the machines themselves were busted open with only some small stubs of wire left poking out.

Reed looked to his right and noticed a small stair set leading to some upper offices that he thought might be a better chance. He walked over and climbed to the upper floor. Before searching the next room, he looked out over the area again from his new viewpoint. There was still nothing in sight, but he couldn't help being impressed at all the engineering that went into a place like this. He wondered if when he was a kid he might have taken a field trip there to see all the machines churning away pumping out lord knows what for the city.

He walked into the next room which was completely torn apart compared to the front desk area. There was a pile of broken down desks and chairs in the corner. Graffiti was painted all over the walls in large letters depicting signs and words he couldn't make out. A circle of rocks enclosed a small spot on the floor that had been used as a fire pit still filled with charred pieces of desk.

Reed shuddered and jumped back when he noticed there was a camo sleeping bag against the far wall that still looked like it had someone sleeping in it. What was he supposed to do in this situation? Surely the man would not take kindly to someone barging in on his hideout. He looked at the ground and picked up a sizeable chunk of wood, just in case he needed something to defend himself, and started very slowly creeping in the bag's direction.

When he got within ten feet of the man in question a horrible smell invaded his nose. It smelt like rotten food mixed with diarrhea to an extreme measure.

Reed wondered when the last time the guy bathed himself was. He could hardly keep getting closer and didn't understand how someone could live like that. When he was only a couple feet away from the bag the smell was almost unbearable. Reed gently pushed on it with his foot to no response.

"Hey!" Reed whispered.

There was no sound or movement from the bag. Reed reached over and pulled down the top. He yelped and jumped back at the sight of an almost completely decomposed body. Most of the skin was already gone and the flesh underneath was nearly down to the bone. A few rats scurried out of the bag between Reed's feet.

He ran out of the room and leaned against the railing of the stairs. His stomach flipped and he couldn't get the smell out of his nostrils. He dry heaved over the railing, his stomach twisting in knots. It took all his determination to keep from vomiting what little he had left in his body.

After a few minutes fighting for his life, he was able to get his body back into check. It drained most of his energy and knew that they needed to find food quickly or he wouldn't have any left to run on.

Something caught his eye in the line of machines that he hadn't seen before. There was an orange bucket sitting directly under one of the skylights at the end of the facility.

If it had rained any time soon then there might be a chance of some water! He felt the dry, cracking of his lips and a thirst that he didn't fully realize was there before. He ran at almost a full sprint, flying down the stairs and turning for the end of the building. As he flew past broken down machines and empty conveyers, he saw some rabbits and mice scurry away from him at the sound of his stomping footsteps.

He reached the bucket and peered inside. There was only a small inch layer of water with some sediment at the bottom. Thirst outweighed his care for clean water, sweeping up the bucket and pouring it into his mouth. After a couple small gulps, he forced himself to stop. He contemplated drinking at least half of it but decided that Dahlia needed it more after what he put her through.

Reed took the bucket and went for the exit. The water helped him regain some his senses and he started to think about the body upstairs. He wondered if the man had starved to death or died of some disease, or if someone had killed him. The thought of some rouge killers around the area didn't sit well so he chose to believe the former.

Before he passed back into the reception area a thought occurred to him. What if he had something useful on him when he died? Reed wanted nothing more than to leave and not go anywhere near the body again, but also knew they had to take any chance at something of use now. Against every fiber of his being, he set the bucket down and started back up the stairs.

Standing outside with his hands on the door, he prepared himself for what he had to do. The door creaked open and he held his breath, running quickly over to the body. Reed grabbed the bottom of the bag and yanked as hard as he could hoping it would just slide off. The man's feet got caught on the inside of the bag and the body was dragged a few inches across the floor. A portion of his skin stuck and ripped some of the meat off the bones.

Reed got up and ran back to the other side of the room before he suffocated and gasped for air. The smell was expanding, filling the room to where he couldn't escape it. He took one more deep breath and ran back over to the body, rummaging through the man's pockets searching for anything of use. His left hand wrapped around something and he ran out door before checking what it was.

Bursting out of the room and running down the stairs, he finally stopped and slapped his hands on his knees attempting to catch his breath. He turned his hand over and opened his fingers to a small match book with at least a dozen matches left in it.

He thanked the universe that it was worth it. Matches would easily come in handy for many nights to come.

Chapter 17

Reed shoved the matches in his pocket and grabbed the bucket on his way out of the building. He looked at the van and saw Dahlia passed out cold in the seat. It was getting later in the day and sunset wasn't too far off. IF it came down to it, staying in the van wasn't the worst option. The fact it was out in the open for anyone to see worried him. If more people from the lab came looking for them then they would have no trouble spotting it from far away.

He walked up and lightly knocked on her window, trying not to startle her. She shook her head a bit and slowly opened her eyes. Once she saw it was Reed, she rolled down the window, "Can I help you?"

"Oh, you know. You just looked real thirsty sitting out in the sun all alone like that, thought maybe you'd like a fresh drink of water?" Reed shook the bucket.

"You found water?!" Her body shot up, "Well get on in here then!" She fumbled for the keys for a few seconds until Reed heard the click of the doors unlocking. He walked over to the other side and jumped into the driver's seat with his bucket in hand. The door closed and he hit the locks before offering up the bucket to her, "It's got some dirt in the bottom, but it still doesn't taste that bad."

Dahlia snatched the bucket out of his hands and waterfalled the rest of it without a second thought. Sediment filled her mouth that she spat out over the dash involuntarily, "I don't know what you were going on about. That's probably the best tasting water I've ever had." She picked out what dirt was left off her tongue, "Nice hint of spices with the last of it."

Reed laughed, "The place was picked clean of any food though. Looked like scavengers even tore the electronics off the machines in there."

"I guess the search continues." Dahlia coughed a small amount of blood in to the crook of her arm.

"I found these too." He pulled the matches from his pocket and held them out.

"Where'd you find those? And why do they smell so bad." She pushed his hand away.

The stench in the room was so intense that Reed didn't notice the smell fuming from the matches. He pulled them back and shoved them in his pocket trying to lock in the smell, "Some poor guy up there had them in his pocket. Well, what was left of a guy anyway."

He didn't notice the effect the whole ordeal in the factory had on him until he opened his mouth about it. A grime felt like it was growing over his skin thinking about what he was becoming. How it hadn't even crossed his mind that he should give some respect to the dead. He rested his head back and looked out over the factory wishing he hadn't said anything about it suddenly not wanting to talk.

"How bad was it?" She looked to him, "By the smell of it he had to be pretty old news."

"Most of his body was turning to mush. I'll just leave it at that…. I don't think I'll be able to get that smell out of my nose for quite some time though."

Dalhia noticed his face had sunken and he was staring at his feet, "I didn't mean to pry."

She reached over and grabbed Reed's hand, lacing their fingers together. Her gesture perked up Reeds spirits enough for him to push out of his slump for the time being. He placed his other hand on top of hers and soaked in her comfort, "We should probably get going if we want to find a place before dark. I doubt we have more than a few hours before the sun starts to go down."

She rubbed his hand with her thumb, "Yeah, you're probably right."

Reed pulled away and grabbed the keys from her lap. He started up the van and drove over the curb to get on what was left of the road that led away from the building. Shrubbery completely over took it and buried the path in a sea of waving greenery. There was a trail of shorter grass that had to be where the road he was trying to follow used to be.

After a few minutes of trying to stay on the invisible trail, he stepped on the gas and drove straight out hoping to find something. The sun was glaring in his eyes making it hard to see. Reed put his arm up to block the it while fighting to stay straight through the bumpiness of the field.

A tightness was mounting through Reed's stomach and working its way up into his torso. With every minute that passed he could feel its grip on his insides getting stronger. It was like a snake that was slowly tightening its coils around him, trying to squeeze the life out before going in for the kill.

Dahlia suddenly sat up straight and pointed excitedly out the windshield, "DEER!"

Reed looked over and saw a few deer with their heads up staring at them intently a few hundred feet away, "Oh yeah, that's pretty cool." His eye's floated to her, wondering why she loved random wildlife so much.

"Cool?" She looked at him like he was an idiot, "If we step on it and hit one then we would have meat for days!"

The thought didn't even cross Reed's mind before she said something. His body was so tightly wound that he'd started to mistake it with his hunger. The gas pedal hit the floor and Dahlia was shoved against the passenger door from the sudden turn. Even with him giving it everything it had the van was picking up speed at an agonizingly slow pace.

"Can't this thing go any faster?"

Reed raised his voice, "I'm giving it all she has!"

They were about a hundred feet away from the deer when they bolted in all different directions. Reed tried to follow the one that seemed to be the closest to them. From farther back it didn't look that difficult to go in the same direction as the animal, but the closer they got the more spastic its movement became, and the van did not turn very quickly in the tall grass.

The deer tried to make one last sideways leap to freedom as they came up only feet away from ramming it. Reed smacked its back end with the front of the van and sent it tumbling in the grass. Only its front half rose from the grass while trying to make a final run for it after the hit.

He felt bad about not killing it on impact and quickly put the van into reverse. He backed up enough to straighten out in line with the injured deer and get some momentum.

They rammed it head on this time when Reed punched the gas. The van lurched to a stop without another sound from the deer.

He opened the door and jumped out to check on it. The deer was still twitching in a pile of folded over grass where it had been struggling before. Reed carefully walked up to it and grabbed it by the antlers. He looked away and jerked them in a clockwise motion as hard as he could trying to break its neck and put it out of its misery. There as a loud crack and he continued to twist with all his might wanting to make sure it was dead before he gave up.

The deer stopped twitching and Reed dropped the antlers. He looked down and saw that he had completely turned the deer's head upside down from its body. He thought it strange that he felt worse about killing the deer in this way than when he killed the guards. The guards at least wanted to do him harm, so he could easily justify any retaliation. This innocent animal was living his life in peace until Reed came by and brutally murdered him with a van.

He tried to shake off his feelings and focus on the goal of dragging this animal into the back of the van. He moved to its back end and grabbed it by the hooves. He was trying to drag it through the grass making hardly any progress. The fatigue from not having anything to eat was starting to ravish his muscles. He lost his grip and fell down only a few feet from where he began. Wanting to conserve as much energy as possible, he started trying to think of a way that was smarter than dragging it along.

If he couldn't bring the deer to the van then why not bring the van to the deer. Reed got up and walked over to the door, jumping back in. He reversed it until the deer was to the side of them and then pulled up beside it on the side with the sliding door.

Dahlia smiled at him, "Didn't want to drag a full-grown buck all the way around?"

"Not particularly." He shut the engine off, "I don't have the energy for that anymore."

"Then let me help you get it into the van at least."

Their eyes met, "Are you going to be okay doing that?"

"I've rested and let you take the lead enough for one day. I'm feeling a lot better now, I promise."

Reed didn't quite believe her, but the thought of not having to lift that animal alone was too alluring to pass up, "Alright, let's get this thing in and get a move on then."

Dahlia exited the van on her side and walked around to meet Reed, being noticeably more cautious of how she was moving. He slid the door open to the back and they squatted down on either end of the deer grabbing whatever part they could.

Reed was trying to hold his head high enough to not be poked by the antlers, "On the count of three we lift and shove it right in. I don't know if I have two attempts in me"

She nodded, "We got this, easy."

"One, two, thr...."

"Wait wait wait." She let go and waved her hand at him, "On one two three? Or one two three go?"

"Just on three."

"Okay." She grabbed hold again.

He glared at her, "One, two, thr..."

"You sure on three?"

Reed was getting frustrated with her now. How many times did he have to explain something as simple as a countdown? He knew she wasn't dumb. Maybe the crash had jumbled her brain a bit, "I'm sure."

"Positive?" The sided of lips were quivering trying to not turn up into a smile.

He dropped his side, "You're fucking with me, aren't you?"

"Me? What? Nooo." She shook her head.

He raised his eyebrows dramatically, "Ha Ha Ha. Let's get this deer in, you butt head."

"Say what you want about me, you're smiling though." Her cheery grin was fully taking over her face.

"Yes, yes. Even when you're messing with me over the body of a dead deer, you're still adorable, I get it." He rolled his eyes while he talked.

"Yes I am." She gave one overly large nod.

"Alright, for real this time. One, two, three!" He grunted putting all of his might into lifting the deer's head.

They both struggled to lift their ends of the animal barley able to shove it in the van. Reed slid the door shut and started wiping the dirt and hair off his shirt. Dahlia did the same and looked up to admire the sky, "It's starting to look beautiful." She stared into space, "The closer it gets to sunset the more it looks like a painting up there."

Reed took the opportunity this time and slid his arm around her waist from the back to share the view. She happily invited him in, wrapping her arm around his back and placing her other hand on his chest. They took in the tapestry that was the sunset in its early stages for a couple of silent minutes enjoying one another's touch.

Dahlia dropped her head, "Of anyone I could have had to go through all this craziness with, I'm glad it's with you."

"I couldn't imagine it with anyone else. I don't think I would have ever lasted without you either." He chuckled once, "The thought of you was all that kept me going a couple of times the past two days."

"Only a couple times?" She allowed herself to melt more into him.

Reed gently pushed her head up by her chin with one of his fingers to look directly in her eyes. The moment he saw them, a fiery jolt of joy and nervous anticipation shot throughout his body like lightning. His stomach became tingly, and his thoughts instantly devolved into how he could mess things up.

"Every time." His lips quivered, "I can't go a minute without you on my mind." He pulled her in and brushed his lips against hers gently. He was about to push away when she grabbed the back of his head and pulled him back. She kissed him passionately before he could get away.

He felt like a man on top of world and couldn't have hoped for a better outcome. A warm fuzzy feeling was racing through his body and bouncing back and forth throughout every corner of his brain. They kept their passionate embrace for as long as she would let him before separating.

"Wow." Reed whispered, "That turned out way better than I had hoped for."

Dahlia chuckled and hugged him, "I was wondering how long it would take you to try that."

"I was waiting for the perfect moment." He kissed the top of her head.

"Good excuse." She squeezed tight, "You found it though."

Chapter 18

Reed never wanted to let go of her. It felt like a piece of him stuck to her when they separated, "As much as I want to live in this moment, we need to find somewhere before it gets dark."

"I know." Her hand was reluctant to let go of his waist, "We need to figure out how to cook up this deer before it starts to rot too."

Reed dropped his arms from her, "Aaaaaand, there goes all the romance."

Dahlia laughed and let him go, walking back around the front of the van to the passenger seat. Reed jumped back in the driver's side and shut the door, "Any suggestions?"

She pointed to the concrete rim of the city, "Probably could follow the curve of the city wall, I bet we'll find somewhere the fastest that way."

"Good idea." He started driving parallel to the city walls following its slight curve keeping a large distance away. It only took a few minutes before spotting a small building in the distance. He revved up the van with a mixture of excitement and fear about nightfall.

A few hundred yards from it, he could see that the building in question was a small, old, rundown farm house. There didn't seem to be any sort of covered area or garage to speak of to hide the van. He would have to resort to hiding it behind the house to conceal it from the city's view. It was better than nothing, however, it wouldn't be enough to calm his nerves about being spotted.

They were getting closer to the house when Reed caught a glimpse of his hands. He was so busy being wrapped up on Dahlia and searching for a place to go that he didn't notice the blood stains on his knuckles.

He turned his head and squinted at them. It was strange to him he hadn't noticed until now and that the blood was still shiny wet. He looked up to quickly make sure they were on track and then refocused on his hands. The blood was starting to form enough that droplets were running down the back of his hands trying to reach his forearms.

What was wrong with that deer's blood? How is it clumping together now?

A light airy feeling shrouded his head making it harder to maintain focus on one thing. Headlights beamed in from his driver's side window almost blinding him. They were about to get rammed from the side and Reed quickly slammed on the gas and turning hard to the right.

"What are you doing?!" Dahlia yelled, burning a hole through him with her stare.

Reed tried to correct his course having narrowly avoided the oncoming vehicle, still running it at full speed. He spun the wheel in the opposite direction of the house hoping for the best. Dahlia's side of the van rammed through the building diagonally throwing glass and splinters in all directions. They were at a complete stop with half of the cab inside the building.

He quickly looked over at Dahlia to make sure she was okay. Thankfully she was wearing her seatbelt and didn't look like she had anything new wrong with her. Reed panicked and threw it in reverse trying to break free from the wall. The front passenger tire was lodged in the house and couldn't get any traction. He put it back into drive hoping to bust all the way through with the tires spinning and screeching against broken wood.

When Reed jumped out of the door there weren't any lights driving through the field next to them. He ran out behind the van throwing his head around searching for the guards. There was no sign of any vehicles anywhere, not even the faint roar of an engine in the distance.

He was throwing his arms around and grabbed his hair, "Where are you?!" Reed dropped to his knees and began to cry when he wrapped his mind around it. He sat in the dim light of sunset until he felt Dahlias hand on his shoulder, "It's okay."

She got down on her knees behind him and wrapped her arms around his torso, resting her head on the back of his neck. The feeling of her support only made Reed cry harder. She held him in silence until he calmed down enough to breathe normally.

She kissed the back of his neck, "What was it this time?"

He sat for a few seconds before responding to her, "Another vehicle." His teeth grinded against each other, "Another vehicle that was about to ram us. It was so vivid. The lights from the side were blinding me and I could hear the engine bearing down on us." He spoke slowly, not wanting to share any of the details but knowing he was safe with her at the same time, "Now we don't have a way around. If they come for us again then we're going to be sitting ducks out here."

She ran her fingers through his hair and scratched his scalp, "We didn't have a car before and we made it through. We'll figure it out."

"I don't know." He punched the ground, "I feel like we're screwed."

"I'd have to agree with you on that one." A man's voice shouted at them from behind.

The two quickly shot up and spun around to see where it came from. A group of three older people, two guys and a girl, were standing behind them by the van. One of the men was tall and lanky with a ripped flannel shirt under his tattered blue overalls. He was carrying a large machete in one hand and leaning on the van with his other. The second was the shortest of the three and wore a full grey sweatsuit that was too tight for his slightly more well-fed stature, with a revolver pointed directly at Reed and Dahlia. The woman stood in front of the two men with jeans that were obviously too large for her, held up by a belt that was tightened down to a notch that was torn out past the premade holes it originally came with. Her bright blue T-shirt also looked like it was three sizes too big for her with the neck hole torn open and draped over one of her shoulders. Both men had long bushy beards with shoulder length brown hair while the woman's long blond hair was tied up in a large bun.

The man with the revolver held it straighter, "Don't move another muscle."

The woman took a couple steps forward looking them up and down, "Curious. You don't look like you work for the government, but I can spot one of those white beacons of a van from a mile away." Her voice wasn't hostel like the other man. She had a more confused and curious sound to her, "You made quite the new entrance into our little home here with that thing."

Reed and Dahlia just stared in silence, both terrified they might get shot if they said anything.

"So, tell me why I shouldn't have my friend there do away with you while we still have a few minutes of light left in the day?" She looked from one of them to the other.

Dahlia forced herself rigid to not look weak, "We're not with any sort of government if that's what you're afraid of."

"Do I look like the person who should be afraid in this situation to you?" The woman put her hand on her hips and gestured backwards with her head, "Where'd you get the truck?"

Reed sighed, "It's a long story."

"Well, it better become a really short story here soon. Not much light left." She nodded at the sunset.

"We were captured and stuffed into this van before we took control and drove it away." Dahila told her.

"Mmhmm." She squinted and licked her lips, "You two were captured, likely bound at the time, and took over the vehicle from at least one, armed officer. Probably two if they were coming for both of you at the same time. You sure that's what you wanna stick with?"

Reed straightened up, "It's the truth"

"You have any proof of any kind to back this claim up?"

"Just look at us." He opened his arm outward, "We're beat up and half starved to death. Does that sound like someone high on the food chain?"

She continued to stare at them intently for a while, moving her lips back and forth every so often trying to decide if she believed them or not.

The tall lanky man pipped in, "They sure don't look like the govern folks."

"Shut it!" She snapped her fingers at him, "There's a reason you don't make the big decisions here."

"Come on Stame, he's got a point. When have we ever seen those vans this far out anyhow?" The short one added.

She stared at him, "So what if they're not? Doesn't mean we can trust em."

"What if we can tell you where to get a load of fresh meat?" Dahlia's eyebrows raised.

Her neck cranked sideways, "Say what now?"

"If I told you I know where you can find a load of good fresh meat as a peace offering, what would you say to that?"

The tall man licked his lips and breathed heavily, "Haven't had some meat in a long while there Stamey."

She zoned in on Dahlia, "Hmm. I'll tell you what. If you can get us that meat you speak of in the next ten minutes before sundown then I'll consider not killing the both of ya's."

Reed tilted his head back to the van, "Open the sliding door."

"Open the door!" Stamey yelled at the tall man.

He slid the door open and looked inside. From where Reed was standing, he could see that the deer had been thrown around in the back and flung blood everywhere. From the small part in his vision, it looked like a murder scene. The man reached inside and drug the deer out by one of its hoofs. It slid out and plopped on the ground in front of him.

The woman looked in awe at the corps, "How'd you manage that with no guns?"

Reed smirked, "Rammed it with the van."

"Well, you should have started with that little bit of information there. No way in hell is one of those officers gunna be hauling around a dead deer they went and hit." Stamey turned back to them, "I'll tell you what. Since you obviously don't have the tools to skin and gut this carcass, and don't look like you would know where to even start with that anyway, we'll do it for you and let you stay for dinner if you give us three quarters of the thing. But then you gotta be on your way after that, sound fair?"

Dalia looked over to Reed, "Sounds good to me."

"Beggers can't be choosers."

"Well great. While we're waiting for Durrian over there to prep the meat, we can talk about how you plan to fix the hole in our house." Stamey told them, turning around and walking to the back yard.

"I ain't doing this by myself if you want dinner tonight." Durrian kicked the deer in the butt, "Grab one end and you're gunna help me chop this guy up Bassel."

The two men grabbed the deer on either side and started hauling it to the back of the house, following Stamey.

Reed looked around, "I guess we follow them?"

"Looks like it."

The two followed the group to the back of the house. Stamey was around the corner walking over to take a load off in a small chair. It was on a porch with a built-in overhang covering the whole thing. The porch spanned the entirety of the back of the house and was decorated with a large wooden barrel they were using as a table and some fraying lawn chairs. The whole thing was lit with some dim string lights. A huge empty square dirt patch that went on for as far as they could see in the shallow light connected to it.

Stamey plopped herself down in one of the lawn chairs and made a motion with her hands for either Reed or Dahlia to take the other.

Reed nodded to it, "You take it, I'll stand."

"Mans got manners at least." Stamey took a drink of something clear from a small glass.

Dahlia smiled, "Well, he did just crash our car."

Stamey pointed to the house, "You get to do the fixing then?"

"I'm really sorry about your house. I don't know much about construction though."

Stamey laughed condescendingly, "That's alright. It's not our house anyway."

"You don't live here? Then what are you doing here?" Dahlia asked.

"I guess you could say we live here right now. Been here a couple months, I think. Them city boys call us scavengers, even though they're the reason no one out here had any work left and had to start fending for themselves, the bastards." Stamey hit the top of the barrel with a clenched fist.

Dahila ignored the outburst, "So, you guys move from place to place then?"

"You spent your whole life in the city there, pretty girl? They keep you sheltered or brainwashed to what's been going on out here all this time?"

She shook her head, "No, nothing like that. We just can't remember...."

"*Dahlia!*" Reed interrupted.

She shot him a disapproving look. "What does it matter? It's not like they're going to tell anyone that would do anything."

Stamey relaxed back in her chair, "What do you mean you don't remember?"

"We got mixed up in something with a lab down in the forest and somehow, they wiped our memories of everything. It's like we can remember how to do stuff but nothing else. Not even our real names."

"Them government scientist can do just about anything nowadays." Stamey took another drink, "Sorry to hear about that."

"You believe us just like that?" Reed was genuinely surprised.

"Why not? You rammed through the house with a dead deer in the back and don't know squat. Pretty strange introduction already, and then there's no reason why you would pretend to not know about scavengers unless you really didn't."

He thought about it from their angle, "Guess that makes sense."

"We've been going from place to place for years now, maybe decades. They all kind of blur together after a while." Stamey pointed to the door leading into the house, "Durrian and Bassel are brothers that were barely making it when I met up with them. They've got good survival skills but don't make the brightest decisions of where to go or what to do."

"Why'd you stop here?" asked Dahlia.

"We were headed over to a farm that sits around the bend there. I've been scavenging around these parts for a long time and that particular farm has always been under the protection of the city. Officers would make their rounds at random intervals, so it was never a good idea to try and steal from there, but then about a month ago it seemed like everyone up and left out of nowhere. No more vans patrolling, no one working on the crops. It was weird to abandon a working farm, but I've seen weirder things. We've been picking the last of the scraps off this farm while scoping it out to make sure no one's coming back, so far it's still clear."

Dahlia looked surprised at her answer.

Stamey's head moved back when she looked at her, "What's that look for?"

Dahlia shrugged, "Just surprised you'd tell two strangers all that information."

"Just cuz we're scavengers doesn't mean we're savages. You're going about trying to survive out here like the rest of us. Besides, us three aren't going to eat a whole field before the crops die out."

Reed took that as an open invitation, "You don't care if we head that way then?"

She sat back and waved her glass in front of her once, "Don't bother me none. Just as long as you know we'll be headed there behind you in not too long."

Reed almost felt grateful that he rammed the van through her house. Picturing being able to be with Dahlia without anyone chasing them on a farm was more than he could have asked for. The thought excited him until he wondered how long it would be before they ended up looking as scraggily as this bunch. Trying to survive on their own out here sounded better than the alternative, though it was still a scary fate to have in front of them.

The three sat and chatted for a couple hours about the places that Stamey and her crew had been, waiting for the brothers to prepare the meat. She had a never-ending batch of stories for them to listen to about their time together and all the ups and downs of life.

Durrian poked his head out of the door, "You wanna get a fire going Stamey? We're almost done in here."

"Sure." She got up and started walking over to a small fire pit that was about ten feet out in the yard. There was a bundle of wood chopped into kindling on top of some newspaper sitting to the side. She reached into her pocket and grabbed out a small black block and a folded pocketknife. After crumpling up some paper and stacking some small pieces of wood on top in the pit she started to strike sparks from the black block with her knife onto the paper.

"You can use these." Reed quickly pulled the matches out of his pocket and walked up to her, "Might be easier."

She took the matches from his hand and lit up the fire, "Thanks." Her eyes never left the flames when she handed them back.

Durrian and Bassel came out of the house with large chunks of meat on some metal roasting sticks. They handed each person one and the group tilted them over the fire to cook up their dinner. Most of the time spent waiting was quiet, the brothers and Stamey chatting it up about this and that every so often to drown out the silence. Dahlia and Reed stood close and couldn't take their eyes off the meal that was slowly cooking in front of them. Having to wait and watch while the grease formed tiny droplets that dripped off to the dirt was like its own small form of torture.

After almost an hour, Durrian pulled his slab back and cut it open with a rusty knife for inspection, "They should be cooked enough by now, go on and dig in guys."

Reed immediately pulled his chunk back and bit a piece off the corner. It tasted better than anything he had tasted before, and he had to hold himself back from burning his mouth by scarfing the rest down.

Chapter 19

The group ate in silence, the only noise being the chomping and chewing of the freshly cooked deer. Reed felt foolish for agreeing to give so much of it up, even if he knew he wouldn't have been able to prepare it as well as Durrian.
The night had fully caught up to them, a full moon cast out light that blanketed the field. If they were still going to be shoved off to find this other farm in the middle of the night, then he couldn't have asked for a more beautifully clear sky.

Reed was the first to finish and walked over to the house to lean his cooking stick up. Peering into the room through a small window, he saw a table surrounded by three wooden chairs that was covered in blood, guts, and deer body parts where they had prepared the thing. The kitchen was completely torn apart with the fridge door removed, gone to who knows where, and all the other appliances wiring dangling out or taken. Nothing else filled the empty space besides one door that led to a back room.

Did they all sleep in the same bed? The thought of all three of those scavengers covered in filth and grime sleeping in the same bed night after night almost made him feel sick. Maybe they weren't savages, but they sure lived like them. It clicked in his head again that he and Dahlia were in the same boat now. How would they look after a decade of scrounging for food and trying to find new places to sleep every few weeks? The thought disturbed him, he'd been so focused on their past and getting away to start a new life that he hadn't thought much about what that life would look like.

"You alright over there?" Dahlia said, walking up behind him.

He backed away from the window, "Uh. Yeah. Just got a little lost in thought is all."

"Okay, just making sure." She squeezed his shoulder before turning around to go back to the fire.

Reed snapped himself back to the present, following behind her to the fire. Everyone except Bassel had finished their dinner now and were warming their hands by the flames. Stamey had her arms crossed staring at it, "So, what's the plan with the truck?"

Reed looked at her, "Its stuck in your wall and doesn't want to budge, so unless we can wedge it out somehow then I'm not sure what to do."

Durrian grunted, "Took a quick peek under the front tire in the house and unfortunately for you, your axle is busted. Even if we pushed that car outta the wall it's going nowhere in a hurry."

Reed had no idea what that even meant, no car knowledge had been spared in the erasing process apparently. A part of him wondered if Durrian was simply making something up so that they could keep the van for themselves. Although he didn't come off smart enough to play those games, Reed didn't think he would be smart enough to know that either. He felt a twinge of guilt for thinking this way about them after being treated kindly with open arms.

"You know where we can find a repair shop near here?" Dahlia asked Durrian.

He laughed, "I'm the closest thing to that I reckon. Used to work on cars a lifetime ago, most of that stuff is still rattling in the ol noggin somewhere."

Her smile went from ear to ear, "Well great!"

Durrian held up a hand, "Before you get ahead of yourself. I could probably fix it, If I had the parts and tools that is. And that's a tall order that no one can fill round here. Sorry if I got your hopes up there."

Reed looked to the open field, "Guess we're walking to the next farm."

"It's not that far." Stamey assured them, "Probably only a few hours walk from here."

"We better get moving then," he nudged Dahlia with his elbow, "before we get too comfortable by this fire."

"Hold on a minute." Stamey left the fire and walked back to the house.

Reed looked at the brothers for any indication of what she was getting. Durrian gave him a small shrug coupled with a confused look. Dahlia and Reed walked over to the porch to wait for her while the brothers stayed by the campfire. After only a minute, Stamey walked back out with a flashlight in hand.

"Here," She shoved it in Dahlia's hand, "try not to use it unless it gets too dark to see. I don't know how much power is left in that battery."

Dahila looked at the light, "Thank you. You didn't have to do that."

"Yeah thanks." Reed added.

"Ah it's nothing. Think of it as a trade for the van."

"What do you plan to do with it?"

"I don't know yet." She scratched her chin, "Bassel will think of something. I know he doesn't sound like much, but he's a wizard when it comes to anything electronic. I'm sure he can pull some doo dads out of there and turn it into something useful."

"I hope he can." Reed reached out and shook her hand, "Thanks again."

"Just keep with the curve of the city and you should spot it before long. It's no farther from the wall than this little plot is. Be careful now, ya hear?" Stamey lowered her head and raised her brows before letting go of Reeds hand.

"Goodbye guys! It was nice to meet you!" Dahlia yelled to the brothers before turning around to leave.

The two walked around the building where they first entered. Reed heard Bassel muttering something about not wanting them to leave yet and Stamey reassuring him that it wouldn't be the last time they saw them. He took one last look at the van as they passed, the door still open with a blood splattered mess in the back. He could feel some of the mixture of emotions he'd been pushing down start to try and make an appearance. Reed did not want to deal with any of that now and sure as hell didn't want to put Dahlia through anything more today. He looked away and gritted his teeth through it.

Dahlia's eyes were at the sky, "The moons beautiful at least."

"Oh yeah. Very beautiful" Reed stammered.

"I hope whoever left that farm in a rush forgot to take their bed."

Reed could suddenly feel the bags under his eyes, "I think I would pass out the second my head hit a pillow right about now."

"Do you think they all sleep together?"

"I only saw one room and no couches so I'm assuming they all sleep in the same bed." A shiver shot through him.

Dahlia pushed her neck forward when she talked, "No, I meant do they all *sleep* together?"

"Ughh!" His gag reflex waved through him, "Why would you want to think about that?"

"I don't want to! Just something that popped into my head! I mean after decades... A girls gotta have some needs, ya know?"

"I mean, I guess yeah. Thanks for getting that image stuck in my conscious forever." A shower had never sounded so appealing to him than after that thought.

Dahlia laughed at him.

The two walked quietly for the most part for the next couple hours, too tired to do much other than focus on wading through the field of waist high grass. Dahlia being the only one to break the silence every now and then making an observation about how the city looked or seeing some pattern in the stars. Reed felt bad about not responding much with her on the walk. He felt like his dwindling life force was being slowly finished off with every step.

"I think I see it!" Dahlia burst out, pointing in the direction of a small black blob in the distance.

Reed squinted, trying to make out anything more than faint shadows in the darkness. Dahlia snatched the flashlight from his hands and beamed it toward the figure. The light from the flashlight was weak and shallow, illuminating barely enough to make out the house from where they were standing. She quickly shut it back off once she confirmed it was the farm and handed it back to Reed.

"That has to be what she was talking about!" She playfully shoved him, "Come on! Let's go!"

She ran for the house, leaving Reed behind. The thought of going at a faster pace felt like an impossibility to Reed. He didn't want to kill Dahlia's excitement and pushed himself as much as he could, not reaching close to how fast she was.

She was fading in with the other shadows and he was suddenly feeling very vulnerable alone in the dark, "Wait for me!"

"Hurry up slow poke! The faster we get there the faster we can sleep!" She yelled back to him, barely slowing down.

Dahlia kept her pace ahead of Reed until she reached the house, it took Reed longer than he liked to catch up in his exhausted clumsy running. He slammed his body against the wall going to lean up and catch his breath, breathing heavily enough that he wasn't able to speak.

She was at least also breathing heavily, "I'm sorry I got ahead of myself. I just got too excited at the sight of the place."

"It's... okay..." Reed forced out through his labored breathing.

They stood there while Reed caught his breath. He turned to get a look at the front of the farm. It was a small one-story house with a large flower garden in the front lawn full of dead or dying roses. The front of the building had one big bay window in the center that looked out over the front lawn, which now was as overgrown as the rest of the area. A wood front door was on a porch covered by an overhang that looked like it wrapped around the other side of the house. Wood shingle siding covered its entirety and was still in unusually good condition. The whole house looked like it had been well cared for and there was no visible damage to speak of.

Reed still needed to lean against the wall, "Well, what are you waiting for? You going to check out our new place?"

"Oh, *our* new place huh?" A giggly smile stretched across her face.

"I mean..."

"No, I like it." She grabbed his hand and pulled him along with her.

They walked up to the front door with a newfound excitedness. Dahlia turned the knob and pushed the door open.

"Not locked. They must have been out of here in a hurry."

"Good for us." Dahlia pulled him inside.

The moon didn't provide enough light to see what was going on inside the house. Reed turned his flashlight on and pointed it down the hallway they were greeted to as soon as they walked in the door. On the right were three doors spaced out evenly down the hall until it opened up to a different area at the end. Directly to the left of the door was an arched entrance to a large area that looked like it used to be their living room. The whole house was laid out with nice brown hardwood floors and had the walls painted with a vibrant light blue color.

Reed shut and locked the door, then shined his light around the entrance to the larger living room area. There was a sizeable couch with a wooden end table on either side of it placed in the middle of the room. In front of it they had a wooden coffee table to match, with a deck of cards thrown around it like someone had tossed the whole thing in a fit of rage. He flipped one of the light switches even though he knew it wouldn't work.

Dahlia gave him a look, "Really?"

Reed quickly shrugged, "Worth a try."

They turned back down the hallway and slowly walked up to the first door. Dahlia swung it open and walked inside in front of Reed while he shined the light into the room. A small bed obviously meant for one person was shoved in the corner under a window that looked out to the side of the house. Other than the bed, there was only a small cloths dresser on the other side of the room.

"It's weird." Reed shined the light around the top of the dresser and the walls.

"What's weird?"

"It seems like people lived here but there's no photos or trinkets or anything personal anywhere."

Dahila looked to him, "They probably took all that with them."

"They had enough time to pack all that up but not to pick up the cards in the living room or lock the door? Just seems like somethings off is all."

"Does it matter?" She slid her hand across his lower back, "As far as I'm concerned this is our house now."

"You're right, I like the sound of that." Reed left it alone and followed her out.

They moved on to the next room. It was another bedroom with a much larger bed, two dressers, and a closet in it. The bed was fully adorned with flower printed pillows and a red flannel blanket.

"Now that bed has my name on it." Without hesitation he jumped on to the bed and sunk in its comfiness. It felt like landing on a marshmallow, begging him to stay and fall right asleep.

"Think we should at least make sure no one is in the other part of the house before we sleep?"

The thought of getting out of that bed was the last thing Reed wanted to do. He felt like he was glued in, becoming one with the mattress, "I'm sure they would have said something by now if there was anyone else in here."

"Here, give me the flashlight and I'll do a quick look down the end of the hallway. You get comfy and I'll be back in a few, you big baby." She grabbed the flashlight from him.

Reed was already half asleep, "You're the best."

"I know." She kicked the bed, "Take your shoes off at least before getting under the covers please. We don't have any way to wash those yet."

Reed kicked off his shoes and stripped down to his white lab underwear before scurrying under the blanket. A minute later Dahlia came back did the same. She joined him and pushed back on his body, morphing into the little spoon.

"Welcome home." He kissed the back of her head just before falling asleep.

Chapter 20

Reed woke up to the sun peering through the window on his face. He felt better with a good, full night's sleep than any other time since the lab. Still a bit groggy, he turned his head to see Dahlia still soundly snoozing, the sun not quite reaching her yet. Unlike when he had turned in for the night, his body was sprawled out across the bed taking up most of the covers.

He turned to face Dahlia and scooted his body back in, tight to hers. She gently scooted back started making groaning sounds.

"Are you awake?" Reed whispered.

"I am now." She said in her pillow.

"You can go back to sleep if you want. I'm going to try and find us some water." He kissed her head.

She didn't move, grumbling back to sleep.

Reed climbed out of the bed as gently as possible trying to not fully wake her. He walked over and closed the curtains by the window to cover the sun from beaming on her. The door creaked and groaned when he tried to slowly close it to reduce the noise. Every move he made sounded like mountains crashing together and his heart skipped a beat when the door loudly clicked close.

Successfully out of the room, he walked to the end of the hallway to take a look around in the light. To the left of the opening was a small kitchen area with stainless steel appliances and jet-black cabinets. The sink was polished white ceramic that matched the tile backsplash, the contrast standing out significantly against the black surroundings. To the right was a small dining area with a round wooden table and three chairs.

Reed randomly opened cabinets to see what was left behind. Rummaging through, he found full sets of plates and cups, stainless steel pots and pans in the lower doors, and an entire drawer of silverware completely forgotten about. It was like a dream finally having some dishware that they could call their own for now. This house was already quite a step up from where Stamey and the brothers were living. He was thankful they let them be the first to settle in.

The idea of sharing the house with those three instead of just Dahlia bogged down his joy of exploring the new space. He knew there was no way to avoid it and without them they may not have ever stumbled upon it, but that didn't stop the selfish desire of wanting it all to themselves.

Reed stepped out of the back door to a wood porch trying to keep his mind off the future and on what they did have right now. It was a continuation of the porch from the front of the house that wrapped around the side and ended at the corner in the back. A swinging chair made of wood for two that looked like it was carved out of either huge branches, or small trees sat to his left. A couple other wicker chairs with red cushions on the right.

He stood on the edge of the porch looking beyond into the gigantic field of crops that stretched farther than he could tell. It was a beautiful sunny day without a cloud in the sky and the air felt warm on his skin stepping into the light. As far as he could see, there were four parceled out square chunks of land, each with its own vegetable filling the space to bursting. The closest square, that was bordering the small grassy backyard, were tall stalks of corn that towered over Reed's head. The corn cobs were so huge that they bent over trying to pull the rest of the stalk to the ground. The one to the right of the corn was rows and rows of smaller, green-leafed plants. They were about five to six feet tall and all growing on to one another. He couldn't tell what they were supposed to be or what the plants in the back two fields were, but he was filled with a grateful joy that he wasn't used to feeling.

They could live here for months. Perhaps indefinitely if they could figure out how to keep the crops alive, although they seemed to be doing fine on their own at the moment. The only sketchy part about it would be its vicinity to the city. Surely, after a while, someone would notice people working a farm that was previously abandoned. They might even come to harvest the crops until there was nothing left or appoint someone else to start it back up.

He decided to stop getting in the way of his own happiness and that he would figure it out when the time came. It was quick work to pick off the low cobs of corn that were hanging down over the small waist high wooden fence. Each one felt like it weighed at least a few pounds. After picking a large arm full, he walked back to the kitchen and began peeling off the husks. They were far more difficult than he expected to rip off by hand. A half hour of struggling passed to get the husks off all the corn, dropping and cursing at them many times in the process.

Dahlia came strolling out of the bedroom and walked over to greet Reed in the kitchen. She went straight to him and gave him a kiss on the cheek.

"Good morning." She said, looking at his harvest.

He smiled up at her, "Good morning, I was going to surprise you with some breakfast in bed."

She grabbed a corncob, "Well then you probably shouldn't have cursed out the breakfast and woke me up then." .

"You heard that?" He looked away, "I thought I was keeping it down."

"Well you didn't do a very good job." She grinned, "It sounded like the corn had personally offended you."

He gave the pile of torn off husks a dirty look, "They're a lot harder to clean up for eating than it looks."

"It looks great, you want to eat at the table like we're a couple of civilized people?"

"I do like to pretend." Reed grabbed a couple plates from the cupboard and handed her one.

They sat down with a plate of three ears of corn each and wasted no time digging in. The corn was so sweet when Reed bit in to it he could hardly believe it wasn't made of candy. He was hoping for a more grounded food like corn to taste like an actual vegetable and not a morning pastry. Maybe that's why they abandoned this place; they messed up the crops so much that it wasn't worth keeping it going. Regardless of the taste, Reed chomped every kernel down until he was feeling almost over filled. The feeling was so foreign and came faster than he'd expected.

He pushed his plate away from him and sat back, "You want to walk through the fields to the back and check things out? Other than corn I can't tell what any of the other plants are."

"Sounds good to me, hopefully we can find some water somewhere out there too."

They walked along the fence line until they reached the second patch of crops. Reed hopped over the fence to examine the tall green plants, "What do you think they are?" He looked all around them like it was going to help him know what they were, "Doesn't look like they're growing anything on these leaves."

Dahlia climbed over to take a look. It only took a few seconds for her to grab one of the plants by its base and trying to rip it out of the ground. After a few good tugs she was able to pull the plant out with some light brown bulbs twice the size of his fist attached to the root.

Reed's face lit up, "Potatoes!"

"Really?" She raised one of her eyebrows at him, "That reaction for a couple potatoes huh?"

He laughed, "Honestly, I don't know where that came from. I must have really liked potatoes before I guess."

"There's a lot you can do with them I suppose. You can mash them up, boil them, even put them in a stew." She sat them back on the ground, "Pretty versatile, if we can find some water to clean these off then we'll be eating good."

They strolled on the fence line that separated the corn field from the potatoes. The vegetables were so overgrown on either side that they were constantly pushing potato leaves out of the way to make a small open trail. It only took a half hour of walking to get to the end of the first two portioned out parcels. The other two fields were cut into squares of the same size with two different crops.

Dahlia pointed to the field behind the corn "That kinda looks like overgrown lettuce there."

large leafy green towers of vegetation that were a couple feet shorter than Reed were in rows that spanned further back than he could see.

"What makes you say that?"

She shook her head looking out to the field, "I don't know. Just what popped into my head."

In the field to the right was the shortest of the plants. It looked more like tall grass in rows covering the field than food. Except this grass was very thick stalked and less bushy than outside of the fence area. Reed hopped over and pulled at the stalks to see what he would get. Unlike with the potatoes, they all immediately broke off and put reed on his butt. Dahlia laughed before climbing over to help him.

Before he got up, he started to dig with his hands around where the stalks broke off. Dahlia came and joined him until they uncovered something with a yellowish shell connected to the bottom. They continued to dig until Reed was able to get his fingers shoved under the bulb enough to pull it from its dirt tomb. They stared speechless at the soccer ball sized onion sitting in front of them.

Reed rolled and sniffed it, "I guess this is the last resort field once we eat everything else."

"Yeah, we might kiss a lot less when that happens."

"I guess I'll have to take advantage of my time before that then." Reed pulled her in for a light kiss.

Her grin started to take over her face, "I guess we will."

Reed stood up and looked around to see if there was anything interesting in sight. While scanning the outer fence line of the onion field he spotted some small brown plants sticking up in the distance. He pointed over to them, "Let's go check those out past the fence line."

She squinted, "What are they?"

"I don't know, could be something worth looking at though. Maybe something more appetizing than some onions or lettuce."

"If you say so." She took a few steps, "One condition though."

"What's that?"

"Last one there has to prepare lunch when we get back!" she said bolting off.

She caught Reed off guard, gaining a hefty head start. They both ran through the onion field as fast as they could, trying not to trip on all the overgrown vegetables. Dahlia tripped on the fence trying to leap over it allowing Reed to catch up. She fell to the ground, mostly catching herself on the way down. Reed climbed over the fence and helped her up.

"Thank you." Dahlia pulled him in for a quick kiss and then shoved him back, turning around and resuming her full sprint.

"Oh, come on!" Reed pushed off the fence trying to pick up speed again.

They were only a few hundred feet off from the plants that he could now see were big rows of cattails. He started to catch back up to Dahlia, the fire of competition pushing him past the speed he normally ran. Dahlia stayed a few feet in front of him until they reached the cattails, putting on the breaks right before the line. Reed ran in to her when she stopped. The two flew through the plants and landed in a small pond on the other side. They both resurfaced quickly, surprised by the water.

Reed swam over to her, "Are you okay?"

"Okay?" She splashed him, "We found water!"

The murky water he was treading sounded less than appetizing, "I'm dying of thirst too, but don't you think it's a bad idea to drink dirty pond water?"

"Not this water. The stream flowing into it!" she pointed behind Reed.

He turned around and saw a small creek flowing into the pond about fifty feet back. Dahlia wasted no time trudging through the water after it. It was up to Reed's chest and difficult to wade through. The bottom of the pond was soft and sucked his shoe down every time he took a step. An itchy burning sensation started to seep from his shoulder wound that he tried to ignore. He was so thirsty that he had to use all his willpower not to suck down every last drop of the cloudy pond water on his way.

After what felt like an eternity, they both reached the mouth of the creek and climbed their way out of the pond. Dahlia tore herself out by clutching onto the bottom of a cattail stalk and pulling out of the water. She extended a hand and helped yank Reed to shore.

The two rushed over to the creek and dunked their heads into the slow running water to drink as much as their bellies would hold. It had a cold clean taste that filled his senses and reinvigorated his body. After they got their fill, Reed laid down in the grass with his feet to the edge of the creek. Dahila laid down next to him and put her head on his chest.

Dahlia closed her eyes and took a deep breath in, "We could eat lunch here and bathe in the sun everyday if we wanted to. Take a nice refreshing dip in the water, fill up some buckets or something to bring back to the house. Sounds like a nice life for the time being."

"Sounds like a dream come true. Although, next time we probably shouldn't dive in with our clothes on."

Dahlia turned her head to him, "Next time if you don't run into me then we won't."

"Sorry about that." He traced his finger up and down her arm, "I got a little too carried away. We should be dry by the time we get back home at least."

The two laid in the grass and laughed the hours away until midday when they both started to get a little hungry. They decided to walk back home and pick up some potatoes and corn on the way. Having lost the race, Reed picked out and prepared their lunch. Dahlia scrounged around the yard and porch areas finding a couple of buckets to carry water back with. After their quick lunch they made the walk back to the creek to retrieve some water. Reed found a small pile of chopped wood on the side of the house with no porch and brought it to the back yard. He bent down a portion of the grass and collected enough rocks to make a fire pit. It was getting near the end of the day by the time he got everything set up and a fire going. Tired of having corn for two meals already, he poured some water into a large metal pot from the kitchen and placed it as well as he could on the side of the fire without it falling over.

Dahlia poked her head over the pot, "You making some corn soup?"

He shook his head, "Thought we could change it up a bit. Gunna try and soften a couple of those potatoes by boiling them. Can't live off corn forever."

The rest of the day passed waiting for the water to slowly come to a slight boil and then for the potatoes to cook enough to become soft. The sweetness of the potatoes wasn't as intense, still retaining some of their earthy flavor. They sat on the porch swing and watched the sunset for a while before deciding to turn in for the night.

Her head was resting on his shoulder with her arm wrapped around his, "Should probably head in before it gets too dark to see."

"Yeah, I'm getting pretty tired anyway." They walked into the house and over to their room. Dahlia opened the closet looking for anything of interest.

"Found some clean sheets." She plopped them on the bed, "I want to change the ones we have, who knows what the last people did in there."

"Good thing we didn't sleep in them already."

Dahia threw the clean sheets at him, "Shut up and help me pull these sheets off already."

Reed pulled the sheet edge from under the mattress when his hand hit something hard. He recoiled at first before digging his hand under to pull it out. It was white floral picture frame sitting upside down out of from under the mattress.

"What's that?" Dahlia asked.

"Looks like a picture they missed before they left."

He flipped the it over to see what the previous owners looked like and instantly turned ghostly pale when he saw their faces. It was a wedding picture under an archway in the backyard with the field of corn behind them looking more maintained. The faces looking at each other were Reed and Dahlia, hand in hand, all dressed up and looking as happy as they could ever be.

Chapter 21

Reed stumbled back with the picture in hand, catching himself on the dresser. His mind couldn't process what he just saw. Everything felt foggy and numb at the same time. Any noise around him was muffled while his head spun. Sweat formed in his palms and his body was on fire. He could barely keep himself upright.

Dahlia quickly walked around the bed to check on him. She grabbed him and tried to get him standing back up straight, "Are you okay?! What is it?"

"Us." He handed her the picture.

Dahlia grabbed it from his hands to see what he was talking about. She kept staring at it, trying to take in all the information this one photo presented. She slowly sat down on the bed with her eyes glued to the picture. Reed sat next to her and joined in the staring, still unable to believe his eyes.

"We look so happy... And healthy."

"We're just shadows of these people now," Dahlia whispered.

He placed his hand on top of hers, "I knew you were important. I knew that I felt a connection with you from the moment I laid eyes on you." He took the picture from her, "I never imagined something like this."

"Are you sure this is real?" She looked out the window, "I don't even know what to say."

He set the picture down, "I don't see why they would fake something like this and hide it in a mattress that we were never supposed get back to."

"A part of me can't believe it. Can't believe I wouldn't remember this. Even after what they did to us." A tear formed in her eye, "Right when I thought that lab couldn't take anything more. I knew you felt familiar. I didn't question it, I just accepted it."

"Me too." His head was starting to clear and he could feel a wave of sorrow crashing over him, "I always felt like I knew you, hoped is more like it. I never would have guessed this though."

"Either way, you won me back again." Dahlia tossed the picture to other side of the bed and faced Reed, "I hate that our lives were taken from us, I hate that I can't remember who we used to be. After seeing this, that hate I felt before is a small drop in the bucket compared to now." She took both of his hands in hers and looked him in the eyes, "We vowed to be together forever at one point, and we've still been keeping that promise. You've captivated me in the best of times and now again in the worst of times. I love you for that."

Reed was taken aback. He thought he had felt the same way at a few different points but pushed the feelings away thinking it was too much too fast. The truth was, he always loved her. From the second they had a moment to relax in the store and she walked out in that purple dress, he knew she was his one.

"I love you too." He looked at the picture, "And I'm not just saying that because we're married now."

She chuckled and blushed, breaking eye contact. It felt like a massive release to get that off his chest. He was glad to break the tension of the serious, albeit, lovely conversation. His skin felt like it was going to rip if he had any more emotions fill him.

She placed her hand on his, "Say that again."

He smiled, "We're married now."

Dahlia grabbed the back of his neck and pulled him in for a deep passionate kiss. They laid down on the bed holding each other in their arms. Their kissing continued for a long time until it started to melt into more. The two spent the night embracing each other's bodies for the first time, or for the hundredth.

Reed woke up with Dahlia still asleep in the crook of his arm. He gently tried to pull his arm out from under her head. Pins and needles felt like they were coursing through his arm from the lack of circulation all night and he was having trouble controlling it carefully. Dahlia's head slipped off him and landed on the pillow harder than he would have hoped when he managed to get free.

She groaned with one eye open, "Are you going to wake me up every morning?"

Reed was shaking his arm around trying to wake it up, "Not on purpose."

She gave him a slight smile and rubbed her eyes. Reed felt connected to her in a way that he didn't think possible before. Surprised but glad that he could still feel that sort of love through all of his damage, "I'll get us some water."

"Just give me a minute to get my pants on and I'll come join you."

Reed turned to one of the dressers and slid open the first few drawers, "Looks like they left our old clothes at least. Can't believe we didn't look in here yet."

Dahlia grabbed a pair of overalls and a black shirt while Reed threw on some extra thick tan work pants and blank grey shirt. Neither were surprised that everything fit perfectly. Putting on their fresh clothes felt like the start of a new beginning, starting in their past.

Reed walked out of the door thinking again about why they would have been picked. It was an unanswered question that tormented him, lingering through any and all of his thoughts. He turned back to look at the front door of the house and the second bedroom door caught his eye. It was right at that moment that it clicked, why they had been chosen and pulled from their house.

He ran into the spare room and pulled open one of middle drawers in the dresser. He picked up a shirt that unfolded with some cartoon mascot on the front that would be too small for either him or Dahlia. It dropped from his hand as he walked back to the hallway. They had a child.

His heart immediately felt like it was going to explode, he leaned against the wall to balance himself. The hall was blurring together while his stomach dropped to his heels. Dalhia called out to him; her voice sounded distorted and slow and he was barely able to understand it.

Dahlia grabbed him by his shoulders and looked directly into his eyes, "Reed! You need to talk to me! What's going on in there?"

"We had a child."

Her words were coming out faster and faster, "What are you talking about? How could you know that?"

"Isaac. The doctor's assistant. He told me that Stintz had another test subject that was too young. We were married and there's a kid's sized bed in the spare room. That's why they took us. We were able to have a baby when generations haven't. It's the only thing that makes sense why they would take us over anyone else." Reed stared at the floor almost unable to believe the words himself.

Dahlia leaned her back against the wall and slinked down until her head was in her knees. Tears trailed down her cheeks. Reed got onto his knees and pulled her in for a hug that he needed as much as her.

"We can't leave our child there." Dahlia pushed Reed back to make eye contact with him, "If that sadistic psychopath has our kid, then we have to get them out."

Her voice sounded foreign and gave him the chills, "How do you plan we do that?"

"I don't know. We need to figure out something, and fast. I can't wait around another minute now that I know our kid could be subjected to the same treatment we were."

Reed thought about what their first move could be. They couldn't walk all the way to the lab and try to barge in the front door. Who knows what they could have waiting for them.

"Stamey and the brothers," Reed blurted out. "We could go back there and see if they know anything about the place, or anywhere we could possibly get some weapons. They've been trolling around here for years. They've got to know something helpful."

She nodded vigorously, "That's a good point. Okay. Let's scarf some corn and water down and make our way back there."

Reed quickly walked out and picked a couple ears of corn. Breakfast was silent except for the sound of fast crunching. They chugged the rest of the water they had before preparing to leave and walked out the front door, headed straight for the other farm. The day was hot, and sweat was draining out of Reeds pours by the time they were a quarter of the way there.

Dahlia pointed ahead of them, "What's that?"

Reed pulled his look from the ground to see what she was talking about. Out in the distance there was a stack of smoke billowing up into the sky. The place it was coming from was far enough out that it was hidden behind a small hill in the valley.

"You think they're cooking up some morning deer for breakfast?"

"Looks like way too much smoke for that." Dahlia waved him up, "Come on, let's pick up the pace a bit. Somethings not right."

They started jogging toward the smoke, still unable to see the cause. After about ten minutes they reached the hill that obstructed the sight and got a full view of the scene. It was still a long way off, but they could see that something large was fully engulfed in flames in the back yard of the house where they had shared a meal the other day.

"Holly shit." Reed said, out of breath.

"We need to get there, now!" Dahlia burst forward in to a full sprint. Reed was trailing behind her, not knowing if he could keep the pace up the entire way. There was still about a mile to go and the sun was beating down on them more with every passing minute.

He managed to keep within ten feet of her the whole way to the house. They approached the yard and hopped over the fence to see what was going on. Reed and Dahlia were both struggling to catch their breath as they looked at the van completely engulfed in flames just feet away from the porch.

"What the hell did they do to it?" Reed wondered out loud between breaths.

"STAMEY! DURRIAN! BASSAL!" Dahlia yelled as soon as she was able to.

They stood there for a minute, waiting for a response that never came through the silence mixed with cackling fire. Dahlia ran over to the house and burst through the door before Reed had time to react.

"STAMEY!" She yelled the second her foot got in the door.

Reed ran in after her and his jaw dropped. The furniture in the main room of the house was completely torn apart and thrown around the place. The table and chairs in the kitchen were smashed and turned over. A couch in the main room he hadn't seen before had the cushions cut open and thrown from it. Stamey was the first to catch his eye. Her body was propped up against the wall with a machete holding her up. Durrian and Bassel were on the kitchen floor with their hands bounded sharing a large puddle of blood.

Reed ran out the door and fell to his knees in the backyard. Uncontrollable vomiting poured out what little he had in his stomach into the grass. Dahlia slowly walked out after him blank faced and silent.

"They're still after us." Reed wiped his mouth, "And I don't think they're fucking around anymore."

"They must have defended us." She stared out at nothing, "If they said anything about where we were we would be as good as captured by now." She paused, "They died for us."

Reed stood up trying to get his arms to stop shaking, "They would never tell any government workers anything, let alone where to find other people."

"We need to get out of here. Who knows how long ago they were here. They might not be that far away. They could even be watching to see if we'd come back."

"Where should we go?" He looked back at the house, "We don't know anyone else out here."

"I don't know! We can't stay here though! I can't be by their lifeless bodies for another second!" Dahlia burst in to tears.

Reed pulled her in tightly. She squeezed him as hard as he could stand.

"I'm sorry this happened." He started stroking her hair.

"I know we didn't really know them, but they showed us kindness when they had every reason not to. They were good people. The closest thing we've had to friends." She choked out between sobs.

Reed was trying to turn her back toward the fence, "I know. It's not fair. Let's get you out of here."

"You were right. What are we going to do now?"

"I don't..." He looked across the field to the wall, "The city. We need to go to the city."

"Are you crazy?" Dahlia pushed out of his arms, "We'll get spotted in a second!"

"Isaac." He grabbed her shoulders, "When I was chatting up Isaac in the back of the van he started bragging about his apartment in the middle of the city. It's one of the four center buildings, on the corner of Burley and Nelson. We go there and convince him to help us. He has to know all about the lab's operations."

"And what makes you think he'd help us?"

"He's a good man. I know who he works for says otherwise. He was forced in by his family. Stintz is his uncle. He had no choice in the matter and sympathizes with us; it's why he let me go the first time."

"Yeah, and look how well helping us out the first time worked for him. You sure he's going to want to go down that road a second time?"

"No, I'm not sure. But I believe in him. And I believe it's our best chance."

"If you believe in him, then I guess I do too." Dahlia wrapped her hand around his arm, "So, what's the plan to get inside the city?"

Chapter 22

His hands dropped, "When we were pulling up the first time we got taken into the city, it looked like they only had one officer on duty letting people in. It shouldn't be that hard to sneak past him."

"You want to sneak past him in broad daylight?"

"I don't think we have the luxury of waiting. Whoever they have after us now, that left that mess in there, I don't think they're stopping until we're found." A lump formed in his throat.

"Let's go then," Dahila started walking while looking at the house, "I can't stand to be here anymore anyway."

They climbed over the fence, wading their way through the sea of hot grass, "Probably wouldn't be a bad idea to hug the city wall." Dahlia was looking at all the buildings tall enough to see over it, "Might be a little harder to see us then being the only two moving things in the middle of a field."

Reed agreed and they headed straight for it. The sun was relentless on his skin as they walked, having him begging for shade. When they made it up to the wall, Reed leaned his hand against it to take a small break. The cement was still cold from the cool air of the night before and Reed pushed as much of his body against it as he could trying to cool off, "We really should have brought some water."

"You're the one who said we had no time to lose." She gave him a snarky smile.

"Yeah yeah." He pushed off the wall, "Let's pick up the pace a little, once we're in the city we should be able to get some shade."

It felt weird wanting to be in the city. Not that long ago he never wanted to step foot in there again, yet here he was trying to sneak in as quickly as he could. The thought made him hate Stintz even more. He couldn't stop at causing all the trauma Reed had in there, now he had to make him want it.

Their child wouldn't leave his mind the whole walk. Was it a boy or a girl? Did they look more like me or Dahlia? Were they okay? Had Stintz already begun experimenting on them? The more he worried about it, the more his anger for Stintz grew. He never wanted to kill anyone, even though he had to. Until now. He truly didn't know what he was going to do when he came face to face with him, but he wanted him erased from existence.

After an hour, they could see where the road entered the city around the curve of the wall. There was no movement by the checkpoint and no cars on the road.

Reed crouched down, "If anything moves or drives by, we need to drop into the grass."

"You sure? You don't want me to wave my arms around and yell at them?" She lightly hit him in the shoulder.

"Hilarious." He couldn't take his eyes off the entrance.

The closer they got to the checkpoint the harder Reed's heart pounded. Keeping anxiety under control was becoming a full-time job and they weren't even to the dangerous point yet. His skin was screaming at him as they approached the checkpoint. They slowed down and ducked almost completely under the grass.

The officer that oversaw the post was slowly pacing back and forth in long stretches across the road, kicking whatever small chunks of rocks or debris he saw. The cement blocks closing the other roadways were only big enough to block oncoming cars, leaving plenty of room to slip past on foot.

It looked too easy. Cars were a rare commodity around here and the officer before said that they keep all means of scavengers and raiders out. How could one inattentive guard blocking one pathway be accomplishing that? There had to be something they were missing. They approached the hard line that separated the ungroomed field from the short mowed grass. Reed grabbed Dahlia's arm and dropped fully to the ground.

"Once we cross that line, there's no turning back." Reed whispered, locking eyes with her.

"I know, we don't have a choice anymore though." She spread the grass enough to peek through at the officer, "What's the play? We make a run for it when his back is turned?"

He shook his head, "I don't know. I can't shake the thought that there's something more than just these cement blocks protecting the entrance."

Dahila looked around on the ground until she spotted a sizeable rock. She picked it up and looked over to make sure the officer was looking away.

"Don't..."

Before he could finish, she stood up and chucked the rock at the closest entrance. Reed yanked her back down the second it left her hand.

The rock flew past the block and activated machine noises cranking around from atop the structure. It only took a second after they heard the noise for a flurry of machine gun shots to replace it. They hugged the ground at the sound of the gun spraying hundreds of bullets a second. Their heads were laying on the dirt, neither of them moving a muscle. The shooting stopped after only a few seconds, the sound of the officer's footsteps stomping closer to them replacing it.

Reed was torn between what to do. He wanted to stay and curl up into a ball in hopes that they wouldn't be seen, also wondering if they should get up to run with whatever head start they could. He had pulled her down in time, hadn't he? Stomping footsteps grew louder as he approached. Maybe he didn't, maybe the officer caught a glimpse of her falling back down, or maybe he could see the parting in the grass and assumed there were trespassers. The officer was almost upon them now, his steps slowing from a run to a walk. No, there's no way he didn't see them. They had to make a run for it, it was the only way to have a chance. What a dumb idea to try and waltz right into a city with a whole force of people paid to keep them out. Why did she listen to him? His stupidity was finally going to be their downfall.

Reed looked at Dahlia, trying to give her some sort of sign that they needed to run. Dahlia locked eyes with him and he tried signaling her by moving his eyeballs in an upward direction a few times. Her eyes were yelling at him while she very slightly shook her head side to side.

He knew he couldn't leave without her on board. Whatever their fate was going to be, it was locked in now. He hoped with all his heart that she was right while a part of him prepared to die. He was glad he'd at least gotten to fall in love again, and with the same person.

The boots came to a complete standstill and Reed held his breath in fear of being heard.

The officer grunted, "Probably a fucking squirl again, quick little bastard got through this time."

He left back to his post, the sound of stomping boots getting fainter with every step. Reed exhaled loudly and tried to catch his breath, almost unable to believe they hadn't been seen. He looked over at Dahlia again and saw that she had a tear rolling down her face.

"I'm sorry." Her lips quivered, "I should have thought more about what could happen before I did that."

"It's okay." He put his hand on hers, "Without you we might have been that rock, blown to bits before we even knew what hit us."

She squeezed his hand, "I thought we were going to die."

"For a moment, I did too."

She sniffled and wiped her tears, recomposing herself, "What now?"

"There's only one way in that I see, with one officer in the way."

"What do you want to do to him?"

He frowned, "I don't *want* to do anything. He's just doing his duty. But we need to get through there, so we need to do something."

They both laid still in the tall grass thinking of possible solutions. There didn't look to be any way around doing something terrible to that officer.

"Did it look like he had one of those strap guns on him?" Dahlia asked.

"I don't know, I didn't take a good look before diving back under the grass."

Dahlia poked enough of her head above to look down at the officer. It only took a couple seconds before she jolted back under the blanket of the field, "He's got one of those rifles strapped to his back. If one of us can lure him over here down the way a little bit, then the other could catch him off guard and get his rifle. Once we have that, we just blast him and leave him strapped up."

"And what if he blasts the one who's planning on being bait?"

"Well... I'm sure he has one of those release controllers too." She paused, "The other person will have to wait till he's taken care of."

"And you're sure it was the same type of rifle, right?" His brows raised, "You're positive it was one of those strap shooting guns?"

She peeked back through the grass the best she could, "Mostly positive."

"Mostly?!" He ducked down lower after how loud he blurted it out, "What happens when we go to blast him and blow a hole through his chest? Or better yet, one of us gets shot down?"

Dahlias face tightened, "Do you have a better idea?"

Reed thought about it before answering, "Who's going to be the bait?"

She had a nervous smile, "I am the faster one out of the two of us."

He rolled his eyes, "Great. Guess I'll go tempt fate a little bit more then."

"I'm sorry," she grabbed his hands, "one of us has to do it and it makes the most sense this way. I promise I'm not saying this so I don't have to, I just…"

"It's okay." Reed interrupted and cupped her face in his hands, "This is gonna work, I love you." He pulled her in for a kiss and she grabbed the back of his neck for the embrace.

"Just don't let me die." He smiled.

She tried to hide her smile, "Why would you say that and ruin a perfectly romantic moment."

"It's what I do," he winked. "Now where do you want me to go?"

She pointed away from the city wall, "I figure you could crawl ten feet or so down the road and then poke your head out until he sees you. Once he's on your case and gets close, I'll rush him and take his gun."

"Okay." He nodded forcefully, "I trust you. This is going to work."

Reed got to his hands and knees and slowly crawled away from her. He couldn't help thinking that he was crawling to his end even with his faith in her abilities. He got a good enough distance away but couldn't bring himself to pop his head out of the grass. It felt like there was a two-ton weight weighing him down to the ground. Everything felt impossible and an uncontrollable feeling of impending doom was spreading through him like a virus. He couldn't get it to stop. He thought about Dahlia and his time at the farm, trying to pull in as many feelings from that day to anchor himself back as he could.

Their wedding picture stuck itself in his mind, followed by the small empty bed in the other room. His head and shoulders raised out of the grass and he stared at the officer. The officer was doing his slow pace back and forth again with his back turned. The rifle strapped to his back looked similar enough to the strap shooting ones for him to feel a little better about his odds. Reed prepared himself when the officer got to the end of his pace and was about to turn around. To his surprise, the officer was mostly staring down at the pavement and didn't even notice Reed in the field.

He made it all the way to the end of the road and turned back around without spotting him. Reed was relieved and annoyed at the same time.

"You've got one job dude" he muttered to himself, "How bad can you be at your one job?

He decided to fully stand up in hopes of being seen. The officer reached his turning point still not noticing anything.

"What the fuck?" Reed involuntarily blurted out.

The officer raised his head and locked on to Reed at the sound of his voice.

"Oh shit." He slowly jogged away from the officer, thinking it would look strange to stand there waiting to be attacked.

"You! Stop or I will have to shoot you!" The officer yelled at him.

Reed froze in place, wondering if by shoot him he meant with a strap or with a bullet. He slowly turned around to face the officer who was closing in quickly. He stopped five feet from the grass line with his gun aimed at Reed, who could now see that the rifle looked very different from the containment guns that were used on them before, "Walk out of the field towards me with your hands behind your head, slowly."

Dahlia was too far to make a move if Reed didn't do something. He tried to think of a solution walking over to the officer. Before exiting the tall grass, he stopped and stared into the black eyes of the officer's mask.

"Yup." He pointed his gun at the ground in front of him, "Just a little further."

Reed slowly walked diagonally, trying to get the officer's back to Dahlia. If she had a longer distance to run, then at least she would have an easier time coming from his back.

"Right here." He pointed a couple feet in front of him.

Reed continued to try and turn his back by walking to the side of him.

The officer aimed down his sights at him, "You fucking stupid or something? I said right here."

Reed continued on his path enough to get the officers back away from her.

"You move another fucking inch and I'm going to blast your head off your shoulders, you got that?" He yelled.

Reed saw Dahlia creeping out of the grass, hoping she would pick up the pace.

The officer looked over the gun's sights, "What are you doing here?"

Reed was shaking, trying not to collapse, "Oh, ya know. Just passing through, seeing the sights."

"Sights huh? The only sight you're going to see is my boot on your skull if you lie to me again."

Dahlia was only a few feet behind when a twig snapped under her foot.

"Huh?" The officer turned his head to check it out.

Dahila and Reed both rushed him from either side grabbing for his gun. Dahlia had both hands on the rife trying to yank it from the officer's grasp while Reed wrapped his arm around his neck from the back. The three struggled against each other until the officer slammed his head back into Reeds. The blow knocked him to the ground and the officer let one hand off the rifle to punch Dahlia in the stomach. Reed quickly recovered and threw a punch at the back of the officer's head. The blow caught him off guard and released his other hand from the rifle, letting Dahlia fall backwards with it taking a blind shot at the officer.

The blast from the rifle was deafening and the bullet tore through his calf. He fell to the ground howling in agony.

Dahlia got back to her feet and screamed at Reed, "Let's go!"

Chapter 23

Dahlia slung the gun to her back mid sprint for the entrance, "What do we do about the machine gun?"

"It didn't shoot at us when we drove through the open lane. It must only attack people trying to slip though the others." Reed shouted. He was glad he didn't have time to overthink it. His heart was pounding out of his chest as they passed through the checkpoint.

Reed heard the officer calling out about intruders running into the city past the checkpoint. Dahlia led and continued sprinting a couple blocks down the road before making a turn on another street. She was zig zagging down every random road and Reed struggled to keep up.

A surge of adrenaline flowed though him when he saw a large van speed down the next road over from them in the opposite direction. He tried to keep his thoughts focused on tailing Dahlia. Any creaking door or gust of wind was putting him on edge.

"Dahlia." His lungs were burning and he couldn't say it loud enough for her to hear.

She was about ten feet ahead of him and continued to bolt her fastest down random roads attempting to lose anyone who would be chasing them. Reed pushed himself with what little energy he had left to close the gap between them. He grabbed her by the arm and swung them into a small alleyway out of view from the street.

Reed was choking on his own attempts to breath, "Dahlia."

"We need to keep moving! They're going to be tearing the city apart!" She was already struggling to get out of his grasp.

"We need to stop and regroup for a second. We don't even know where we are." He let go and leaned against the wall behind him.

Dahlia's voice was running quick and verging on breaking into tears, "I didn't mean to shoot him. It just happened so fast, and I couldn't let him win and…"

"It's okay. We did what we had to do. We didn't even know he had a real gun. He's going to be okay, you only got him in the leg."

She wrapped her arms around him and let out a few tears, "I don't want to lose ourselves trying to get to our kid." She buried her face in his chest, "Defending ourselves is one thing…" She swallowed hard and caught her breath, "This was different. We attacked him. He was just doing his job and now he might never walk again because of me."

He hugged her tight, kissing her head and rubbing her back, "It was an unfortunate mistake. And they're the protectors of city so I'm sure they have the best healthcare people can get nowadays. He's going to be okay."

She pushed herself back enough to look him in the eyes, "No more mistakes. Promise me that no more innocent people will be harmed by us."

"I promise. No more." He smiled.

She nodded her head and tried to pull herself together, "So which way do we go?"

"Well, we can't see the center from here" He poked his head around the corner, "I guess we keep following the taller buildings until we reach it. Any noise or sight of anything suspicious and we dive into the nearest alley."

She nodded, "Sounds like a plan."

He did a quick sweep of the area from the alley before returning to the street. The tallest building was directly across from where they were. The layout of the roads confused them and looked nonsensical from street level. They ran down roads without seeing anyone or anything for ten minutes until they heard an engine roaring around the area somewhere. It felt like a maze that they could be cornered in at any moment.

Dahia pointed to a corner building with the lights on the bottom floor, "There's a store, lets duck in until it sounds like they passed us."

Reed agreed without saying anything and immediately changed course to the open storefront. *Mobius Electronics* was plastered on the door. They burst into the store and crouched under the windows that looked to the street. Reed tried calming himself and sat with his back to the wall when he noticed two very confused older women staring at them.

One wore a long dress that was covered in small mirrors in the shape of diamonds, all strung together in an orderly grid-like pattern by a bright yellow thread that stood out against the darker green under cloth. The second had a golden tiara like crown with small spikes sticking out of it made to look like the sun's rays and another long dress that was showing an open field on a sunny day with mostly blue skies like a tv screen even though it still had the same characteristics of fabric. The grass and the small clouds even moved along the dress being blown around by the wind.

Reed looked up at them, "Uhhh, Hello."

Dahlia turned to see who he was talking to and looked stunned at the sight of other people. Everything they heard about how bad the population was getting made them not even think about the fact that they might run into someone else.

"What are you two doing?" asked the woman covered in mirrors.

Dahlia put her hand on Reed's chest, "We went for a run down the road. Just taking a little breather."

The second eyed the barrel sticking up from behind Dahlia, "In an electronics store, with a gun?"

Reed looked around and took in their surroundings before answering. The store was relatively bare compared to the cheese place. The vibrant green walls were lined with shelves filled with various electronics that he didn't immediately recognize. In the center of the store was a circular desk that completely enclosed three robotic arms with cameras attached to them in the middle. The cameras made him recoil a bit, thinking about what happened at the cheese store.

"Uhhh, yeah. Just wanted to get out of the heat and....." Reed started, fumbling an excuse that would make the women leave them alone.

Before he could finish, the woman's dress that acted like a screen went black. A high-pitched noise blared from the store's speakers and big red letters rolled across her dress along a voice that read it out, "*Attention citizens. Two trespassers have entered the city. They are a man and a woman traveling together and should be considered armed and highly dangerous. If there is any sighting of the assailants, please report it immediately.*" The speakers cut out and the woman's dress changed back to the sunny field with blue skies.

Reed put his hand up to them, "I know what you're thinking and it's not what it looks like."

"Incident report!" The woman in the mirrored dress yelled.

Her words sparked life in the cameras and all three turned to look at the woman. She pointed at Reed and Dahlia and they centered their focus on the two.

Reed knew what was coming the moment those cameras spotted them and wasted no time. He grabbed Dahlia fast as he could ramming them through the door. Bars jetted downward to lock them in, clipping Dahlia's arm on the way.

She winced in pain and tripped into Reed, knocking them over. They looked back at the store from the ground, metal bars blocking every inch of glass and door.

Reed looked at Dahlia's arm, "You okay?"

"I'm fine." She rubbed it, "I'm thankful for your quick thinking."

"I wasn't about to fall for that one again." He looked behind him, "We need to go, now. They're sure to be here any second."

She nodded and they climbed to their feet. Reed took the lead, trying to follow his original path. They ran down the road and made a few turns looking up at the building tops for guidance, hoping to not get lost.

An engine roaring and screeching tires in the distance bounced off the buildings around them. They came to a stop and looked around to try and locate it.

Reed's head was snapping in all different directions, "I can't tell which way it's coming from!"

"I think it's from that way!" Dahlia yelled, pointing to their left.

"You sure?"

"No, but we don't have time to argue. Go!" Dahlia pushed him to the right and started moving.

They ran down the road until they reached the end of the building. Dahlia grabbed Reed and pulled him around the corner where they wouldn't be spotted. She pressed herself close to the wall and moved her head far enough out to see around the edge. They waited for about ten seconds before she saw the van turn a corner and come screeching down the road. It was only in her sight for a split second as it almost drifted down the street to the electronics store.

She sighed and flipped her back to the wall, "Well, we have a little more time now. They turned down the road to the store."

"Thank God. I think we're getting close too. I don't remember the buildings getting much taller than these ones." Reed was breaking his neck looking upward.

"How do we get in without being spotted when we get there?"

He shook his head, "We'll deal with that when we need to. One thing at a time."

She closed her eyes and quickly nodded a few times, "Ready?"

He looked to the road, "As I'll ever be."

They continued to sprint as fast as they could without immediately running themselves out of breath. Dahlia allowed Reed to continue taking the lead, thinking he had a better idea of where they were going. They ran down road after road for the next fifteen minutes without hearing the van anywhere near them. He couldn't tell if there were people in the few open stores they passed but there wasn't anyone on the sidewalks to report them for now.

Reed's chest was burning up from the run. Every breath felt like he was shoving hot coals in his lungs and blowing fire back out. His legs ached and he could feel the dryness of his lip starting to crack open. The adrenaline was wearing off and now it was only the thought of his helpless child that pushed his body forward.

They turned down another road and that's when Reed saw two buildings that looked different from the rest a few blocks down. The sliver he could see were mostly made of glass with one being lined with a shiny silver metal that took up all the small spaces in between windows and the other being lined with gold, both reflecting brightly off the sun of the clear day.

"That's got to be it!" Reed slowed down to try and catch his breath.

"Not out here." Dahlia pointed to a small alley. It was barely big enough to comfortably stand in between the two buildings to their right.

They ran over and leaned against the wall desperately trying to breathe normally again. Reed didn't realize how far he had pushed himself until he stopped. They were in a full sprint almost the whole time they ran through the city and his body felt like it was about to collapse under the weight of gravity. At least this time it looked like Dahlia was having the same issue trying to collect herself, so he didn't feel so bad about his condition. They both took a long time to get to a place where they could even manage a conversation.

Dahlia was stretching her legs out, "Before we get any closer, we should have some sort of plan."

"I don't know which one it is from here but it's on the corner of Burley and Nelson"

"I saw the signs running down. We're on Nelson Road now, so it's got to be one of those two."

Reed couldn't see any finer details on either of them with the blinding glare shooting off, "One of us should go down to check it out and then come back to make a plan. The broadcast said a man and a woman so maybe no one will think twice if they only see one of us."

"And what if everyone is wearing a crazy get up like those two old ladies were." She threw her arms out looking down at her clothes, "We'll stick out like a sore thumb."

He rolled his eyes with his whole head, "Unless you have a large dress in your pocket or you want to go back and mug those old ladies for their cloths then I think we have to take our chances."

Dahlia glowered at him.

He put his hand on his chest, "I can go and check it out, maybe the men around here don't dress as lavishly as the women."

"I don't like this." She squeezed his hand, "Please be careful."

"Of course." Reed said softly, bringing her in for a kiss.

They parted lips and she pressed her forehead against his, "And don't get too close to anyone if you don't have to. I doubt we smell great at this point."

Reed chuckled, "I don't see that happening but good advice."

He broke out of their loving hold and looked around the corner before leaving. There still wasn't anyone on the street and he heard no sound of vehicles in earshot. Reed jogged over to the building at first before forcing himself to slow down to a walk. There couldn't be any reason for someone to take a second look at him. It was painful to go so slow and it made his chest tight.

The walk down the next few blocks to the buildings felt like it took hours. The closer he got to them the more paranoid he became. At first it was about his appearance before it started to increase to the way he walked being different, or the look on his face, or the officers in their vans darting around the corner for him. His skin was crawling as he reached the first silver-lined building, every step ahead like a new mountain he had to climb and push his body over. The street sign on the corner read, *Valley Rd.*

He shook his head. Of course it was the golden building.

He looked in the silver lined building as he passed. There was a grand entrance full of silver themed archways and chandeliers. It looked more like a decorated ball room with a reception desk than an apartment entrance.

He paid little attention to the atmosphere of the place, instead scanning the floor for people. Only one person, who was sitting in a chair at the reception desk, was present on the entire floor. This time it was a man, who was wearing a fairly simple silver suit that shinned brightly off lights that were directly pointed to focus on him. The only oddity in the outfit, other than the lights made to make him shine so brightly for all to see, was a crown like headpiece with three silver spikes jetting up toward the ceiling at a forward angle. There were two smaller spikes coming off either ends of the piece with a large one that was almost twice the size of the other two coming straight out of the center. The man didn't notice Reed walking past and instead was focused on a small tv that was held up by a metal arm attached to the corner of his desk.

He continued on to the golden building, slowing his walk to have as much time to scan the inside as possible. It held a spherical shape opposite to the square one outside of the building. Any empty space made by the rounding of the interior was hidden from the outside with golden panels that cut off the window. Golden balls of various sizes hung from the ceiling at different elevations providing the lighting. The front desk was a rounded half circle with a golden top and a teal front that looked like bubbles. A marble trail of teal that gently flowed back and forth connected the desk and the front door. The man sitting at the front desk was wearing a golden suit with an equally golden sphere on his head. The sphere had a circle of smaller gold balls wrapping around the top of it but didn't seem to have any spot where the man could see out of. Above his head suspended by wires was a large sign that read *Golden Globe Apartments*.

The lack of a face confused and concerned Reed. Was there even a real person under there or was he some kind of android that didn't need to see. He almost laughed at the ridiculous notion. The elevators were sitting to the left of the reception desk and didn't look like they needed any special way to use them.

Reed circled back to Dahlia in the alley having done as much recon as he could from the outside. She looked happy and almost like she had been holding her breath the whole time Reed turned the corner, "How's it look?"

"Looks like a pretty straight forward entrance to a building. Well, a way over the top entrance." He looked at the vibrantly colored building surrounding them, "These people are pretty ridiculous."

"So we just walk right in and hope for the best?"

"I think we go in one at a time but.... yeah." He shrugged, "Unless you want to stick up the place."

She formed a half smile, "This seems like a really dumb idea."

He grabbed her hand, "It's the only one we have and there's no turning back now."

"Alright," She gestured to the sidewalk, "lead the way."

Chapter 24

He stood firm and looked back to her, "Probably best to leave the gun here, I doubt that will fit in with their fashion sense."

"You don't think so? I thought it was very fashionable," She did a small twirl, then slung it off of her back and leaned it against the wall in the alley, "If you insist."

"I think I'll go in first and talk to the front desk guy to distract him before you stroll in and walk directly to the elevator."

"What are you going to say?"

He squinted and looked up for a second, "I don't know. I'll improvise. Just remember, top floor. I'll be coming up right after you if I can't make the same elevator."

She pushed his shoulder, "You better."

The two started walking down the street to the Golden Globe, stopping before they were in view of the windows. Reed looked back and gave Dahlia an inquisitive thumbs up before continuing. She slapped his thumbs up and grabbed him in for a kiss before shoving him off. They both smiled to each other and Reed turned for the door.

The large handle looked like a quarter of a golden sphere attached to the large thick glass door. It was much easier to pull open than Reed thought it would be with its size.

The man at the desk straightened his posture when he heard him enter the building. Reed slowly walked over to the desk, his skin feeling tight again and his breaths were becoming more shallow. The golden globe headpiece that completely covered the man's face was not helping his nerves. It was very unsettling approaching a faceless suit.

When he reached a few feet from the front desk a square portion of the headpiece became translucent and Reed shuddered at his face appearing.

The man stood tall with his hands laced together loosely hanging slack, "Are you okay sir?"

"Yes. Just uh. Wondering if you had any apartments available at the moment?" Reed was questioning everything, from how he was standing to the unsureness of his voice.

The man looked him up and down with a disapproval, "These are the highest end luxury apartments in the city, are you sure you're in the right place sir?"

"Excuse me?" Reed raised his voice.

"Sir?"

He heard Dahlia walk into the building and knew this was the time to make a bigger distraction.

Reed started to get red in the face, "My family owns and operates the majority of the farms that supply *your* city with all the food it has. Just because I came here from a morning of inspections around the fields you assume that I don't know where I am?"

"I'm sorry sir, I just.." The man started.

He sliced the air with a hand, "No, you listen here! My family helped found this city and has taken care of it ever since, so I'm not going to be talked down to by some receptionist who thinks he's in the top class because he has access to the bottom floor of the building. You got that?!"

Dahlia walked right past him, completely unnoticed by the frightened front desk worker, into the elevators.

The front desk worker put his hands up, "I'm incredibly sorry sir. The people who live in these apartments usually don't look so much like the workers that they employ. Please, accept my deepest apologies, it will not happen again."

"I would hope not!" When the elevator door closed, he lowered his voice, "I suppose it was an honest mistake though."

"Thank you, sir. Now, you wanted to see what apartments were still available?"

"As a matter of fact, I do." He pointed a finger upward, "The higher up the better."

He tapped away at a screen that was embedded into the desk, "Let me pull up a list of all the available spaces."

Reed heard a faint rumbling from outside. He wondered if it was the officer's van pulling up, finally finding him. The front door swung open violently with a loud thud from the glass door slamming against the wall. Reed flipped around and saw four fully equipped officers rushing in his direction with guns aimed down at his chest. He stumbled backwards toward the desk as they fired their guns simultaneously, the bangs of the ignition flooding his eardrums. His hands instinctively went to his chest and eyes closed while he fell to the floor screaming. When he opened them back up the officers had vanished and there was no trace of an injury or van out on the street. Even the door wasn't open like it was a moment ago.

The receptionist leaned over the desk, "Are you okay sir?!"

Reed patted his chest and looked around. What the fuck was that? The realism of his delusions was starting to really frighten him. They were getting more and more difficult to tell from reality each time.

He shouted while pulling himself back up, "Yeah, I'm fine! Your damn floors are so polished that I slipped and fell is all."

The man looked at him through scrunched eyebrows.

"Where's that damn list?" He threw his arms out.

The man looked at his desk, "Right here in front of me sir."

"What's the best you have open then?"

They shared a look, the receptionist not moving.

"I haven't got all day!"

"Before we continue," He pulled out a scanner from behind the desk, "could I do a quick scan to confirm your information please?"

"Why do you need to do that?"

"It's just policy sir, I'm sure a man of your stature understands."

Reed crossed his arms, "You don't believe me?"

"Like I said," he set the scanner on the table, "it's policy before we go deeper into the logistics of our leasing agreement."

Reed felt trapped, he had talked his way into a corner and would be done the second that scanner hit his face. He looked into the eyes of the front desk worker searching for any excuse to not have to go through with it and came up with nothing.

"I don't need this!" he shouted.

"Excuse me?"

"I was merely curious about the accommodations of this place on my way to see a good friend of mine but am no longer interested with how I've been treated. If you'll excuse me, I'll be on my way now."

"I see." He tapped a few keys on his desk, "and to whom might you be visiting today sir? For my records of course."

Reed rolled his eyes, "Isaac, top floor."

The man pushed away at his screen before stopping and sighing his shoulders in a slump, "Ah yes, right here. Isaac Stintz, top floor penthouse." He put the scanner back under the desk, "I'm sorry for the interruption sir, have a lovely visit."

The mention of that name immediately put Reed on edge. He'd forgotten that they could share it. It amazed him that someone raised from people in that same psychotic lineage was the person they were going to for help. He left the desk for the elevator, "Thanks."

One of the doors opened almost immediately after the button was pushed. Reed stepped inside and pressed for the fourteenth floor, the top of the line. The front desk worker and him locked eyes while he waited on the elevator. The translucent part of the headpiece faded back to gold and broke their stare down as the doors were closing.

The elevator was dead silent rising up the building, the slight pull of gravity as they rose being the only indicator that it was actually moving. Unlike the entrance, the elevator was nothing special in sight; a gold box with rows of buttons on either side of the door and a small screen that showed what floor they were on that currently stated, *going up*.

It only took half a minute to get all the way to the top. The elevator dinged and the doors opened when they reached the floor. Reed walked out into a small red walled hallway with gold trim that only led to one door at the end. Dahlia jetted out from beside the elevator and almost tackled him into the wall with a strangulating hug, "You were brilliant!"

"Thank you." He thought about his delusion, "I almost lost it at the end there."

"You made it though," she squeezed him harder, "and that's all that matters."

They kept hugging for another minute before breaking off and looking down the hallway.

Dahlia kept his hand in hers, "I guess this is it."

"You know what we didn't take into account in this plan." He looked over his shoulder at her.

"What?"

"What if he's not home?"

She slightly smiled, "Why would you say that, now of all times?"

"Just something I thought of."

"Only one way to find out." Dahlia pulled him down the hall.

Dahlia's muscles stiffened in front of the door before knocking on it. There was shuffling on the other side and footsteps that heading their way. The door opened and Isaac's face immediately turned ghost white.

"What are you guys doing here?!" Isaac whispered.

Reed was less than quiet, "we need to talk."

"Come on," Isaac ushered them in, "get in before someone sees you."

They were surprised by the simple esthetic of the interior compared to the rest of the building. He had a huge sprawling open apartment that was fairly empty of furniture or decor. The kitchen directly to the left of the door was lined with stainless-steel countertops and appliances surrounded by thick glass cabinets full of different assortments of white dishware. The large island matched the counters steel tops with a frosted glass underside. Straight ahead of them was the living room with a large U-shaped black leather couch facing a fully transparent glass walls that looked out over the city. There was a staircase with a black railing that went up to an open loft area where Reed could see the corner of his bed frame.

"You can sit on the couch while I get us some water." Isaac walked away into the kitchen.

They went over to the living room and sat on the oddly stiff couch that surrounded a glass coffee table with a single mug sitting on the corner. Even though he hated the city for all it was worth, Reed couldn't help but marvel at the view that Isaac would wake up to everyday. It was mostly empty rooftops over the view that him and Dahlia shared on the roof from before. He could see the farm that Stamey and the brothers were murdered at in the distance. The van fire had died down with smoke still billowing upward on its way to the sky. The other farm, their farm, was far enough to one side that they could only see a quarter of the first corn field and the house.

Reed wondered if Isaac had sat up here and watched everything play out from his penthouse. Seen them crash the van, trudge across the field, and then ultimately see the squad of men make their way to the farm and kill anyone that had come in contact with the two. Just the thought lit a fire in his chest.

"Here, I'm sure your thirsty." Isaac handed them each a large glass of water.

They each drained their glasses to nothing without coming up for air. The water tasted so pure and clean compared to the stream water they were drinking the past day. It was like a completely different beverage with a new taste.

He took the glasses back, "I suppose I'll get you some more."

If Isaac couldn't help them, Reed was still glad they made it all this way to have the memory of how that water tasted.

"Here you go." He set newly refilled glasses on the table in front of them.

Dahlia grabbed them and handed one to Reed, "Thank you."

"I see you've been looking out at that smoke cloud, there was a fire at that farm earlier. Sometimes something random like that pops up in the area and I always wonder what's going on down there." He said to Reed who was still looking out the window.

"I can tell you what happened. Your uncle happened." Reed kept his eye on the rising smoke.

"Oh." Isaac's face dropped.

"There were a few good people who were living up there for the time being. They helped us out and even showed us where we could find some food." Reed paused before continuing, "then when we went back, they were brutally murdered and thrown throughout the house. The fire was that van we stole, up in flames." his voice was rising while telling the story.

Dahlia clamped his leg, "Reed."

Reed was almost shouting, "No, Dahlia, he needs to know exactly what his uncle is doing! He needs to understand why this can't continue!" He stood up, pointing out the window, "those people did nothing but help us, and what did they get for it? Propped up by a machete and tossed in a puddle of blood, that's what!"

"Reed! Calm down!" Dahlia pulled him down by his arm.

He sat back down next to Dahlia and she started rubbing his back.

Isaac set his glass on the table and shook his head, "I'm so sorry. I didn't know anything about what happened after that accident. I called it in after you two left and was told that I should go home until further notice. They didn't even send someone to drive me home. I had to walk the entire way back." He looked at Reed curiously, "Why did you come here? To me?"

Dahlia sat back, "Because we need your help getting into the lab."

"Why the hell would you want to do that?"

She nodded at him, "Because of you."

"Me?"

Reed put his elbows on his knees and closed his hands together, "Because of what you said to me in the van, about another test subject. One that was too young for now."

"Why would that matter to you?"

He put his hand on Dahlias, "We're married, and we think that might be our child in there."

"What are you talking about? How could you possibly know that? If that is true, then it's information that I didn't even have access to."

Reed looked at Dahlia, "We found a wedding picture wedged in our mattress at the farm that those good people pointed us to." He switched to Isaac, "everything else from our lives was stripped away, but they missed a spot. Why else would they take two people who ran one of the biggest farms in the area that was located right next to the city."

"No, no way." He was shaking his head, "There has not been a recorded natural conception in decades before even I was born."

"I don't know if we hid him away or if we had some sort of deal where they left us alone. There was another bed and dresser, with clothes clearly not meant for an adult, in a separate room at our house. What other reason would we have that for? It's not like we would need a guest room nowadays. Just think about it, it makes sense."

Isaac looked down at the coffee table with a blank stare trying to process all the information.

"I know you don't want to be a part of this, on either side. you need to make a choice though. We're going to go there with or without your help." He pointed at Isaac, "You could be the reason that someone gets to live a full life."

"What about my life?"

"You can do whatever you want to do." Reed looked around the apartment, "I'm sure you have the money to start over."

"Are you going to kill him? My uncle?"

"I can't answer that."

Dahlia looked past him, "We don't want to kill anyone. We can't let him stop us either."

"He's not a monster. He really does believe everything he's doing is to save us." His eyes went to the window, "However, I understand. It's too much, maybe he's too diluted now. I don't know."

Reed sat up, "Will you help us?"

Isaac stayed silent for a minute, Dahlia and Reed staring at him. He looked up and made eye contact with them, "What do you need?"

Chapter 25

"For starters, we need a way in that doesn't involve the front door."

He sat back and thought about it before answering, "The only other entrance to the building is a back door that's unlocked by keycard."

"Sounds just as bad as the front door," said Dahlia.

Isaac had a blank stare, "It's not like they have that much security left after what you guys have done since you got out."

"They can't find any more people who want to guard the mad scientist lair?" Reed lifted his brows and tilted his head, "How strange."

Isaac gritted his teeth, "Society doesn't have many people to do those kinds of jobs anymore. And that mad science liar could still be the reason that humankind doesn't collapse completely. Maybe they will find a way with the research they have already done." His body relaxed, "They have to."

Reed could see Isaac's pull to his uncle's work, that what he was doing was justified on some level. If he was honest with himself, he questioned whether or not their lives were going to cost humanity's collapse sometimes. He couldn't believe that, he didn't know if he would be able to push on if he did, "People always find a way. Dahlia and I are good examples of that."

"We're really running the clock down to the final seconds on this one."

Dahila's lips went straight as an arrow, "I'm sorry you don't have much hope. If you don't believe us or in people, then at least believe in your uncle."

Reed's forehead scrunched. Any mention of the doctor in a good way, especially from Dahlia, made his skin crawl. He couldn't believe that she would stick up for him after everything he'd done. She had to be trying to manipulate him through his family. No, she wasn't a manipulator. Some of what she was saying had to be true to her or she wouldn't say it. He couldn't and wouldn't support her on this.

She continued on, "Even though you don't agree with his methods, it's obvious that you think he's a brilliant scientist and our best hope. Believe in that feeling, that he can overcome this problem without people like us."

"He is an inspiration when it comes to science." The edge of Isaacs lips curled upward, "He obtained his medical degree and a doctorate in genetic engineering at the same time like it was nothing. He hardly even had to study, briskly skimming through the material once or twice retaining every last bit of it. I'm considered higher than most on the IQ scale and even I had a hard time with the genetic engineering course, and I only have my master's in the field. "

"See," she smiled at him, "that's the type of person who can find a way above all else. You just have to choose to believe that he can."

"You're right. If anyone can figure this out, it's him. You need to promise me that you won't kill him then, no matter what happens. If he dies, then we all die." Isaac looked directly at Reed.

He didn't want to kill anyone, he never did. The more they talked about how amazing this man that took everything from him was, the more a dark desire tried to float up from the depths. He was reluctant to make the promise with the thoughts floating around his head. Maybe that's what separates them. The willingness to resist those dark urges.

Reed met his eyeline, "I swear it."

"Just like that?" Isaac leaned back.

He nodded, "Like we told you, we never wanted to hurt anyone."

Dahlia grabbed Reed's hand and brought it to her lap, gently placing her other one on top, sandwiching his hand between hers.

"Sorry about the tangent. Let's get back to business." He was audibly more upbeat, "There's one other way you could get in, but it's far less glamorous."

"We haven't been living in glamor, I'm sure you can smell us from there."

He sniffed once to check, "That's fair. The old building that they repurposed for the lab had a garbage chute they haven't gotten rid of yet. It runs down the side of the building and opens into a service room on every floor. The chute itself would be plenty large enough to fit in if you could shimmy up it. It leads into an underground vault where everything would sit until it was picked up on garbage day. The trap door leading into the pit is activated with the same key card as the back door so it shouldn't be a problem to get in."

"How deep is the pit?" Reed asked.

"No idea."

"And what if it's too deep to be able to reach the chute?"

"If you go that route then I guess you better hope it's not." He pointed to his lab coat hanging off a hook by the door, "I'm a scientist, not a garbage man, I don't know the intricacies of how the trash pit is built."

Reed felt the fire and had to take some deep breaths before continuing. He knew Isaac was risking a great deal even talking to them. Anger wanted to creep in with every word Isaac said to them regardless of what they were.

Dahlia looked to Reed, "Unfortunately, that might be our best bet right now."

He grunted loudly, "The worse option usually is."

"Take this before I forget." Isaac reached into his back pocket and pulled out a blank white card from his black leather wallet.

"This will open the back or front doors as well." He handed it over to them.

Dahlia took the card, "What if you need it?"

Isaac exhaled everything he had and put his hands on his head, "I don't even know if I have a job anymore honestly. Besides, by the time you two do whatever it is you're going to do, I'm sure I can figure out a solid alibi." He stood up, "If you guys want to get cleaned up or eat something before you go then feel free to use my shower and kitchen."

Dahlia beamed, "That would be amazing. I literally can't remember what it feels like to take a shower."

Isaac chuckled before the realization of what she said, his face sunk and he turned away from them, "I'm sorry. It's right over there if...." Isaac was cut off by a loud knock at his door.

"Shit!" Isaac whispered.

Reed shot up off the couch, "What do we do?!"

"I have a small safe area under the counter in the island, go, now!" He started to shove them in its direction.

The door knocked three times again, like a ticking clock counting down the time to an inevitable explosion taking them all out.

"You mean behind the glass?" Reed was having trouble keeping his voice down, "I think they can see through glass!"

"I'm not an idiot, it's one way glass! you can see out, but it won't show any shadows from inside."

They rushed over as quietly as possible to the kitchen. Isaac knelt under the countertop and pushed on the frosted glass underside until it opened enough for a person to slide through.

"Go!" He ushered them in, "And stay quiet, it's not soundproof!"

Reed and Dahlia hurriedly squeezed though the opening into the space under the island. The small box did not look like it was built to house two people in it. Reed and Dahlia had to shove at each other to make enough room. They pushed the door closed sealing them inside the box. The only saving grace to his claustrophobia setting in was the fact there was a handle on the inside.

The two crouched together and watched Isaac rush over to the door. He opened it up as the third round of knocking was starting. Reed couldn't immediately see who it was and the look on Isaacs face told the story of something terrible waiting behind that doorframe.

Isaac was almost shaking, "Uhh. Hello, what are you doing here?"

"I was in the neighborhood. Are you going to invite me in?" That voice echoed throughout Reed's being. He knew right away that it was Dr. Stintz.

"Of course, sir. Come on in, take a seat on the couch if you like. Do you need anything? Like water or something to eat?" He was already on his way to the kitchen before finishing the sentence.

"A glass of water will be fine." He held up his fingers, "Two ice cubes."

Stintz slowly followed Isaac to the kitchen wearing the same lab coat he always had on, stopping with his legs directly in front of Dahlia. The pulsating feeling of their impending doom was seeping out of reed head into the rest of his body. Dahlia covered her mouth and he held his breath to conceal their breathing as much as possible. It felt like he was going to explode like a grenade, destroying everything in its path. The blood in his veins felt like ice running through his body while his skin acted as a heat blanket burning him up. He needed to get out of this glass coffin they were forced to be silent in before he lost his mind. All he could do was focus on the ground instead of the doctor's legs and try to hold on until they made it through.

"Here you go." Isaac put the glass on the counter with a loud thud.

"Everything alright?" He picked it up and drank almost all of it at once, "You seem nervous to see me."

"Yes, yes. Everything is fine." He was nodding too much, "I mean I'm a little nervous about my job."

"Yes. Well, that's actually why I'm here. Come take a seat on the couch so we can talk."

"Okay. Sure. Good news?" He was visibly barley holding it together.

Stintz walked toward the couch, "It can be."

Isaac followed and sat on the opposite side of his uncle, the couch blocking everything below their shoulders from view. Reed and Dahlia both let out a slight sigh and tried to catch their breath as quietly as possible.

Isaac and Stintz sat on the couch in silence while Stintz stared blankly at him like he was peering into his soul, digging out all his secrets. "Do you still want to work under me at the lab?"

"Of course, there's no one better that I could possibly learn from."

"Mhhm." Stintz looked around the room.

"Is that still on the table after the crash?" Isaac asked.

Stintz tilted his head, "The crash? You mean the botched transport of two already confined individuals?"

"Err, yeah, I suppose."

"Please, elaborate on that incident." Stintz squinted. "For instance, how did you end up being the only one unharmed at that grizzly scene?"

"Well, uhh," he took a quick drink from his glass, "after the male broke from his restraints, he looked to take out the driver and left me in the back."

Stintz frowned, "And you did nothing to try and stop him?"

"I'm an academic, not a fighter. I thought the guard would be more than a match for him." His eyes dropped, "Regrettably, I hid in the back until the van came to a stop. I jumped out of the side to assess the situation and the male took off in it before I could do anything."

"Very shameful of you, to be outsmarted by a piece of lab equipment." Stintz paused before continuing, sitting farther forward, "even more shameful though, to lie to me about it."

Isaac recoiled, "What are you talking about? That's the truth of what happened."

"I'm going to ask you bluntly so we can be done with this facade. Where are they and what did you tell them?"

All the blood rushed out of Isaacs face, he began mumbling and muttering nonsense under his breath attempting to piece together a coherent response. He looked up at Stintz "I have no idea whe...."

Stintz put his hand up, "Before you tell me you don't know anything, allow me to inform you that I tapped in to the lobby cameras and saw them both walk into the building. After your miraculous survival above all of the guards, I suspected you had something to do with the escape. With no subjects to continue my research, I opted to return to the city and keep an eye on things. Just in case. So, I'll ask one more time." Stintz paused, his voice lowering, "Where are they?"

Isaac threw his hands out, "Uncle, Christoph, please. I don't know."

Stintz frowned and gave a slight nod of his head. He pulled his coat open just enough to stick his hand in to grab something. He smiled, "It's okay Isaac."

Bang!

A gunshot echoed through the apartment. Reed and Dahlia had to watch silently as the back of Isaacs head exploded into a barrage of red paste, coving the floor behind the couch.

Chapter 26

Dahlia squeaked and her body scrunched in the corner. Reed clasped his hand over her mouth with his other on the back of her head. He focused his eyes on Dahlia to try and keep himself from screaming.

Stintz sat still at the scene before standing up, looking at his deceased nephew, "All over some faulty hardware. Shame it had to end like this."

Another one dead. Another person who tried to help them, dead. Reed never considered the danger it would put on Isaac, only what it could do for them. The scale of worth was getting too heavy on the wrong side.

Stintz didn't move for a long while, almost as if he was admiring his work before he walked around the couch and stared out the window. He gazed out over the city and the fading smoke cloud. It didn't take long for him to search the apartment being completely open with mostly glass walls. There wasn't much effort put in either, mostly peering around corners and looking up the stairs at the loft area. After he was satisfied, he walked back over to the couch and grabbed his glass, finishing it off and placing it in the sink on his way out.

The moment they heard the click of the door Reed and Dahlia let out huge gasping breath followed swiftly by tears. The tears weren't just for Isaac, they were for everyone that had died by being associated with him.

"We should stay in here a bit longer. Just in case he's waiting for us." Reed whispered.

Dahlia nodded, unable to bring herself to say anything.

Reed put his arm around her and they shifted to a sitting position the best they could, Dahlia sitting on Reed's lap with both of their legs almost able to fully extend out the other way. They sat in the box and cried until there were no more tears left, neither feeling like enough time would ever pass for them to feel safe to leave. The emotional exhaustion they both felt took its hold and they drifted off to sleep.

Reed woke up only able to hear the pounding from his heart, looking around wildly for something bad that was going to happen. His rapid movements woke up Dahlia who was much more relaxed, "How long do you think we were asleep for?"

She groggily looked across the room, "It's still light out. So probably only an hour or two."

They shifted their bodies enough to pry the door open and shimmy their way out. Reed stood up slowly, his joints cracking and aching from being bound up for so long. His eyes immediately focused on Isaacs body. The pool of blood was large enough to take up a large portion of the floor.

He couldn't break his eye contact with the body. Everything in him wanted to turn away but something kept him glued to the tragic sight. The iron warm smell of blood filled his nostrils the same way it covered the floor. He had seen so much horrific death in the past few days that he was already instinctively pushing away all the feelings he used to associate with it. Numbness began to overtake and he knew that it wasn't how he was supposed feel. It wasn't an unwelcome guest, washing over and diluting the bad feelings in him. He welcomed it in like an old friend and turned away from the body, "What now?"

She couldn't look at Isaac, "We go to the lab and get our kid back. End this madness and start over somewhere new."

Starting over. It seemed like such an impossible feat at this point. What he would give to go back to the time when their wedding picture was taken. A time he couldn't even remember but longed for, when everything was figured out and they could just live their lives, "Do you believe that's still possible?" He wondered if he would ever feel the happiness that was on his face in that picture, if he could ever get past all the trauma he'd gone around and collected.

Dahla grabbed him by his shoulders and looked directly into his eyes, "As long as we're in this together, we can accomplish anything we want. No matter how daunting, okay?"

Reed's lips hardly twitched trying to fake a smile, "Okay."

Dahlia let it go, not looking convinced. She walked to the sink and chugged another glass of water. Reed went directly to the fridge and opened it up to see what they could eat before going on their way.

She looked back and her eyes closed, returning to the fridge, "I can't eat with his body sitting right there."

Reed half closed the door, "We need to eat something to keep our strength up if we're going to make it all the way to the lab on foot."

"let's just take something and go then," she leaned against the counter looking at the wall, "I need to get out of this room."

"What if they're waiting outside the door? Or in the lobby? I'm sorry. It's difficult, I know, but we need to be extra careful. Stintz saw us come in and not leave, so I'm sure he's going to keep an eye on that lobby camera." Reed looked across the room, "Why don't you go and shower off this whole scene while I figure something out for food. As much as you want to get out of here, I saw you light up at the thought of a shower."

"I don't know. Using a dead man's shower just seems wrong."

"Please," he rubbed her arm, "he already said you're welcome to it. I know you'll feel better. I'll be right here waiting for you when you're done."

"Okay, I'll just take a quick one." She pulled him in and kissed him before walking to the bathroom, "Thank you."

Reed turned his attention back to the fridge. The shelves were mostly empty, other than six containers full of mixed vegetables over rice all stacked neatly in a corner. Reed lifted some tin foil on a plate that was covering up a half-eaten steak. Any sight of meat flashed Isaacs head back into his mind. He covered it back up and grabbed a couple containers of the vegetable rice mix, not wanting to check in anything else.

Reed opened drawers randomly until he found the utensils. He grabbed a couple forks and walked up the steps to the loft area. The upper area was very minimal; a small bed with a black headboard, white blankets and pillows, accompanied by a single glass dresser. Through the glass, he saw one drawer filled to the brim with multiple pairs of the same blue pants and another with a bunch of identical white T-shirts. New clothes were a luxury he couldn't pass up and he grabbed a new outfit for each of them. He sat on the top step and waited for Dahlia while staring out over the city.

Twenty minutes passed by before Dahlia emerged from the bathroom, her glistening skin a welcome sight wrapped up in a white towel. She stood out like a shining example of what beauty was supposed to be all fresh and clean.

"Up here."

She walked over and up the stairs combing her fingers through her wet hair. Reed handed her the clothes when she got to the top and she gladly walked behind him to get dressed. Reed gave her the container and fork when she sat down beside him before opening up his own. She opened her food and shook her head when she caught a glimpse of Isaac in the corner of her eye. The food was gone as fast as the container was opened. She ate quickly out of disgust more than hunger, "Do you think it's a little strange that there was a gunshot in one of the rooms and no one came to investigate?" She set the container down on the step.

"I hadn't thought about that to be honest." Reed was savoring every bite and talking in between mouthfuls, "It wouldn't surprise me to know that Stintz has a way around that. I'm sure he came with everything already prepared. He knew there was a possibility of killing Isaac and wouldn't leave something like that up to chance."

"You're probably right."

Reed went to grab a couple more containers out of the fridge and offered one to Dahlia while walking back up the stairs. She shook it off and he placed it on the floor of the loft. After scarfing down another container full he was overstuffed. Not knowing when their next meal might be had him wanting to keep going until his stomach popped.

Dahlia leaned in to him, "You're turn for a shower."

He hadn't thought of taking one himself until now, only wanting her to have whatever she needed to feel a little bit better.

"That actually sounds amazing." He hoped up and walked down the stairs with his new attire in hand.

The bathroom was tiled from floor to ceiling with white hexagon shaped tile. It brought back memories of how the lab made him feel, blinded by white painted everything. He shook it off and stripped down, walking into the glass lined shower and turning the water up until it was burning his skin. The heat from the water and the relaxing feeling of the body wash scrubbing over his skin washed away a lot of his stress. If he wasn't keeping Dahlia waiting, he would have stayed in the hot steamy cocoon for hours. The cut on the back of his shoulder ached and he attempted to scrub it clean the best he could, not knowing what had gotten into it. He finished up rinsing off and dried himself with the small hand towel that was left hanging by the sink. Putting on new clean clothes felt like he was getting a fresh start, like he could leave all his trauma from the past few days lying on the floor with his old dirty ones. If only it was that easy. Reed walked out the door to Dahlia still sitting on the top step waiting for him.

Reed stretched the front of his pants out a little, "Pants are a little loose around the waist, guess Isaac had a few pounds on me."

"Good thing for that, otherwise I probably wouldn't be able to fit in them. It was already a tight squeeze." She looked down her shirt from the collar, "If only he had a girlfriend I could have stolen a bra from so I didn't have to keep wearing this thing from the lab. Even after scrubbing it clean in the shower, it will never feel clean to me." She paused and spun Reed so his back was facing her, "'Your cut is bleeding again. I'm sure he has something in his bathroom to put on it, come on."

She riffled through his cabinets until she found some antibiotic ointment and gauze wrap. She tapped his shoulder, "Shirt off."

He tossed the shirt to the side and she started carefully spreading the cream on it, "That's definitely infected. Hopefully this will help." She placed a pad of gauze on it and wrapped more around his chest and over his shoulder to keep it in place.

Reed looked at her with raised eyebrows, "A little over kill, don't you think?"

She patted his cut just hard enough for him to feel it, "I think the words you're looking for are, thank you"

He smiled, "Thank you."

Reed left the bathroom and took another shirt without a blood stain on it from the drawer. He looked to Dahlia, "You ready to see what's waiting for us?"

"No. We can't stay here any longer though." She turned to the door, "If he is looking at the cameras, then we need to run as fast as we can the second those elevator doors open."

Reed nodded as they walked to the door. They left the apartment and got on the elevator, the doors closing and sealing them in. Dahila pushed the lobby button, the robotic *going down* chiming from the speakers. The ride down felt impossibly longer than the ride up, both of them wound up tight ready to bolt. There was the gentle upward push of the elevator settling on the ground floor.

The doors opened and they both broke in to a sprint for the exit. The lobby worker was barely able to react while they rushed past him. Reed tried to bust the door open with his momentum, barely budging it slamming his shoulder on the glass. They both forced it open and ran down the road in the same direction they came from. A few blocks up, Dahlia snatched the rifle she had left in the alley, hardly slowing down.

The two continued to run down roads trying to follow the path of descending rooftops. The confusing layout of the city baffled him. From the outside it looked a lot more cohesive and linear than the roads were on the inside. All the different bright colors faded by time and dust accompanied by the mostly destroyed screens made it hard to tell if they had already been in an area before. Everything was such a vibrant contrast from one another, and it all stood out so much that it made them blend together.

An hour passed by the time they reached the bottom line of buildings next to the outside wall. Reed slowed to a jog followed by collapsing with his back against the wall as Dahlia came and sat next to him. They both were struggling to catch their breath, unaware of their exhaustion until they stopped.

"Seems like they gave up the search." Reed puffed out, starting to regain his composure. "Or they're so far in the wrong direction that we didn't hear them driving around at any point."

Dahlia raised her head from her knees, "Either one works for me."

Neither was able to fully catch their breath in a short enough time that they thought was safe. The paranoid itch creeping around the corners of their vision. Dahlia was the first to rise, "Ready?"

He didn't know if his lungs would ever be ready. Sitting in one spot was too much for him though, "Yup, let's go."

The buildings along the wall were still six stories tall and too far for a jump down. Every color that was fighting for the spotlight stood out even more against the grey cement of the big circular barrier. If time and dirt wasn't fading them out, they would have been too much to stare at for long. There were a few screens that still functioned lining a few of the buildings, broadcasting lines of advertisements over and over for any product you could think of.

It only took a short while before they could see the checkpoint. With buildings blocking most of the view as they walked, they were only a few hundred feet away when it popped up. They both slowed down and tried to get a better look without saying anything to each other.

There wasn't any extra security or officers in sight on the inside of the wall. From where they stood, Reed could see the large machine gun turret sitting on top of the structure, putting him on edge. If that thing went off when they got close, then they had no chance of getting through.

"We should walk down a block before we get to the main road leading out for a better view of what's on the other side."

"Good idea," Reed was fixated on the checkpoint rooftop, "I'm not a fan of the look of that turret though. We need to be extra careful."

They started to cross over to the main road at the next intersection down. Dahlia led the two and stopped him before turning the corner. She looked back and put her finger in front of her mouth before slowly looking around the corner. Nothing jumped out as abnormal.

She waved him on and they walked onto the main road. An alarmingly loud voice came from checkpoint, *"Citizens must remain clear of exit points. The city is under a temporary lock down."*

Dahlia took one more step forward and the machine gun jumped to life and aimed down the road at them. She pushed Reed back and retreated behind the building. After a minute of waiting, she stuck her head back out from hiding.

The moment her head poked out into the open the machine gun came back to life, directing its attention to her. Dahlia shrieked, pushing backward into Reed. A flurry of bullets tore apart the corner where she was standing. The two crawled backwards watching the brightly colored red wall turn to a mist of color and concrete dust. It only took a few seconds for a huge chunk of the building to be completely disintegrated and the bullets to stop.

Dahlia was still half on Reed, "That's going to be a problem."

"Yeah. A big one."

"Any ideas?"

He shook his head, "Not any good ones."

She stared at him, "What's one of your bad ones?"

He watched the dust start to settle in front of them, "We throw a rock or something to distract it and make a run for it."

"I don't think we can run that fast." Dahlia got up and brushed herself off, "The first part isn't so bad though. I think we can figure something out with that."

"Like what?" He pulled himself up with her hand, "Throw a lot of rocks?"

"I was thinking something more permanent." She put a hand on the rifle strap, "I'm thinking if we throw something and it distracts it long enough, then maybe I can get a shot off and cripple it."

"How many shots do you have in that thing?"

Dahlia slung the rifle off her back and fiddled around with it until she found the button that released the magazine. She emptied it and looked down at the three bullets in her hand, "Not much room for error."

"No, it's not." He took one from her and looked at it closely, "Are you sure about this? Once we use those, we've got no defense."

"You have a better idea?" She snatched the bullet back.

"Good point." He put his hands on her shoulders, "You've got this. I believe in you."

Her eyes lifted up to meet his, "That's a better answer."

"Wait here, I'll grab something really quick."

Reed walked back around the block looking for something to throw. It didn't take long to find some old tin cans rolling around by a sewer grate surrounded by smaller rocks. Reed grabbed a couple of cans and filled them halfway up with rocks to give them some added throwing weight. Dahlia had the rifle reloaded and was practicing looking down the sights when he came back.

"Hopefully something shiny will be more of a target." Reed shook the cans, "You ready?"

"As I'll ever be."

"Three, two, one. Now!" The can left his hand and flew out into the open.

The turret locked on before it even flew halfway across and unleashed its barrage of death, shredding the can to pieces in midair. Dahlia flung her body around the corner enough to aim towards the turret and immediately let off a shot. Before Reed could register the gunshot, Dahlia threw herself backward and tripped to the ground. Another volley of shots tore out more chunks of wall until rebar was showing.

Reed helped her to her feet, "Did you hit it?"

"No." She put another one in the chamber, "I got too scared and shot before I could even aim at it."

"It's okay. We've got two more tries. Just take a deep breath and collect yourself for a second. Let me know when you're ready."

Dahlia took his advice, unable to shake fear from her expression. She looked at Reed and nodded, "Ready."

Reed felt a burst of adrenaline shoot through his body. A real fear of losing her was trying to push its way through. It felt strangulating, like someone was holding his arms down to keep him from a second throw. A deep breath caged them in enough for now.

"Alright. One, two, three!" Reed said again as he threw the second can.

Dahila whipped around the corner and took aim before the turret could start its volley of bullets. The strangulating fear burst through the cage forcing him to pull her back to safety. Dahlia took her shot before reed was able to get his hands around her waist. The machine gun had obliterated the can and was on its way to her by the time he got to her.

Reed slammed down with Dahlia on top of him. He got out from under her to check if she was alright and his soul dropped from his body.

There was red.

Too much red.

Chapter 27

He burst into tears and let out a blood-curdling scream wrapping, her in his arms. His vision tinted white, and he could hear ringing in his ears while he rocked her limp lifeless body back and forth on the sidewalk. A muffled voice was trying to break through in the background, like yelling at the volume of a whisper.

Someone's hands grabbed his shoulders and pulled him away from the body. He desperately clawed at Dahila, not wanting to leave her there. The person laid him down on the pavement, his eyes still glued to her. They put their hands on his head and pulled it down into their lap, forcing him to look up at them.

He couldn't believe his eyes. Dahlia stared back down at him, cradling his head in her lap and brushing his hair with the sound of bullets breaking off concrete in the background.

"It's okay. I'm right here with you." She whispered it again and again until he could wrap his mind around what was happening.

Reed couldn't process what his eyes were telling him. Everything went numb and shut down for a minute while he laid and listened to her sweet calming voice bring him back. He sat up and looked to the sidewalk. The body had vanished and left no trace of ever being there. It took a minute longer before he was able to peel his eyes from the empty spot on the sidewalk. Dahlia was sitting on her knees quietly waiting for him when he turned back. He clasped his arms around her and started to cry, "I thought." He tried to say between sobs. "I thought I'd lost you!"

She rubbed his back, "You'll never lose me. I'll always be right here waiting for you."

Still laying his head on her shoulder, Reed opened his eyes and looked over to the intersection. Bullets were taking off chunks of buildings and shredding through glass and monitors all around the place without stopping for a second or having any specific target.

"You got it this time?" Reed sniffled and tried to straighten himself out.

"I think so." She tilted her head to see a little more of the road, "I couldn't tell because you pulled me back, but it's been firing off nonstop since I shot at it."

Reed looked confused, "I did pull you back? I didn't imagine that part?"

"Yeah. You pulled me back so hard that you lost grip and threw me few feet away. I heard you screaming the second I hit the ground. You were sitting down cradling nothing, rocking back and forth until I grabbed you."

Reed's gaze fell to the pavement, "I'm sorry."

"No." She pulled it back up, "I'm sorry you had to go through whatever you did. Just remember that none of it was real."

"Thank you. Thank you for never making me feel bad about any of that stuff. I don't know what I would do without you."

"Well, it's a good thing you never have to find out. You're stuck with me." She gave him a smile that he immediately returned.

"Thank goodness for that."

The barrage of bullets came to a sudden halt, and they could hear a loud repetitive clicking in its place. Reed looked around the corner to see the turret moving around aimlessly still trying to shoot from an empty barrel.

"It's got to be out of ammo." He grabbed her hand, "Let's not waste any time and run for it."

"Alright, let's go." Dahlia took the lead, running past him.

Reed followed behind her. They ran through the checkpoint with no resistance after the turret. The woods down the road felt like a safe haven and they didn't stop to check anything out on their way. The sooner they could be in the shroud of trees again the safer Reed would feel about slowing down. He couldn't help but feel like something bad was going to happen on the way to the woods, like waiting for the other shoe to drop. Even with the hang up of a machine gun, it felt too easy to escape.

As they started to pass into the first thin layer of trees Reed could feel himself becoming more relaxed. Even at the pace they were running his muscles loosened up a bit in the beginnings of cover. A couple miles from the city and a thick layer of trees that shaded most of the ground finally allowed them to take a break.

Dahlia slowed to a walk and got off the road into the woods. Reed followed her, thankful that she slowed down. He didn't know how much longer he could have kept running without collapsing. They were walking side by side in the shade of the trees with nothing but the sound of branches lightly rustling against each other and the occasional bird tweeting above them.

"Reminds me of when we first got out together."

"Me too." She looked at the canopy, "When I could barely breathe with my mouth burned shut. It seems like so long ago."

"I know what you mean. I don't even feel like the same person after everything we've had to go through." Reed told her.

Her forehead scrunched, "We're not the same people. We were changed in the lab and then changed again by all the shit they dragged us through trying to bring us back."

He sighed, "I guess you're right."

It was mostly silent the rest of the walk until they reached the convenience store an hour later. Everything was left exactly as it was since the last time they were there. The bars in the store still up all throughout the windows and even the glass from the vending machine was still scattered all over the ground, pushed around from one of those cleaning cars spraying everything without care.

"You hungry?" Reed asked, looking at the store.

She didn't notice her stomach screaming at her until he asked, "One last meal before the final stretch sounds amazing."

"Probably should go in the way we came out, just in case."

"Course, I'm not stepping through that archway again."

They walked around to the back of the store and crawled through the hole in the wall, carefully peeling back the torn aluminum siding trying not to get cut. It was eerie being back, the lights still on brightly and the broken clothes hanger they used as a pickaxe still lying on the floor. Reed grabbed Dahlia by the hand and started guiding her over to the clothing area.

"What're you doing?"

There was a giddiness to his step, "I wanted to look at something with you."

He stopped her a small way back from the changing room and tried to stand in a particular spot next to the shelf of jeans. Still hand in hand, he looked over and pointed to the changing room doors.

Dahlia struggled to make sense of anything he was doing, "What? The doors?"

"I was standing right here when you first came out wearing that amazing purple dress with the bow, it completely blew me away. I knew right then that you were way more to me than just some other escapee. I didn't know the depth of it, but I could still feel our vows in my bones when I saw you." He looked to her, "I just wanted you to know where I fell in love with you for the first time again."

Her cheeks flushed and an ear to ear grin took over the rest of her face, "I don't even know what to say."

"You don't have to say anything. Only know that I was always in this one hundred percent."

Overwhelmed with love she pulled him in close and crushed her lips against his. Reed pulled her closer wanting to savor every moment. His hands slid down to her waist as she laced her fingers in his hair. Reed wasn't sure how many times they've kissed like this, but he was sure he got the same electricity pumping through his veins every time. After a long time, she reluctantly broke apart from his lips, looked at him with heavy eyes, and whispered, "you may not be the smoothest man, but at least my husband knows how to do that."

Reed chuckled, "Clearly I didn't need moves to get you either time. The second time all I had to do was save your life."

Dahlia laughed and pulled Reed in for one more lingering kiss. "I think we're even on the lifesaving by now."

Reed allowed himself to be lost with her without the weight of the world holding him down. He wished this was all there was, all there had to be. After it began to pass, his mind sharpened back on what they were there to do.

"Let's get some food in us." He said, changing the tone.

Dahlia sighed quietly, "Yeah, for a second I forgot why we came in here."

"Me too." He brushed her cheek with his finger, "The longer we stay the more we're delaying the inevitable."

"I'll grab us some water if you want to get some food." She walked off, "Not more chips please, something a little more substantial if you can find it."

"Okay."

Finding something other than chips was going to be harder than he thought after turning down the aisle. The first half on his side was all various brands of chips and chip like snacks. He scanned the shelves on the way down for anything worthwhile. Near the very end of the lane, after a mountain of salt and candy, there were a few bags of beef jerky left hanging up and some other various meat sticks. Reed grabbed a hand full of snacks and a couple bags of jerky, "I think this is the best we're getting out of this place."

"You only went down one aisle, you sure about that?" Dahlia smiled.

Reed grinned back, "I think it's the best *I'm* getting us from here then."

"It looks perfect. Here, I'm sure you're parched from the run." Dahlia held out a bottle of water for him.

Reed drank it like it was the first time he'd ever had the taste, emptying the entire thing in one go.

"This might come in handy too." Dahlia held out a small pocket flashlight.

Reed grabbed it, "Were you able to find batteries?"

She rolled her eyes, "No, I'm going to bring a dead flashlight with us."

"Okay, okay. Dumb question."

He handed Dahlia some jerky and snacks and grabbed another water from the cooler. The two walked over to the wall from where they escaped and sat down with their backs against it, ripping into their bags of food. The only sounds coming from them were ripping meat and starved chomping until they had devoured everything. Reed stood up and offered a hand down to Dahlia, "Ready for the final stretch?"

"Let's go get our kid back."

They carefully climbed out of the hole and walked around to the other side of the building. The woods on the store side would give the same amount of cover as the other side of the road but Reed and Dahlia both felt a higher sense of safety with the latter. One side was where they ran for their lives from Jack, and the other is where they hid out and slept for their first time together. Without having to discuss it, they walked across the street and entered the tree line into the forest.

Walking along the road in the woods Reed noticed that the shade was getting darker around them. He couldn't see the sun through the treetops and knew that it wasn't going to be long until they were completely shrouded in darkness.

Maybe that's for the best, he thought, looking up at the branches. The moon usually kept it light enough to see what they were doing without being so bright that someone would see them from far away.

They walked for a couple hours in the fading sunlight. Reed took in every last drop of warmth while the cool shade of night took over and caressed his skin. The dark blocked them from seeing very far ahead, especially in the cocooned cloak of trees. Not long after the sun had fallen, they saw the harsh cut tree line that butted up against the pavement parking lot. The lab was fully in sight from a few trees back.

Floodlights on both corners of the building illuminated the majority of the lot and the entire pathway leading to the front door. Reed noticed the stain of blood on the pavement from where the back of his shoulder had almost been ripped off. Anger felt like a stove burner turning up in his chest. The sliding glass doors showed an emptiness of lit space behind it surrounded by the menacingly white outside of the walls.

"If I already didn't want to go in the front door, I really don't want too now." Reed said quietly.

Dahlia touched her lips, "Going back in there has been my worst nightmare, yet here we are."

Chapter 28

"Did Isaac say which side of the building it was on?"

Dahlia raised her head higher, "Not that I remember."

Reed shook his head, "I guess a fifty-fifty chance isn't the worst odds."

"You want to choose?"

Reed tried to remember anything that might tip him off to which side it could be. Thinking back was harder than he expected. He had been pushing away all those feelings and memories for so long that it was throwing his mind for a loop doing the opposite. All the same feelings started to cycle through his body passing the memories they were attached to. His body started to shake and skin felt like it was vibrating off trying to process everything. It was a horrible means to go through and he was about to give it up until something sparked in him, "All of our rooms were on the one side. If we were facing the elevator, they were all on the left."

She flipped her hands, "Okay?"

"If we were all on the left then I bet you any storage or extra rooms would be on the right, and facing the elevator was the same as facing the front of the building I think," Reed pointed, "so I bet you anything it's on the right side."

Dahlia looked at the building and then back to Reed, "We're going right then."

The shadow in tree line covered them until they reached the road connecting to the parking lot. They froze at the crossroad, even in the night neither wanted to step out of the woods. Dahlia grabbed Reed's hand and gave it a slight squeeze before bolting out from safety. It took him off guard and he stumbled going to follow her. They both sprinted across the road and into the trees on the other side, ducking down and waiting to see if there was any movement or alarms sounding.

Nothing made a sound and there was no one coming from the building. They stood up and walked the tree line until they were far enough on the right side of the building that they knew they wouldn't be in danger of the lights.

Reed noticed the sharp sting of cool night air. It felt restricting instead of refreshing for the first time while they looked out at the field, "Once we step out, there's no stopping until it's done."

"I know." Dahlia said quietly.

Reed pulled her in for one last kiss before they left, "I love you. We got this." He almost couldn't bare letting go of her waist.

She squeezed his arms, "I love you too, and I know we do."

Reed forced himself to let her go and walked out of the woods onto the small groomed grassy area that surrounded the building. Dahlia followed close behind him, creeping slowly, leaving ample room between them and the last glimmers of the flood light. As they got to the side of the building Reed could make out the silhouette of the garbage chute running down its side.

From the outside, the chute did look large enough for a person to shimmy up. They approached the glossy white metal chute and saw the trap door in the ground at the bottom of it. Dahlia reached into her pocket and grabbed out the keycard. There were no clear signs of where to swipe it, especially with how dark it was. She pressed it up against the door in random spots until they saw a small green light appear and heard the click of the lock opening. The door wouldn't budge no matter how hard she pulled on it. It had been closed for so long that the grass and dirt around it had grown onto the outside rim, sealing it down tight. Reed grabbed the handle with her, and they both pulled with all their might. The hinges squeaked and the ground came apart around the edges. In the silence of the night, it sounded deafeningly loud when it finally broke loose. When it fully released and swung open, they were thrown to the ground, landing with a loud thud.

Reed sat up, looking for someone coming to capture them, "I sure hope those walls are thick."

"If we're lucky, no one will be here." She pulled out her flashlight and shined it in the pit, revealing a heap of large red garbage bags covering the entire floor and going down for who knows how far. All the bags had the same biohazard symbol and words plastered on them. Small rungs of rebar created a ladder that went from the trap door all the way down to the bottom of the garbage pit.

Reed looked down the ladder, "I don't know what else I was expecting from a medical garbage chute, but this doesn't look great."

"It'd be best we just take the plunge before thinking too much about it." Dahlia said climbing in the pit's door.

Reed inhaled deeply, "Awesome."

They climbed down the ladder and stepped out on the garbage pile. It smelled like rotting eggs and roadkill, sticking in his nostrils like barbed hooks. He almost gaged but thought it was still better than what he had imagined. Dahlia shined her flashlight at the top of the pit where the chute was attached. It was at least five feet higher than either of them could reach. Reed was relieved to at least see small metal parts sticking out on the inside wherever two pieces of the chute connected, giving them something they could grab. He had major doubts if he would have been able to get all the way up with nothing to grab and the full weight on himself held up by pushing outward.

"Come here, I'll hoist you up" Dahlia placed her flashlight on a bag facing upward.

He looked at the chute and then back to her, "Then how are you going to get up?"

"I'll stack some trash bags or something, it won't take long." She laced her fingers together and crouched down.

Reed put a foot in her hands, "If you say so."

She boosted him up and he was barely able to get his hands on the first grabbable spot a couple feet up the chute. His fingertips had to be like claws around the ridge and felt like breaking with his weight under them. Dahlia was able to give him enough of a boost to hoist himself in and wedge his legs against the sides. He pushed upward until he was able to pin his foot on the first spot, allowing for a minute of rest waiting for Dahlia.

"Alright," she brushed her hands off against each other, "I'm going to move the flashlight, so it might get dark in there."

Reed stayed silent when she moved the flashlight, fearing that his voice could be heard on the higher levels. It was pitch black without the light beaming through and Reed could only hear the shuffling of bags being thrown against the wall. A few minutes passed until he noticed the movement suddenly stop.

"You okay?" Reed whispered loudly.

"Yeah, just one little problem."

"What's that?"

The light shined at the stack of trash under the chute, "Amazingly, there's not enough trash in here to pile up for me to reach."

"What? What are we going to do now?" Reed could feel his heart revving its engine.

"I know how you're going to feel about this when I say it," She paused, "but you should keep going up and I'll go around back and get in from there."

"What?!" Reed covered his mouth, fearing how loud he blurted it out, "There's no way I'm letting you go by yourself into the back entrance!" He dulled it back down to a loud whisper.

"Reed, listen to me. Isaac said it himself. There's not much security left to stand in our way, if there even is anyone here, and I still have one shot just in case. Besides, we can cover more ground in this place separately anyway. We'll find our kid and whoever else is left in this hell hole and get out of here. I didn't want it to be this way, believe me, but I think it worked out for the best. I'm sorry." The light left the chute.

It took everything in him to stay where he was, "And what if I drop down and follow you?"

"Please don't make this harder than it needs to be and just trust me and trust in my abilities."

All Reeds feelings were pulling him to not accept her proposal. The thought alone made his stomach turn over. He already saw and felt what it would be like to lose her and the hopeless dark pit it would immediately drag him into would be too much for him to go through again. Tears trailed down his face with that image forever painted in the back of his head. He did trust her though and knew how amazing she was. She would have an easier time going through the building that way than he would. Even with everything in him screaming no, he knew he had to let her do this.

"Okay." He tried to hide the cracks in his voice, "Promise me we'll have dinner at the farm again after all of this, just the three of us."

"I promise. It's a date." She threw the light up to him, taking him by surprise and almost falling out of the chute trying to catch it. "I don't think I'll need it to get around back."

Reed desperately tried to catch a glimpse of her face one more time before she left him but couldn't see her. He heard her shuffling through the bags on her way to out and waited for the last step of her feet on the ladder before turning back up to the chute.

The climb had to be his focus, everything else was bottled up like fine wine. The metal parts he could grab were close enough to easily reach. He had the light in his mouth shining through the whole thing. Every misstep or shuffle that made a noise or moved the chute paralyzed him with fear. Any moment could be his last step if someone heard him coming.

His foot slipped and the light fell from his mouth, banging on the sides of the chute the entire way down. His fear came to the crest of a tipping point, now being in total darkness.

The metal felt different when he went to grab the next piece. He pulled himself up and saw that it was the first sliding door into a room. Wanting to get out of this garbage box, he had to force himself to pass it and keep going, knowing that the third floor was probably his best bet. If Stintz only had one person left for his experiments, he knew they would be on his deranged floor of fun.

Reed was getting the hang of climbing in this peculiar fashion and sped up quickly. It wasn't long before he was passing the second floor opening and moving upward. The closer he got the more his heart pounded on the inside of his chest. Forcing himself to keep his momentum going was turning into a harder task than the climb itself. A few minutes passed until his hand landed on the cold bare metal of the third-floor opening.

He pushed it open just enough to peek through and make sure no one was waiting on the other side. It was a small storage room that they were still using. Through the slit, he could see various types of medical equipment stacked in cabinets next to hooks with guard uniforms hanging from them. Even slowly pushing it open caused the metal door to scrape loudly against its frame. Reed climbed through as carefully as he could, accidentally letting go of the door as he fell in the room.

It slammed down with a loud *thunk,* giving Reed a heart attack. A storm felt like it was going to be upon him while he scrambled to his feet. He waited in silence ready to fight for his life without a sound in return. After a few seconds passed, he decided that he was safe for the time being and looked around for anything useful.

The thought of dressing up in the guard uniform crossed his mind but it would be pointless without one of their helmets. Scalpels and anything sharp that could be useful were locked up tight in a caged cabinet. He placed his hand on top of a shelf above the guard uniforms and ran it across in hopes of something helpful. His hand hit something hard and cold toward the end of the shelf. Grabbing it and pulling it down, he was shocked at the sight of a handgun.

Immediately Reed pushed the magazine release and it fell out to the ground. Adrenaline spiked and he rushed to pick it up. Reed emptied it out to see what he was working with. Five shots in total. That should be plenty.

Chapter 29

Reed's hand was trembling on the door. Every new milestone on their way here felt like a new point of no return. He slammed through with force, frantically spinning his head and gun around in all directions. The unnatural penetrating whiteness was the only thing that looked back at him. He stood up straight and tried to collect himself. Looking down the hallway to the last door where Isaac had inadvertently let him slip away brought back all those feelings of confusion and helplessness crashing back down on him like a tsunami engulfing a city.

He pushed himself through it and started walking down the hallway, almost being drawn back in by forces bigger than himself. In the back of his mind, he knew that it was unlikely there would be anything in there, but he had to see it again. If for nothing else than for some closure.

The entire walk his eyes were locked in on the double doors. The white of the walls reminded him of when his eyes would start to fade out with his delusions. The entire place was inhuman, not suitable for anyone normal. A hornets nest was stirring up in his gut and slowly uncorking his wine rack of pushed aside memories. Sweat formed in his pours as the thoughts came flooding back. There was someone whispering from nowhere in his ears and small black dots speckling his vision.

Nothing is real, none of it can hurt you.

The thought played again and again like a broken record in his head to try and keep him in the moment. He blinked and suddenly the floor was riddled with the bodies of all the other people who hadn't survived after encountering them. The entire hallway floor was shrouded in red and Reed could feel the warmth from the thick pooled blood on his feet as he stepped.

Nothing is real, none of it can hurt you.

The whispers grew louder the closer he got to the doors until they were almost screams. At first they sounded like random people until he was able to make out his own voice penetrating through the rest. He looked down and saw Dahila's corpse at the foot of the doors

Nothing is real, none of it can hurt you.

There were only a few more feet to go. He closed his eyes.

You can do this.

Reed kept walking with his hand stretched out and the screaming intensifying every step. His fingers made contact with the door and everything went quiet. He slowly opened his eyes and looked back down the hallway. Everything was gone, leaving only the cold white emptiness to stare at.

He took a deep breath in through his nose and held it before blowing back out of his mouth.

The double doors were lighter than he remembered as he stepped into the room where it all started. His muscles tightened him into a statue at the sight of Dr. Stintz hooking up an IV of the familiar golden fluid to Dahlia's unconscious body. A guard stood by with his weapon already pointed at him.

Reep pointed his gun at Stintz, "STOP!"

Stintz made the final connection and Reed saw the fluid flow into her arm.

"I will shoot you!" Reed screamed at him with his finger on the trigger.

Stintz slowly took his medical gloves off and set them on a rolling tray before putting both of his hands in the air.

Stintz turned around to face him, "You shoot me, this kind gentleman guns you down, and then what?"

Reed stared at him, not knowing how to answer. He didn't think of anything afterwards, he just wanted to get Dahlia out of here. His hand was trembling and mind was bending with all the horrible outcomes swirling around mixing into each other. It took all his self-control to not open fire on the man who put his love on a table.

"I'll tell you what happens." Stintz continued after waiting for Reed to respond, "We both die here in an unnecessarily painful and messy way with the guard unable to wake the subject, who will then die of dehydration in the coming days."

Reed was holding back tears, "Dahlia."

"Excuse me?"

"Her name is Dahlia." Reed looked at the guard and then back to Stintz, "And who's to say I don't get both of you?"

"It is a possibility, although an unlikely one with his training." He pointed at Reed with his hands still up, "In fact, the only reason you're still standing here talking to me is because I have instructed him to not fire at you unless you do something rash."

Stintz lowered his hands back to his sides in a robot-like fashion. Reed couldn't see a flicker or ember of soul behind his eyes. Stintz's dead eyed stare didn't show an ounce of fear with the gun pointed right at him. Either he didn't think Reed had it in him or he did not fear death, neither option helped Reed's confidence.

"You see, you are extremely valuable to me. I know you think I'm some monster, but the truth of the matter is that I am all that is standing in the way of humanity blinking out of existence. *We* are all that stand in the way, because I can't do this without you."

"Why me? Why us?" A tear rolled down his cheek, "Why can't you find someone else?"

"That's a fair question." He paused and took a single step closer to Reed, "You see. Your family, and her family.." Stintz started before being cut off.

"Dahlia. Dahlia's family, say her name when you speak about her."

He cleared his throat, "Very well. Your family, and Dahlias family, have both been farming for generations. With the population of this planet growing at an exponential rate we had to make changes to how we grew our food, or we would have fallen behind. Over time those changes began to affect us in unforeseen ways, primarily in men, creating the problem we face now." He paused and focused more on Reed as if trying to see if he was understanding him.

"I know all of that already, I'm still not seeing where Dahlia and I fit into this."

"Yes, well, along with growing food for everyone else and abiding by the new guidelines, your families both had entire separate patches of land that were completely untampered with for themselves. Your family and Dahlia's both grew and traded this food with each other, presumably how you two met, both the only children of each of your families. As luck would have it, you fell in love and started a farm of your own."

Reed felt his anger pushing his finger closer to the trigger, "Then we had a baby and you people took us all away from our nice lives to be guineapigs."

Stints picked up a scalpel and examined the blade in the light, "Yes and no. We knew about your child even though you tried to hide him. We let you live your lives until there was no other option left."

Reed choked up, "Him? I have a son?" Knowing this information made Reed feel the gap between them shrink.

"Yes," He placed the scalpel back down, "sixteen now I believe."

"Sixteen?! And I can't remember anything?!" Reed yelled moving closer to the doctor.

The guard took a step forward and aimed down his sights, stopping Reed when he noticed.

"It's okay." Stintz waived off the guard. "This is precisely why I developed the serum that would block out all those pesky memories. Out of mercy. Without it you would be in this amount of distress every time we had to wake you up."

"Where is he?" Reed shook the gun at him, "Tell me right now!"

Stintz raised an eyebrow, "How am I supposed to know?"

"You have him here. Somewhere in this damn place, and I'm going to find him!"

"I'm afraid not, you can turn this entire building upside down and not find a trace of him."

"Bull shit! Your nephew Isaac told me you had a younger person locked up here, stop lying!" Reed shouted.

Stintz silently smiled, "I told him that just in case he decided to keep you from me, as a safety net. After his inability to complete the simplest of tasks and transfer you from one table to the next, I saw weakness in him. I could tell that he wouldn't have the stomach to do what needed to be done, so I lied. I lied hoping that if he helped you escape, he would mention it, and the thought of a child in my care would draw you back to me. And it turned out better than I could have hoped for." Stintz got some twisted enjoyment out of being right that his face couldn't hide.

Reed's voice started to trail off, "No. No, that can't be true."

"Your boy is as slippery as you are. The day they came for you he disappeared and was never found." Stintz shrugged, "I have no idea where he is."

Reed didn't know what to do, his heart was telling him to kill them both and take Dahlia to search for their son. He couldn't get Stitz's voice out of his head though. That, in doing so, he was singlehandedly setting the human race up for extinction, "You must be able to find someone else for this. We can't be the only people alive that you find useful."

Stintz turned to the side and fiddled with Dahlia's IV, "There have been a few anomalies over the years that we've investigated, but they were all just that. Anomalies. The only reason we allowed you to stay in your little bubble for so long was because farming has been a long dying, necessary, industry. There are just not many people around anymore that know how to keep a large-scale farm afloat I'm afraid. So, we waited. Waited until we felt like we could wait no longer. Really you should be thanking me for all the years you were able to live unharmed."

Reed's gun lowered a few inches, "We're it then. Us or nothing."

Stintz nodded, "It's what we have been reduced to, yes."

He looked at Dahlia sitting on the table and lowered his gun, "Do it with just me."

Stintz stopped messing with the IV and faced him, "Excuse me?"

Reed pointed the gun at his own head, his hand solid as a rock. He knew they weren't both going to make it out, but maybe he could save Dahlia. Maybe he could give her a chance, "Figure out a solution with just me. You said yourself that the problem is mostly in the men. Let Dahlia go or I end it all right here and blow my own brains out."

"It would be near impossible without the both of you. If you..."

"So, not impossible then." Reed interrupted, "Good, get her out of here."

Stintz stared at Reed intensely, trying to decide if he would actually go through with it. The two were locked in to each other, each hoping the other one would break. Finally, after what felt like eons, Stintz buckled and broke the silence, "Have it your way then, if you must."

Stintz turned to Dahlia and unhooked her IV tube, carefully removing the needle from her arm and replacing it with a small chunk of cotton under a wrap of gauze, "She will wake in about ten minutes."

They needed to move quickly, "We need to wheel her out of the building and lock the doors behind her."

"And why is that?" Stintz asked.

"Because." He couldn't keep his lips steady, "There's no way she would ever walk out of here without me. I can't give her the option."

"Very well." Stintz gestured to the guard, "And be quick about it."

The guard exited the room in a frantic walk before returning a half minute later pushing a wheelchair. He awkwardly picked up Dahlia and set her in the chair the best he could on his own, having to readjust her limbs to be sitting in a normal fashion.

"Let's go." Reed instructed, pointing them out the door.

Stintz and the guard exited in front of Reed and the three continued to the elevator in silence. Even with a gun to his own head, all the feelings of fear and anxiety bled away and were replaced with the thought of Dahlia. He stared at her hair as he followed them, taking in every second of her presence, drinking up their final moments before he would forget again. He wondered how he could forget something like this. How this feeling could be blotted out by any drug. It felt incorruptible, everlasting, but that's probably what he thought the first time.

The time it took them to ride the elevator down and walk around corner to the sliding glass doors felt like the blink of an eye. How unfair it was, that the seconds wrapped in fear felt like an eternity while this one was fleeting.

"I'm assuming you already took her key card?"

"That's correct." Stintz told him.

"Then roll her out and lock the door behind you." Reed felt a tear fall from his face to the ground.

The guard rolled her out and turned her around facing the door, giving Reed one last look. As the guard walked back in and pressed a button on the wall to close the doors and lock them, Reed was memorizing every detail of her face. He hoped if he could print her in his mind hard enough, that maybe there was some way he could remember her.

Just before he was going to turn around, he saw her twitch. Her eyes squinted open trying to figure out what was happening. She locked onto Reed and her face sprang to life. Dahlia almost jumped out of the chair and started banging on the glass.

"Don't do this!" She yelled, "You can't let them do this to you!"

"I'm so sorry." Reed walked up to the glass doors, "This is the only way."

She burst into tears, "We can figure this out! Please don't do this! I can't live without you!"

"*I* can't do this without *you*." Reed smiled, "But you're stronger than me, it had to be you."

"Please don't. Please don't," she started to chant between sobs.

He held his hand up to the glass, "Find our son. Live the life we dreamed of. I love you." He couldn't take any more of it. The sight of her falling apart was too much for him to watch. He turned around and started to walk back to the elevator.

"REED!" Dahlia screamed at him banging on the glass door.

Her screams slowly faded out as he turned the corner. Every hit he took and all the damage his body sustained over the last few days paled in comparison to what he had just endured. They rode back up and walked into the room at the end of the hallway and he could feel his soul cracking. Reed climbed onto the table and laid back, handing the gun over to Stintz.

"For what it's worth, humanity has a chance at survival again. Focus on that while I hook you up." Stintz stabbed a needle into his arm.

He wondered if it deserved to be saved. If these were the type of people left, then what was the point of pushing forward? It was all such a grey area to him that had no clear answer. Stintz finished hooking up his IV and started flowing the gold liquid into his system.

It didn't take long for Reed to feel drowsy. He closed his eyes and pushed all the philosophical questions out of his mind and focused on Dahlia. His brain began to shut down little by little and he wanted love to be the last emotion he felt. Her face lit up and smiling was the final image his mind held onto as he drifted back into the dark.

Acknowledgments

A gigantic thank you to my wife, Katie. She is a huge reason that this book exists in the first place. From pushing me to get back in to reading when she did, and then supporting me when I decided to try my hand at writing a novel. I couldn't have had a genie craft me a more supportive, loving, and incredible woman from his cosmic powers. She lifts me up when I get knocked down and helps me keep my mind on the important things in life when I start to drift into my own spiraling thoughts. We bounced ideas off of each other and she was always happy and excited to be my first reader with a strong enough will to tell when something needed fixing. I love her beyond anything I could have imagined when I was younger and am truly grateful.

A second thanks to my children. They both have taught me more about life then they could ever know while still trying to get the hang of talking. Two more of the brightest lights in my life and I can't wait to see who they become.

About the author

Joseph Gleason grew up on a small five-acre farm in a little town that you would miss if you blinked while driving through it. He lives with his amazing wife, wonderful two children, two cats, and two dogs in a house that he refurbished primarily on his own. After two years in the electrical trade and seven in the fire sprinkler industry he sparked the idea to try something new, which ended up as the book you read today. This is his first published book of many more to come.